PICTURE THEM DEAD

PICTURE THEM DEAD

RONALD HIGGINS

ARPress LLC
45 Dan Road Suite 5
Canton MA 02021
Hotline: 1(888) 821-0229
Fax: 1(508) 545-7580

Ordering Information:
Quantity sales. Special discounts are available on quantity purchases by corporations, associations, and others. For details, contact the publisher at the address above.

Printed in the United States of America.

ISBN-13:   Softcover   979-8-89330-485-5
           eBook   979-8-89330-486-2

Library of Congress Control Number: 2024901204

Contents

ONE...1

TWO 30

THREE....................................... 49

FOUR 77

FIVE.. 96

SIX 132

SEVEN....................................... 146

EIGHT 168

NINE 181

TEN 206

ELEVEN...................................... 235

TWELVE...................................... 244

THIRTEEN 261

FOURTEEN 279

FIFTEEN 302

SIXTEEN 321

SEVENTEEN. 331

EIGHTEEN 355

NINETEEN 376

TWENTY 388

TWENTY-ONE 403

TWENTY-TWO 410

TWENTY-THREE 430

EPILOGUE. 435

ONE

Well, another death that hit me harder than any of the ones in my case files and here I was, clattering my way to Los Angeles in compassionate response.

As I sat on the train, watching the cities and towns go by, I could see my reflection in the window. What I saw was a pair of bloodshot blues telling me to close them and get some sleep. Instead, I sat wondering what this trip would be like. I had just closed a case I wished I hadn't taken in the first place.

I guess I shouldn't have complained; it paid the rent and a few other bills. Better yet, my night surveillance gig left my schedule flexible enough to accommodate any auditions my agent set up, but I was still glad it hadn't lasted longer than it did. I mean, eight weeks of haunting meat-packing plants was enough. When it was over, I was ready for anything that would get the smell of blood and bone against band saw blades out of my nostrils.

I had always dreamed of being an actor. Los Angeles and its glittering heart, Hollywood held an irresistible allure. For me, the silver screen represented all that was good and bad about people, and I wanted to be part of it all. Growing up in Burbank probably set my feet on the thespian's path, but the thought of returning under current circumstances tarnished the shine of Tinsel Town considerably. I had been wallowing around in all that was good and rotten about people, with emphasis on the rotten. Too bad most of it wasn't on film.

The only good thing about this trip, besides seeing my Aunt Gladys, would be the weather. August in New York was the pits. It was the time of year when you could take three showers a day and still be sticky. It made looking presentable at auditions nearly impossible. I was glad I was leaving, and so were my sweat glands.

As the train rattled west, I thought about my bruised body and how I was glad my temple was still in one piece given the abuse it had taken. My latest souvenir was a five-inch scar, punctuated by a tinier mark from a bullet hole on my stomach. At that moment though, my biggest concern was getting some food in my stomach. An audible rumble told me it was time for lunch. After almost two weeks on IVs, I was thrilled to get back to solid food. The thrill hadn't worn off yet, and my bathroom scale could prove it.

In the dining car, the waiter who welcomed me looked as though he enjoyed his job. He was about six feet tall, neatly dressed, and had shoes sporting a shine that would have melted the heart of a seasoned Marine. It wouldn't have surprised me to see him as the headwaiter at Club 21.

"I'm sorry, sir, you'll have to wait to be seated." He shot me a sly look. "Unless you wouldn't mind sharing a table with a young lady."

I gave him a smile that said, "Thank you," and hoped the young lady was good looking as I said, "That would be fine."

I followed him through the dining car. When he stopped and pulled out a chair, I did a double take at my dining partner. It was as though he read my mind. Now, if only Miss Lovely looks would be captivated by the idea of a short, dark, and handsome lunch partner. At five foot eight inches, I couldn't count on height to be my selling point. Luckily, it had been said that my eyes are Paul Newman blue, but then again, agents have been known to say lots of things to keep actors going and find them work. They also said my jaw was reminiscent of Cary Grant, my hair was charmingly wavy, and my smile was Rock Hudson meeting Doris

Day for the very first time. I also have always had a bit of an Irish accent that I come by quite honestly when I care to let it show through years of work with a diction coach.

"Excuse me, Miss," the waiter said, "Do you mind if this gentleman joins you for lunch?"

Surprised, the woman looked up from her menu, glanced nervously around the room for a moment, and then looked at me, "No, of course not. Please sit down."

I sat and tried not to make too much of her hesitation. I had lacked great press; my co-conspirator was a waiter, not an agent. The waiter smiled, handed me a menu, and walked away. The woman looked a little uncomfortable.

"If you like, I could sit someplace else." My gentlemanly personality was putting my baser instincts back in their box; I just had to offer.

She looked around with hesitation again. "No that's alright. It is pretty crowded."

She had beautiful, ocean-blue eyes and long, silky blond hair that made me forgive her qualified acceptance of my company. She glanced back at her menu. I kept my eyes on her. As an actor, I'd seen a lot of beautiful women. The business always brought them flocking from all over the world. This woman was right up there with the best of them, a real heart-stopper, at least mine faltered a beat or two.

The waiter brought my water and her vodka collins. She took it, drank it immediately, and then gave a not-quite-concealed sigh as she put her glass down. The lady had needed that drink. I could tell by the relieved look on her face as she reordered another. The waiter nodded at the lady and spoke, "Can I bring you something from the bar, sir?"

"Yes, a screwdriver. Thank you."

"Are you ready to order?"

I listened as she spoke, noticing her soft voice, the slight mid-western accent. I gave my order, and we looked at each other in silence for a moment. This was one of the few times in my travels I had ever been happy with the eating arrangements. I was glad I had chosen not to have my meals brought to my compartment.

"Are you going far?" I asked.

"No, just to Denver." She looked around again as if she was expecting someone.

I was trying to make conversation; she was looking out the window. I tried not to let that shred my self-confidence. As an actor, I had a lot of practice in that department. It had always been nearly impossible to go through an audition and come out whole. An artist friend of mine and I always argued about which was worse, his portfolio reviews or my auditions. He thought it was worse to stand there and have someone who can't draw criticize the most creative and delicately rendered children of your artistic soul. I said they can't hold a candle to the barbarians who tell you to your face that your nose is too prominent, your eyes are too deep-set, your smile's too nice, your teeth are too good, and "Who ever told you, you could act anyway?" Rejections like this were especially difficult to handle when they came on the heels of another audition one hour earlier, where they told you your nose was too insignificant and your teeth not good enough for you to play a dentist in a soap even though they liked the confidence-inspiring openness of your blue-eyed stare. The memory of those two very recent auditions was not a good one to be mulling over just then. It was certainly more pleasant to contemplate my table companion.

There was something compelling about this woman. She was troubled. In both of my lines of work, I was trained to pick up on the smallest of clues; hers were at least medium-sized. Maybe that's why I wanted to draw her out, get her to talk. Hell, who was I kidding? My motives were strictly selfish. She was gorgeous. "I'm going through to Los Angeles. Is this a business trip for you?"

"Yes."

So much for my masterful way with a conversational gambit, I thought. Where were my loquacious Irish ancestors when I really needed them? "My name is Sam, Sam Ryan." Maybe guilt would work where guile had failed.

"Oh, sorry. Marilyn Williams." She looked back toward window. She seemed to have a lot on her mind, and it wasn't our chat.

"Do you make this trip often?" I asked.

"Do you always ask so many questions?"

Whoa! Direct, wasn't she? "Well, it's an occupational hazard," I said, hoping to work on her curiosity. Every other angle had failed.

She looked more interested now. A hint of a smile peeked through the glorious blond curtain that half-hid her face. "Oh? What kind of work is that?"

I did a quick mental calculation and came to a decision. "I'm a private detective. You?" Now her expression softened somewhat. She seemed a little more attentive.

"I see. And are you on a case?" She still seemed edgy.

"No, this is sort of a vacation." I could tell that made her relax.

"Have you been to L.A. before?"

"Yes, a lifetime ago." I tried to give the line a poignant reading. If she were still curious, maybe I'd seem mysterious to her. Besides, it was true.

The waiter brought my drink. We both sat for a moment and glanced out the window. When I looked at her, I noticed she was looking at me.

"Is something wrong?" I asked.

A delicate blush tinted her cheeks; she knew she had just been caught. "I'm sorry, I didn't mean to stare. But you look a little familiar. Have you been in the newspapers a lot?"

I gave her a grin. I hoped it was suitably boyish and appealing. An actor spends a lot of time practicing expressions in a mirror, so I was pretty sure I'd achieved what I wanted. "You mean as in big-city crime stopper or something?"

The blush deepened. It was a nice, wholesome coloring of the cheeks. "I'm sorry." She looked at the tablecloth.

"Don't be embarrassed." Maybe I should have strung it out more, but I had my own weaknesses. "You ever watch 'Cliffs of Carlton Place'?"

She looked hard at me for a moment. "You're Jeff!" Her squeal gave me a gift of delight.

"Was Jeff! The writers killed me off about four months into the series."

She grinned. "I thought you made a marvelous villain."

"Thank you, loyal fan," I said, dropping into the accent I had used as Jeff on the short-lived daytime soap.

Her smile faded. "But you just told me you were a private detective." Her voice escalated in anger if not volume.

"Hey, I figured you to have too much class to dine with an out-of-work actor."

Now her expression really iced over. "Too much to sit down with a bald-faced liar," she said evenly as she started up from her chair.

I put out a hand. "Wait. I didn't lie to you. Security work keeps my days free for auditions. Even actors have to eat, and it beats bussing tables."

She looked hesitant, but at least she sat back down. "You said a private investigator. That's not the same thing."

I smiled. "The security firm I work for gives me a good shot at more lucrative jobs. After a couple of cases dropped in my lap and I found out I could problem solve, I put in for a PI license." I pulled out my wallet and offered her proof. It seemed to help.

"What about acting?" She was still wary.

"Any job that allows me to set my own hours is compatible with my acting. If it pays well, it's super compatible."

She smiled then, a real sun-coming-out-of-clouds smile that told me I'd mended our fences. "So, why are you taking the train? I thought all your movie people jetted everywhere in private planes."

There it was again, this time right out of left field. "Well, let's just say, I'm in no hurry." I started rearranging my napkin and silverware, not wanting to say any more about it. "Besides, four months on a New York soap doesn't make me 'movie people.'" I'd done other things, but this was no time to list my credits.

"Do you like your work? I mean, isn't it dangerous?"

"Oh, I guess acting can be hazardous, if you get trampled in a cattle call, but usually…"

Her laughter cut me off. "Not the acting, the detecting," she said.

I smiled. "It can be dangerous." I felt the scar tissue in my stomach tug. "I don't work-out every day when I'm not traveling for nothing. I stay in shape, because sometimes my cases are real killers. Right now, I'm between jobs." I wanted to change the subject. "What kind of work do you do?"

"I'm a model. I missed my flight out of Chicago. This was the only other way to Denver in time for my next shoot."

"Have I seen you on billboards or something?" She smiled, and I knew she was relaxing. She had the grace of a lady that was taught such things. I watched her pick up her glass. Every move she made seemed to be orchestrated. I wondered if the image was anything like the real thing.

"Probably, I do mostly magazine ads, and I have been on some covers. Denver is my last stop, and then I head home to L.A."

"Have you been modeling long?"

"Five years now, but I just started working out of the Taylor Brown Agency in Hollywood a year and a half ago. My roommate, Debbie, got me on with them. They've been really good for my career; they got me the cover shots."

I held up a hand. "Don't tell me that. You got you those covers. Agents only get you a chance to try for it. Same with auditions."

She gave me a pleased smile. It was all the reward I needed. The waiter brought our orders, and the conversation lessened as we both enjoyed the meal. I was glad he'd seated me here; I decided to reward our waiter later for his insight. After we ate, we ordered another drink and talked some more.

"So, tell me, Sam Ryan, are you a PI who acts or an actor who does PI work?"

"Very perceptive lady," I smiled. "I'm an actor who still has to do other things to make a living."

She nodded. "I did a lot of weird jobs before I got my break in modeling. It'll happen."

"Like all things, one wants it sooner rather than later?" She looked into her lap.

"You're making fun of me."

"No. I just don't know if it's still what I want more than anything else. I just know I keep turning out for the auditions. I keep being glad when my agent calls, that sort of thing. But it could be habit, the old fire horse syndrome."

Her head jerked up, and she stared at me. "You're not sure if you want stardom or fame?"

"I had a piece of fame once before, in Shreveport Louisiana, when I had my own television show. I gave it up to get to New York and the Academy of Dramatic Arts. But I don't know if that's what I'm about anymore." I wasn't telling her the whole truth on that one. I had help giving it all up. Death lending her spotty aged hand again.

"Is detecting what you're about now?"

I shrugged. "I haven't fired my agent."

She seemed to think about that for a moment. I could almost have loved her for that.

So many people just follow suit, treat your life as glibly as you do. "What kind of detecting do you do, Sam?" She grinned at me and winked, a lowering of one eyelid so deftly managed I wasn't sure if I'd seen it.

"Husbands cheating on their wives and lots of damsels in distress?" Her smile had a little challenge thrown in like the proper English on a cue ball.

"I think people have this vision of detectives just running after criminals to get the girl in the end," I smiled. "I guess we all grew up watching too much television."

"Do you get the girl in the end?" Both pleased and a little embarrassed over what she said, her long lashes covered her eyes like dew on morning grass. She looked through them at me. I could feel my face turning red, like the one time I proposed marriage, and the woman who would become my wife asked, "Why me?" It was one of the few times I ever heard myself saying, "I love you." Saying it always made me blush. I couldn't remember the last time I'd used those words, other than with Margaret. And with her, as it turned out, I hadn't used them often enough. I pulled myself back to the train, the dining car, and the present company.

"I don't know. Get the girl? I guess I'll just have to wait and see. Interesting thought."

She sipped nervously at her drink and abruptly said, "Well, I have to go. It was nice talking to you, Sam."

I didn't want the conversation to end. Few women had interested me since my wife's death in a car accident in Shreveport Louisiana. I wondered if Marilyn was going to be one of them. I wanted to know more about her. "Maybe I'll see you again."

"It's a small train, Sam. You never can tell."

It was obvious she intended us to meet again. I felt like a man whose boss told him he was getting a raise, but not when. She reached for the bill. I got to it first. "Let me catch this, Marilyn, my pleasure."

She smiled, "Thank you."

I watched her leave. She had that familiar walk that men have been looking at for centuries. It was hypnotic, inviting. It was grace personified. She was a tall woman, taller than I, so many of them are these days. That was okay. I was used to it. Alan Ladd was short. So was Kirk Douglas. They may have been teased, but they got the ladies, got paid, and worked regularly.

Unable to top lunch, I spent the rest of the day in my compartment reading the newspaper. I checked the sports section first. I liked to keep up with the start of football season. How long I followed it depended on who led the league. If it was the Giants, I stuck with it.

It didn't seem to matter what I read, my mind kept coming back to what Marilyn said about an actor who detects or a detective who acts. It was an embarrassing subject when it came up, much more embarrassing than being asked why I wasn't taking a plane. Sooner or later, I had to resolve that conundrum; I knew too well what had been so validly said about a thing divided against it.

When I looked out the window again, it was dark. I rang for the porter.

"Good evening, sir. Is there something I could get for you?"

Maybe it was the uniform, but all the porters had that same way about them. It made me think the railway owners only hired one great employee and cloned the rest. He was in his late forties, and he had grayed hair and a smile that made me want to give him my last dime. "Yes, would you please make up the bed?"

"Very good, sir." He stepped into the small compartment and pulled a key from his pocket.

"Have you been working on trains long?" I asked.

He dropped down the berth and continued making up my bed as he spoke. "Yes sir, going on twenty-two years."

"You must have seen a lot of the country."

"Yes sir, and the people. You wouldn't believe some of the people just on this train alone. I have some stories."

I smiled. "I'll bet. I'd love to hear them sometime." I slipped a bill into his jacket pocket. "Whenever you next have some time off." I was too tired to get into a long conversation at the moment, but the actor in me wanted to pick his brain and his experience. "Where are we now?"

He had one of those pocket watches with a gold chain, the kind they probably gave him after twenty years of faithful service. He held it at arm's length. "We left Omaha about ten minutes ago, sir." He turned to leave.

"You let me know when you have some free time."

"Thank you, sir. And anything else, just ask for me, Jason."

"I'll be sure to do that." As he was leaving, he almost bumped into Marilyn and side-stepped to let her enter.

"Good evening," I said. "Would you like a nightcap?" She nodded, and I called after the porter. "Hang on a moment, Jason, please."

"Vodka collins," she said when I nodded at her.

I gave Jason our order and leaned back into the room. Marilyn was eyeing the bed he had just turned down.

"Were you about to call it a night, Sam?"

"No, not quite yet. Make yourself comfortable."

Marilyn looked different somehow. I studied her body language. She had definitely come to some sort of decision. Her interesting nerved-up edge had transformed into vulnerability. She sat at the front of the chair seat and kept her weight forward over her feet as if she might bolt. She was wearing a short skirt and a matching lavender sweater. Lana Turner had nothing on her. I was glad she'd stopped by. "You look lovely."

"Thanks, you're sweet to say that."

Her smile left as quickly as it came. She stood nervously and paced to the window and back. Given the size of my compartment, that wasn't much of a trip. Yes, she had made a decision, and she was about to try it out on me.

"What's wrong, Marilyn?"

"Well, you did say you were a private investigator."

So much for a social evening. Whenever people say things like that, I know it's going to be business. "Yes."

"I need your help." She turned her frightened blue eyes to me. "I can pay you."

The tone in her voice was telling me she had no one else. I knew I was going to listen. I'm a sucker for pretty eyes. "I'm on a vacation, not after a fee," I said gently. She looked so stricken that I added, "But you can tell me what's wrong."

"Someone's following me. I can feel it."

"Is it a man or a woman?"

"I don't know. I haven't seen them. I just know." I could tell she was scared witless. She believed what she said, and she thought I didn't. "You think I'm crazy," she accused, a hurt in her eyes that went clear to my gut.

"I didn't say that. Is there any reason for someone to follow you?" Other than the obvious, I thought, knowing I'd have followed her quite a few places myself.

"I have something they want."

"What?"

"I can't…" It seemed for a moment as if nothing would ever follow that opening. She took a deep breath, all the way from her diaphragm. I enjoyed it. "I'll tell you when I feel more comfortable, when I know you better."

"You don't give me much to go on." I knew I was going to get involved in this, no matter what. Hell, I knew I'd plunge into this one just for another one of her deep breaths.

"I need protection, your security services." She looked desperate. I knew desperate when

I saw it. I'd been desperate before. I'd even acted it a few times. She wasn't acting. There was a knock on the door, and Marilyn came up off her chair like Jesse Owens off the starting blocks.

"Relax, it's only Jason with our drinks." I opened the door and took the tray. He left. I gave Marilyn her vodka. Again, she drank it as if she needed the comfort or strength — even false strength it could give. Not a good sign. I'd tried that route once. It only got rockier the farther it went, and it could lead straight to an AA meeting.

I took the glass from her and pressed her cold fingers into the hollow of my palm. "That won't fix anything," I said with as much compassion as I could muster.

She broke down. I looked into her beautiful blue eyes awash with tears. "Now, it can't be that bad." I cringed inwardly. Trust me to sound as avuncular as 'Travels with My Aunt' when I wanted to come off like Matt Helm. My hands squeezed her shoulders. Fortunately, she knew the blocking better than I did. She slid into my arms, and I brought her body to mine. I held her for a few minutes until she stopped crying. "Do you want to tell me about it?"

"I'm sorry, Sam, I didn't mean to fold up on you. It's just that I'm so furious with myself for what I've gotten myself into. I feel so stupid for…" She stopped in midsentence and looked up into my eyes. We gazed at each other for a moment, and then it happened. I knew it was going to happen from the first time we met, or I had hoped. We kissed. Oh, it wasn't anything earth-shaking, but it sure felt good. It must have felt good to her too, because she did it again. I would have invited her into my bed right then and there, and she would have accepted, but I'd had enough of frightened and grateful in the sex department. If Marilyn and I were going to go anywhere, I wanted it to be more than fear that brought her to me.

"Marilyn, why don't you get some sleep, and we'll talk it all out in the morning. I'll buy breakfast."

She stiffened in my arms. "It's all right, Sam. I'm a mess. I wouldn't want my company either." She started to push away and reach for her drink.

I stopped her and pulled her close. "You're dead wrong, lady. I want you. I want your company. But I don't want either of us to look back and regret it. There will be a better time." I took her face in my hands and kissed her very gently. "You need rest. If I'm going to help you, I need a clear picture of what we're up against. You can't give me that when you're strung out on nerves and vodka."

She was a charmer, but I was beginning to think it might be just lust on my part. I didn't need problems unless I got paid to solve them.

She smiled and said, "Yeah sure, you're right." She tossed back her thick blond hair and continued, "I don't even like that stuff. I can't force enough down to get a good drunk anyway. And I know it doesn't help anything." She held up her right hand. "Sober by morning, rested and ready to talk. I promise." She looked like an ad for the Girl Scouts of America. I'd have joined. I took her in my arms one last time and offered to walk her to her compartment.

"No need," she said, giving me a tipsy grin. "I'm next door." She eased across the room, unlatched the connecting door, and let herself out. I heard the bolt on her side slide shut. Damn. I could hear my Irish grandfather snicker.

Suddenly, she opened the door again and tossed a key through the doorway. "Hold this for me, Sam. I'll explain in the morning." She closed the door. "Don't lose it," I heard her say from the safety of her room.

I stood looking at the key. It had a tag with the letter W, followed by the number 313 and another letter, D. Underneath the numbers were the initials C.S.U.N.

I was wondering what I had just gotten myself into. It seemed like forever until morning, but a long, lonely night had been my idea. I was going to have to try to get some sleep, in spite of it. I climbed into bed and didn't spend another second wondering about that strange bit of metal she'd tossed me. I spent more than a few minutes thinking about the lovely woman on the other side of that thin wooden panel.

TWO

 $\mathbf{M}$ orning came abruptly, with a hard knock on my compartment door.

"All right, keep a lid on it," I yelled. I didn't like people waking me like the world was coming to an end, unless it was. I got up, threw on my robe, and reached for the door.

"Yes? What is it?"

"Mr. Ryan?"

"Yes?"

"May we come in?"

I sidestepped and let the two men pass. One was tall and on the thin side; the other was about the same height and stockier. I knew right away they were cops. You don't last as a P.I. without learning to recognize a couple of cops when you see them. Sure enough, the thin one flashed a badge in my face. I put out a hand to stop him from flipping the case closed before I had a long second look. Nobody really examines those badges, but they should. The fakes are looking better and better, but, like I said, I wouldn't have needed a first look to peg these two.

"My name is Callahan," said the thin one. "I'm with the Denver police. This is my partner, Detective Rogan." He stepped closer, invading my space. I didn't give him the satisfaction of stepping back. "Did you have lunch with a Ms. Marilyn Williams yesterday?"

I didn't like cops. Certainly, I had no faith in them. If I ever did, that faith died a few years back in Shreveport with Margaret. "Yes." I could feel my blood pressure rising and hoped it didn't show. He knew the answers already, he was testing me.

"Anything else happen?"

He was beginning to sound like the father of a girl who had been kept out past curfew. "I told you; we had lunch together. What's the point of all this?"

"Did anyone see you two together?"

"Yes, the waiter in the dining room." His partner was writing while I talked. "He sat us together."

"You know her from before?"

"Before what?" I couldn't help it. Something about him made me want to make him work for every morsel. The look on Rogan's face made me regret my attitude slightly, but only slightly.

"You met her for the first time at lunch?" Rogan put in. He was determined to make the question clear; I had no option except a straight answer.

"Yes." I gave it to him.

The ball bounced back into Callahan's part of the court. "Jason, the night porter for this car said you and Ms. Williams had drinks in your room. What time did she leave?"

I was fully awake now. I wanted to ask a few questions myself. "Suppose you tell me what's going on here."

"Why should we? You were the one with a broad in your room." This from Rogan. I had a feeling I'd be sorry I'd slid a sliver under his skin.

I faced him squarely. "What the lady and I were doing in my room is none of your business."

"Look, Mr. Ryan," Callahan said, "There's been a murder, and we've been called in. We'd appreciate your cooperation."

I remembered when I was a kid, and my dad was going to tell me something I didn't want to hear. I used to cup my hands over my ears and start singing "Lalalalalalala," repeating it over and over. It always seemed to make what he was going to say much less believable and a little bit easier to swallow. But I couldn't do that here. I had to ask, even though I was pretty sure of the answer. "Who was murdered?"

"Marilyn Williams. She was found dead in the next compartment."

I felt like I'd been kicked hard in the stomach. He kept watching me as he talked. I knew he was waiting for my reaction. I didn't want him to think there was more to this than there was. This was one time I wished I hadn't slept so soundly.

"I'm sorry. She was a nice woman." I was hoping he wouldn't ask any more questions. I wanted him to go away. I wanted to feel something more than I felt for that lost beautiful girl who had asked for my help and had been put off until a morning that, for her, never dawned.

"Did you see or hear anything unusual last night?"

"No." Go away, Callahan, I thought.

"Did you notice Ms. Williams talking to anyone else on the train?"

"No. I wasn't with her every minute." But his partner tapped on the connecting door.

"You know this led right into her room?" I nodded.

"I offered to walk her back to her compartment last night about 10:10. She said it wasn't necessary and let herself through there."

"Pretty convenient."

"What are you implying?"

Callahan shrugged. "What are you inferring?"

I sat down on the bed. "When she left, she slid the bolt shut on her side. I heard it. In fact, I believe she meant for me to hear it."

"Why, you getting too friendly? Maybe she made you angry when she shot you down?" His thin face looked as if someone had pressed it from sheet metal. The lines around his mouth deepened as he set his jaw.

"No, nothing like that. She was just fooling around. You know… teasing." I certainly wasn't going to tell these apes she'd come onto me in an alcohol-induced weak moment, and I'd turned her down and sent her home to sober up. One didn't speak ill of the dead if one could help it. She'd probably meant the sound of the bolt as a "see what you missed, sport." Well, now there'd be no second chances. Not for her.

"And so, you locked your side?" Detective Rogan pulled back the bolt on my side. "Afraid of being taken advantage of?" He smiled. It wasn't a pretty sight. His teeth were a dingy smoker's yellow, and the front ones pushed forward as if he'd be thrilled to be fed a carrot.

I shrugged. "Habit. Reflex."

"You habitually lock yourself in at night?"

"I'm from New York." That should cover it for him. In New York, you locked your doors when you were wide-awake, in broad day- light.

Privately, I thought about my action. Maybe it had been my non- verbal message to her that she was safe from me but, unfortunately, not from others.

Rogan spread a meaty palm flat against the interconnecting door and pushed. As the door swung open easily, silently, I noticed the dark wiry hairs that sprouted from the backs of his fingers.

"You said she locked it?" It was Callahan's turn at me.

"Yes. I heard her shoot the bolt." I stood up.

Callahan pushed me down again. "Seems you were wrong."

I shook my head. "It was locked. I know it was."

"You try the door after she left?" He had a sleazy smile on his face that made me sick. Everything about these guys was ugly after a while.

"No. I told you …"

"You heard her slide the bolt," he mimicked, cutting me off. "I know. You going to let me search your things, or do I have to get a warrant?"

I gestured around the compartment. "Make your day, Lieutenant Callahan."

The two of them swarmed over my things like ants at a picnic. They found my gun, and I showed them my permit and my P.I. license. They weren't impressed. My gun was broken down for traveling, and the clip was in a different bag from the pieces of the weapon. There wasn't much he could say, but his actions told me a lot. If Marilyn had been shot, he'd have bagged the weapon. Besides, I didn't have a silencer.

"See," I said, definitely pushing my luck. "No smell of cordite, no bloody handkerchief, no dripping axes, no blood-spattered clothing."

Detective Rogan stepped up until he was only a sour morning breath from my face. "And maybe you weren't wearing clothing when you paid Marilyn a visit. Maybe you cut her and came back in here stark naked and showered off. Maybe…"

"Maybe you need to sell those screenplay rights, Rogan." A knife. Nothing is more frightening than a blade in the hand of someone who looks as if he can use it. That I knew from personal experience.

Callahan put a hand on Rogan's arm. "We'll have the lab check both showers for blood residue. Mr. Ryan, the porter will help you move your things to another compartment. Please give him and us your full cooperation." He smiled like a shark closing in on a surfer.

I nodded. Jesus. They were actually going to check my shower drain for blood! The hope that it had been quick and painless for Marilyn fled. I wondered how badly they'd cut her up trying to make her talk. A blade against that beautiful magazine cover face, her career as well as her personal life in scarred tatters, after that anyone would have said anything so they would stop. But did she?

Rogan leaned out into the corridor, and Jason appeared as if the cop had waved a wand. Together, we folded my suitcases closed, and Jason carried them down the hall. I scuffed into my slippers and followed, Callahan was at my heels like a spaniel, or a pit bull.

"That'll be all for now. Oh yes, I'll need to know where you'll be staying while you're in California."

I gave him the information he wanted. He left me in the new compartment, three doors down from Marilyn's. I was alone with my thoughts once again, and it wasn't pleasant. If only I had invited Marilyn to stay the night, she might've still been alive.

Well, I didn't, dammit, and she wasn't. That was the problem with being noble and with all of life for that matter. You never knew if what seemed right was right, unless it was wrong.

I dressed and shaved and headed to the dining car for some coffee. Drinking coffee always made me think better. I saw Jason coming out of a compartment ahead of me.

"Jason?"

He turned. "Yes, Mr. Ryan?"

"You remember Ms. Williams, the girl I was with last night?"

"Yes sir, a shame thing like that happening to such a nice young lady. And what they did to that compartment! Makes my job a whole lot more work, I tell you that and moving everyone around." He shook his head.

"The murderer teared up her things, did they?"

"Oh, sir, I never saw such a mess. Not even when that writer lady came on with a portable typewriter and what must have been a carload of bags and papers. Every day I went to clean, there was a roomful of crumpled paper, empty plates, and half-eaten food. Didn't tip too well either, if you know what I mean."

I smiled. Hint taken. I slipped him a bill.

"You think I could take a look, Jason?"

"Oh, sir, I couldn't do that. Those cops, they said to lock it all up until we get to Los

Angeles. I spent most of two hours in there this morning already. Them and the guys with the little plastic baggies and the big flash camera. Now this train is going to be nothing but late."

I added another bill. "Maybe you could just check that door to make sure you locked it."

He looked down at the money in his hand and grinned. "And maybe you could just happen to be looking over my shoulder when I check it?"

I laughed and nodded. "You're a quick study, Jason."

"Yes, sir!"

I followed him down the corridor. Jason cracked the door, and I leaned in. He hadn't been exaggerating. Not a bit. It looked like the stage set for 'Catch Me If You Can.' I did the Community theater production of it in Shreveport. I played Sidney, the Jewish sandwich shop owner from the Catskills, who looked into a room recently vacated by a honeymoon couple who hadn't bothered to put anything away on their rush to the nuptial bed. I'd won a best supporting actor award for the part. No one was giving any awards for the mess in Marilyn's compartment.

The dark spray up the wood paneling behind her bed told its own story. I'd have said from the blood patterns she'd had her throat cut at the end. The bed clothes were gone, probably already on their way to the police lab, but there was an ominous dark splotch where Marilyn's life had leaked right through the blankets, sheets, and mattress cover.

Whoever had killed her had torn the place up, searching, probably for what she had already given me. Did that mean she hadn't told them what they wanted to know? Could anybody hold out against a knife? All I knew was, she was dead, and I could end up the same way if they guessed or knew she'd passed me something.

Jason had given me a long slow ten count. He stepped back and pulled the door shut after us. "The police have already been through it. They want me to keep it locked." He turned the key. "So that's what I'll do." He winked. "You can be my witness."

"Thanks, Jason." I started to walk away.

"Jason, you see anybody talking to her?"

"No sir, only you."

"Right, when would we have normally pulled out of Denver?"

"Sometime around noon would have been the right time, sir," Jason replied.

I nodded. Marilyn would have told all at our breakfast meeting and then headed to her shoot. As it was, the Denver P.D. had come to us. I felt an involuntary shudder work its way up my spine. Maybe coffee would help. But as, my Jewish landlady was so fond of saying, "It couldn't' hurt."

When I got to the dining car, there weren't many people there. My wakeup conversation with Abbott and Costello had ruined my appetite, so I just ordered some dry rye toast with my coffee. It wasn't my landlady's Jewish corn rye, and it wasn't' from a New York deli, but it would do. I pulled out my notebook and sat, watching the other diners.

An elderly couple at the next table held my attention for a while. The gentleman was so precise, I thought he was going to count the sugar grains he put into his tea. He had dipped the bag up and down exactly five times. I watched him mouth the numbers. Odd duck. Then, he borrowed his wife's spoon and used it, paired with his own, as tongs to squeeze the bag. He set it carefully on his saucer and took a sip. He smiled, so he must have done it right. I jotted notes about the procedure. It was a habit I had acquired at the Academy. One of my professors sent the whole class out to take notes on the mannerisms of everyday folk. Then, he'd made us play off the information in improvisations. After two years in his classes, I had become compulsive about people watching. Writing down my observations always clarified them for me. Even if I never looked at my notes again, the act of writing seemed to seal the information in my mind forever. Even after years, a key word or two could bring it back; I could quote it almost verbatim.

The old couple left the car, and I glanced around, looking for other quirks to record. The place was clearing out. I finished my toast and thought about Marilyn some more. I had the feeling I was forgetting something important. Suddenly, it came to me. I had seen someone watching us during lunch. If I hadn't been so taken with Marilyn's beauty, and, let's face it, with making a good impression, I'd probably have been writing about him in my notebook. I took a moment now to jot down everything I could remember. Then I paid my check and returned to my room.

When I opened the door to my new compartment, the sight of it was a shock. The porters were supposed to clean for you, not have a party and leave a mess for you to take care of. It reminded me of an old girlfriend I use to know. She kept her place a mess all the time. I guess that was one of the reasons we never really hit it off. Lord knows, I'm not Suzy Homemaker, but I don't drop my chicken bones in my sock drawer, and I pick up what I let fall long before the roaches show up to take possession of it. I was beginning to dislike the room service around here. Somebody had been looking for something, and I was pretty sure it wasn't a helpful conductor needing my train ticket. I rang for Jason and started straightening up.

They had emptied my suitcase all over the room. The tweed sports coat my late wife had given me was on the floor, but it wasn't torn. It was one of the last things she had bought for me. The pockets and sleeves were turned inside out, and the bottom of the lining was ripped loose. I could get that put back together, and it would never show.

The suitcase hadn't fared so well. The locks were popped, and their linings littered the floor. At least I hadn't bought new luggage for the trip. It was undeniable. They had to be looking for the key Marilyn had given me. Either she had told them what they wanted to know, or they were guessing because they had seen her come to my room. I took the key out of the fold of my wallet. It had C.S.U.N. on it. I tucked it in an envelope, addressed it to my Aunt in Burbank, and when Jason arrived, I gave it to him to mail. It would catch up with me in Los Angeles. I felt better about letting the mail hold the key until I arrived in Los Angeles. I knew somebody wanted that key enough to kill for it.

THREE

As the train pulled into Union Station in Los Angeles, I tried to put Marilyn out of my mind and think about my reason for making this trip. It wasn't any more pleasant, nor was it all that different.

I was there for a funeral. My Uncle Hobart had passed away, and Aunt Gladys had sent for me. Uncle Hobart and I had never been what one would call close, but Aunt Gladys was everything a boy could ever want in a mother. And both of them were as close as I got to parents after my own had an untimely death.

There were times when I thought I knew Uncle Hobart, and then something would happen to change my mind. He was a hard man to get to know, and as far as I could ever tell, he just wouldn't let anyone get very close to him, except maybe, Aunt Gladys.

My aunt was supposed to meet me at the station, but I wasn't sure I would recognize her. It had been twenty years since I'd seen her or my uncle. I began to wish, not for the first time, that I had come back sooner, that I could have returned under better circumstances. It would have been nice to play a round of golf with Uncle Hobart again.

There had been a few things we'd shared. Golf was one of them. I wondered if he'd ever lowered his handicap from his embarrassing thirty over par. No matter, he played it because he loved it. He loved walking the greens in the fresh air and sunshine.

When you haven't seen someone for a long time, you remember them as they were. I was sure Aunt Gladys had changed a lot; time and tears tended to tear women apart, and she'd had her share of both. I pulled the ancient, cracked photo from my wallet. She had to be in her sixties by now. My mind refused to add wrinkles to that kind face and rebelled at dimming the life-loving sparkle in her eyes. For that matter, I wondered if she would recognize me. I put the photograph away and picked up my bags. My early acting composites didn't show a lot of change in the basics when held against the current photos my agent sent around, although my few years in the bottom of a bottle after Margaret's death had added their share of lines around my eyes and mouth. "Character," my agent said. I thought fond things about my agent as I decided that I was at least recognizable.

I worried that Gladys hadn't called the station first and found out about the time we'd lost around Denver. I'd been so wrapped up with the Hardy Boys, I'd completely forgotten about trying to send her a wire. My aunt was a patient woman, but no one wanted to spend empty hours in downtown L.A. all alone. Even when I was there twenty years ago, Union Station hadn't been the best of areas.

As I stepped off the train and walked down the platform, a tall bald-headed man with a handlebar moustache passed, turned, and looked at me. He was the guy who had been staring at Marilyn and me in the dining car. I'd seen that look before. It was as if he were trying to memorize my face.

He saw me notice him, and he hurried through the gate, disappearing too quickly in the crowd. I noticed a little old lady standing to one side of that same gate. She was staring at me. I wasn't sure it was Aunt Gladys until she smiled. It's funny how smiles never change even though faces do. As I started toward her, she threw her hands out and called my name.

"Sam! It's me, Gladys." She hurried forward then continued talking. "It's so good to see you."

Then she threw her arms around me and started crying. I gave her a great big hug.

I replied, "Now, now, stop that. You know the Irish, you'll have me in tears, and won't that look silly? Two grown people crying in the middle of a train station."

"I'm sorry. I'm just so happy." She wiped her eyes and attempted a half-laugh to cover her embarrassment. "I was getting worried, even though they told us the train was going to be late."

"Sorry about the delay, Aunt Gladys. The train was held over at Denver. I didn't get a chance to send word. I was worried about you being all alone in downtown Los Angeles."

She waved away my anxiety as if shooing flies from a fresh apple pie. "Oh, I just walked over to Olvera Street and looked in the shops. I got this really nice bit of lace that I thought I'd use as an inset in an old blouse I couldn't bear to part with. Your uncle bought it for me for our anniversary three years ago."

She started rummaging in her bags. "There were a few other things I just couldn't resist, and I found a great Batman piñata for the little boy down the block. His birthday is next week." She pulled a crepe paper nightmare in a black and metallic blue from a sack. I had to laugh. Blessedly, some things never changed. She still couldn't throw anything away, still sewed her heart out to fix and patch and mend, and still bought frivolous things for others before buying necessities for herself. I squeezed her hands in mine.

"I remember the denim jacket I had in high school, the one you cut a new collar for out of the leg of an old pair of jeans, just so I wouldn't have to throw it out."

Aunt Gladys smiled. "Well, you loved that jacket. It broke my heart to see you put it in the Goodwill bag."

I gave her another hug, for then as well as now. "It's so good to see you, Aunt Gladys."

She started to cry. At that point I was glad that I had thought about buying a package of tissues knowing I was going to see her and that there would be tears. As we walked through the station, I noticed that the high archways and tall columns on each side of the station gave the appearance of entering a great hall in early Rome. The building of Union Station must have cornered the marble market for some time, that and the leaded glass windows. It was still an impressive place to enter Los Angeles through and must have been awesome in its heyday, everything clean and bigger than life and that endless marble polished to a reflective shine.

Aunt Gladys looked at me and shook her head. "Still don't like flying, I see."   There it was again, I couldn't seem to avoid it. "Yeah, Well, I never could get comfortable in a plane." She let it slide, but we both knew it was craven cowardice. "C'mon, my car's out front."

I kept looking at her and noticing how the years had dealt with her. I remembered how when I was growing up, she was always smiling and seemed so happy. She looked tired, and her eyes no longer held that lust for life that had been her trademark through both the good times and the bad. I was surprised to think that Hobart might have been such an important part of her life. Even though she'd lived with him for so many years, it had always seemed to me that they had sort of gone their separate ways under that same roof. I had never seen any overt demonstrations of affection between them. A certain fondness, but not passion. I never thought his going would have taken the life out her like that. I guess I had wanted to believe that Margaret and I had a corner on passion in our marriage. I guess every young couple does.

When we reached the parking lot, I remembered my aunt's '65 Mustang; there it was: the very same. It looked brand new. Someone had taken very good care of it. "Aunt Gladys, is that the Mustang?"

She smiled, "Yep, it sure is. Only I'm not as young as I used to be, so now I have some kids come by on Saturdays and spruce it up for me. I give those cookies and a little pocket money to them."

Yes, those cookies. "Those great oatmeal ones with the raisins?"

She looked up at me and smiled, saying, "Oh Lord, I haven't made those things in years. I buy them ready-made in the stores now. Less of a bother."

I felt an indescribable depression mire me. We may have come a long way, but I think we lost something on the trip. It was sad. I used to love coming home from school to a house filled with the scent of those cookies baking.

"You're welcome to use the car while you're here," she offered.

I guess she'd seen the disappointment in my eyes and was trying to make it up to me. "You'll probably want to go to some auditions while you're near Hollywood."

"Thanks. Although I think out here, you have to have an agent just to get into an audition. I might need it to pick up some work in my new sideline, though."

"Sideline?"

"I've been doing some security work and a little gumshoeing now and then."

"Gumshoeing? You mean like Magnum?"

I smiled. "Well, something along those lines, but no glamour, no Ferrari, no island paradise. Strictly hard, boring work in a hot, sticky city."

"Isn't it dangerous, Sam?"

"Nah! Most of it is research and sometimes a bit of surveillance."

She squirmed a little and glanced at me as she drove. I knew she wasn't too happy with the news.

"I'm sorry about Uncle Hobart. Is there anything I can do? I mean with the funeral or anything?"

"Well, your uncle wasn't much on funerals. He used to say, 'Glad, when I die, have me cremated. There isn't enough ground now for the living, let alone the dead.'"

"That sounds like Uncle Hobart. Do you need me to make some arrangements, or is that already done?"

"I've taken care of that, but there is something you can do for me. As you know, your uncle had a problem saving money, what with his betting at the track and all."

I was suddenly sick with the dread of knowing that I couldn't help her in that department. After Margaret's accident, making money didn't seem like a very high priority, nor was success. Now I was kicking myself. All those wasted years. Then, she surprised me.

"But in the last few years, he managed to get lucky, and he started putting something away. He would never tell me how much."

"I'm happy for you, Aunt Gladys, but what do you want me to do?" I certainly wasn't a money management wizard either.

"You know how fond of you he was. He was sorry when you went off on your own. He knew you would someday, but I guess parents never look forward to that day."

"I never knew he felt that strongly."

Aunt Gladys spoke. "You know your uncle, he wasn't much on words." She paused, but neither of us hurried to fill the silence. At last, she went on. "You knew we could never have children. We kind of saw you as the son we never had." I was afraid her eyes were tearing up again. She sniffed and shook off her emotion. "Anyway, it wasn't long after you left that he started to make some sound investments. The long and short of it is, he left you some money in his will, and I'd like you to go to the lawyers with me."

"Aunt Gladys, I don't know what to say. I mean… I can't take any money from you."

"Oh, yes you can, and you will. And it's not from me. It's from your uncle."

There was no mistaking that look. I recalled seeing it many times growing up. The look meant she wanted me to do something, and she wasn't going to take no for an answer. "Why don't we just wait and see what happens when we meet with the lawyers?" I suggested, putting off a known confrontation. There was no way I was going to take anything from this woman who had been all I'd ever known of a mother.

The look on her face softened as she spoke. "Your uncle loved you very much, and he knew how hard you took it when you lost Margaret. When we first heard you were married, we were so happy for you. She seemed like such a lovely girl. We had hoped you two would visit. Your uncle showed those wedding snapshots to everyone he could collar for more than a minute. Fate was finally giving you a break, Margaret and that television show all your own. Next time we heard, Margaret was gone, and you'd given up the show. Then, you started drinking." She glanced over at me and then back at the road. I felt ashamed knowing they knew, but she went on, "He found out. I remember him telling me that he was going to set money aside, so when you finally put your life back together, you'd have a little something to start over."

I swallowed a lump in my throat. "It sure was a nice thought, Aunt Gladys. But like I said, I'm fine now, and I have a good job. Two jobs, if you count acting." We both laughed at that.

"You'll need money for a comfortable old age. You'll get there, someday, you know," I teased.

She reached out and slapped my arm without taking her eyes off the traffic. "My needs are small, and my mortgage is paid. I've taken a cruise with Beth, and I got seasick. I've flown to Orlando with your uncle when he wanted to play that golf course at Disney World, and I got airsick. Believe me, your uncle was no fool. He left me better off than I ever expected." She gave me a smile that was almost sly. "And he did it before he died. No inheritance tax and such. He wanted to do the same for you but… Anyways, what would I do with any more money except help my only living kin? Besides, your uncle wanted it this way."

"Aunt Gladys —"

"End of conversation."

I couldn't believe Uncle Hobart had been able to really leave her set for her old age, not like I'd like to see her set up. I'd have to think of a way to win this one, maybe later. As we got closer to home, I could see how the neighborhood had changed. Glendale, as I remembered, was a pretty quiet community. I didn't know if it really had changed all that much or if I was looking at the same things with older eyes and a new perspective. If Gladys had blindfolded me and drove me there, I wouldn't have known where I was.

Aunt Gladys seemed to know what I was thinking. "A lot of the people you knew have moved away. You remember Joe Gallo and Karen, don't you?"

"Crazy Joe? How could I forget him? He was always playing practical jokes on us."

"Well, he and Karen finally got married, and they have two girls. I bought them matching dresses while I was on Olvera Street." She gave one of the bags a pat.

"That's great. I kind of thought they'd get hitched. He was always in love with her. I'd like to see them while I'm here."

"That's easy enough. He still lives in the same place. He and Karen took over the house after his folks moved to Florida."

Pulling into my aunt's driveway brought back fond memories. I could see my bedroom window. The vines running along the sill and down the side of the house were my way of sneaking out at night and coming back late without getting caught.

"Your old room's ready. You settle in. Then you can come on down. We'll have coffee and catch up. Oh, by the way, those vines aren't as strong as they use to be, so use the stairs." She smiled, and I think she blushed.

"I never could put anything over on you."

I could hear her laughter all the way up to my room. Inside the house, things hadn't changed a bit. There was Aunt Gladys' favorite Norman Rockwell print, the one of the little boy sitting at the soda fountain, still hanging on the wall on the first landing. He hadn't finished his soda, proving that some things are too good to end.

The wallpaper in the hall was the same, faded, but still there. She'd never changed phones either. She had one of those old original designs with the dial on the face and the straight black cord. It was sitting on a little table by the stairs with a doily under it. Everything looked worn, but neat and clean. It felt good to be there again. I considered it home.

After settling in, I started thinking about Uncle Hobart and the good memories I did have with him. I went downstairs to the kitchen. I could smell my favorite meal: meatloaf. I remembered the first time I'd had it there. Aunt Gladys had to practically shove it down my throat. She told me a real witch gave her the recipe when she first married and promised that if she fed it to her husband once a week, he would never leave her. I was only eleven. I was easy to fool.

As I inhaled the sweet scent of it in the oven, I remembered that she told me she would cut small pieces of celery and onions and mix in some sage. That was about as much as I could remember of the ingredients. I never did get the full recipe. I was always too busy eating.

Aunt Gladys was putting some plates on the table when I came into the kitchen.

"Oh good, you're here, I made your favorite."

"I know I could smell it upstairs." I leaned over her shoulder. "Hmmm, looks good."

Without even thinking about it, I walked over and sat in my old chair, like I had done so many years before. I was beginning to think I was in some kind of time warp.

Aunt Gladys brought a platter to the table and sat across from me. "So, tell me, how long do you plan on staying?"

I started filling my plate, "Trying to get rid of me already?" I took a big piece of the meatloaf and reached for the potatoes.

"Heavens no. I want you to stay as long as you want." That little hesitation was the first hint of the loneliness she must have felt now that Uncle Hobart had gone. We both tried to ignore it.

"Thanks, I appreciate that Aunt Gladys."

I took my first bite of meatloaf, smiled, and spooned homemade gravy over my potatoes. It was not the kind that comes in cans, pale beige and gluey with cornstarch, more suited to pasting in bookplates than gracing a china plate, but real pan gravy from the beef, a dark rich brow, thickened on the stovetop the old-fashioned way.

Aunt Gladys spoke, "How long can you stay?"

"I don't know." I thought of my dwindling finances. I knew I'd probably have to get a paper route to stay more than a month or two.

"Do you have some milk?" I asked partly to change the subject.

"Sure thing."

I continued. "Something happened on the train, and I want to look into it."

She stepped to the refrigerator and got the milk. "Did you know the woman?"

I felt like I was in seventh heaven with the food. I'd forgotten what a great cook my aunt was. "Aunt Gladys, this meatloaf is out of this world. As a matter of fact, I… wait a minute. How do you know there's a woman? I didn't tell you."

She smiled at me. "Well, whenever you talked about something that involved a woman, you always sounded a little anxious and got a certain look on your face."

"Still can't get anything past you, can I?"

"Nope. So, tell me, who is she?" Aunt Gladys leaned forward like a fan at a spectator sport.

"Oh, just someone I met on the train. She was a model living here in Hollywood."

"Lot of them out here."

"Yeah, well she gave me a key to hold for her. She said it was very important." I didn't want to bother her with the details right then. I knew how upset she would get.

"You know, you're just like your father. He always brought home strays too. He couldn't let a sleeping dog lie. Whatever he started, he had to finish. You're the same way. I'd be willing to bet that's why Margaret left you."

Suddenly my appetite vanished. I don't think she meant to hurt me with that statement, but it did hurt just the same. "Margaret didn't leave me. She was killed."

Her face turned white as a golf ball fresh out of the package. "I don't know what to say. I mean I didn't even think… and these days, almost everyone is divorcing."

"That's okay. How could you have known what happened? I never kept in touch after that. You certainly didn't need to hear about my problems. You'd had enough."

"Nonsense, we're family. We always wanted to know how you were doing. We loved you."

"I couldn't talk about it at the time."

"We guessed as much and let you be. How did it happen?"

"Well, you know I went into the Air Force. My last hitch was at Barksdale in Shreveport. I liked it there and stayed, kept flying for a while. When I got out, I started working some jobs for a security firm, and I kept pursuing acting. Then, I met Margaret. I guess we'd been married about a year. The acting took off, and I got the talk show." I sipped at my milk, but thoughts of what I'd lost curdled it on my tongue.

"I was still holding down two jobs, trying to save for a house. One rainy night, I was working surveillance at an electronics supply house near the airport. Margaret knew where I'd be. I guess she just wanted to surprise me, bring me dinner. We had enough money for the down payment, and this was my last night of security work. No more two jobs and more time to be together. She was crossing the street and waving one of those old black arch-top lunch pails when a drunk driver came down the block and hit her. I saw it all. Couldn't do a damn thing. I'll hear that sound until I die." There was nothing like the sound of a fender smacking human flesh or of human flesh smacking wet pavement. For night after endless night, that hollow sound, followed by the clatter of a rolling lunch pail, filled my head and hardened my heart."

Aunt Gladys gasped and clutched my hand across the table.

"Oh, Sam." All the sympathy in the world was in those two words and in her eyes.

"After that, nothing mattered anymore. I lost the talk show within four months. It was a local television station. I found the bottom of a lot of bottles." I shrugged. "Eventually, I had to get away from Shreveport. I picked New York because of the Academy and the career. The rest, as they say, is history."

"Did the police ever get the person?"

I wanted to tell her they had, but the truth of the matter was, the police didn't think it was likely they'd ever find a hit-and-run driver, despite my description of the car.

"Nah, they had better things to do." I couldn't meet her eyes.

Aunt Gladys knew I was holding a lot back. One of the things I loved about her was that she always knew when to leave a subject alone. "So, what's going to happen now?"

I looked up at her. "Well, now I'm going to enjoy your company and maybe see some sights. When do we have to be at the lawyer's office?"

"Tomorrow morning at ten. Tell me what you've been up to since you moved to New York."

"I'd rather listen than talk, Aunt Gladys. Tell me what you've been doing."

"Oh, you know, just taking care of your uncle and staying around the house mostly."

"What about your cruise with Beth?" I asked.

"We went to Mexico, but I didn't like it much. As I said, I got seasick. It was hot and humid, and every town was dirty, with worse smog than we have here. I put on five pounds and got out of my exercise habits. Then, I had to get home, discipline myself all over again, and lose five pounds." She sighed. "Guess I'm just not a globe trotter." As she talked, I could see by the look on her face that she was disappointed with her life.

"Aunt Gladys, do you ever regret marrying Uncle Hobart? He wasn't an easy person to get along with. I often wondered why you stayed with him."

"I loved him very much. But you're right he was never a joy to live with, not until he quit the gambling."

"But that was a relatively short time ago, wasn't it?"

She nodded. "Oh, I don't know. I suppose he was sort of like my bad habit. I might have wanted to break it, but I was just too hooked. So, I stayed. Then things got better, and those last years were everything I could have wished for."

"I guess I just wanted to know, if you had it to do over again, would you change anything?"

"I married Hobie and never looked back, especially after you came to us." She smiled. Then, she looked at me and let her eyes sort of slide out of focus. "Oh, there was a time when I wanted to be a dancer. You know, like on Broadway, in musicals."

"No kidding? Did you ever take lessons?"

Suddenly she had this excited look as she spoke. "Sure, when I was a little girl, my mother sent me to a dance school. It was down the street from where we used to live. It was called Madame La Rue's Dance Studio."

"Were you good?"

"Well, I thought I was." As an afterthought, she added, "And so did Madame La Rue. She used to tell Mother all the time that I should go professional. Sometimes I think my mother wanted that more than   I did, but Father wouldn't hear of it. He always thought a woman was supposed to grow up and marry a respectable man and raise a family. That's what women were expected to do back then. So, I met your uncle. We fell in love and got married. But the family never came." She smiled and patted my hand. "Until you were sent out to us."

Aunt Gladys turned and looked at the clock hanging over the doorway. "Land sakes, I didn't realize it was so late. You run off to bed; you must be exhausted. I'll just clean up a bit. See you in the morning. Have a good rest."

As I lay in bed, a lot of things went through my head. I was thinking about Marilyn and the key she gave me. Sooner or later, I would have to tell Aunt Gladys about Marilyn's murder. I just didn't want her to have anything more to worry about at that moment. My conscious mind started losing its memory as my subconscious mind took over. I could see Margaret downstairs in the kitchen with Aunt

Gladys and Uncle Hobart. Aunt Gladys was showing Margaret how to cook meatloaf, and they were all laughing as I entered the room and walked over to Margaret. I put my arm around her waist and kissed her cheek. She smiled and looked at me. My conscious mind had drifted too far to interrupt it with the fact that Margaret hadn't live long enough to meet them.

FOUR

When I awoke, a bird was pecking at my window. A long time ago there had been another bird that pecked on my window every morning at the same time, and I used to call him 'Clock.' I wondered if this was a relative. I could smell coffee brewing downstairs, so I got dressed and went to fill up on life's gasoline for the day.

"Good morning, Sam, did you sleep well?" Aunt Gladys looked rested and pretty.

"Yeah, I guess I was more tired than I thought, but I feel great now."

"Good, I'm glad. I wasn't sure the bed would be comfortable. We replaced it years ago, when we thought about getting a border to help with expenses. Then, your uncle started getting lucky with his investments, so nobody ever used it."

"It was fine."

"Well, sit down, and have some coffee and a doughnut. They're fresh from the store."

As I sat there enjoying a messy cinnamon crumb and coffee, the front doorbell rang. "I'll get it, Sam. Finish your breakfast."

Aunt Gladys returned looking dazed, like she did when I came home after a fight with a wise guy at school and looked like I had lost. Back then, that was usually the case.

"Sam, you're not in any trouble, are you?"

"No, why do you ask?"

"Well, there's a Lieutenant Terrana at the front door. He wants to see you."

The guy was about six foot one. He had a moustache. His wiry build sported a business suit, and he had a spot on his tie that I didn't think would vanish when it dried. Sure enough, it was a cop. I hadn't expected them this soon. Callahan must have had some pull somewhere. I reached my hand out and shook his, "How do you do? I'm Sam Ryan."

"Mr. Ryan, I'm Lieutenant Terrana from Burbank Homicide. A Lieutenant Callahan gave me your name."

"His first name isn't Harry by any chance?"

He didn't crack a smile. Callahan must have loaned him his sense of humor. "I'm here to investigate the murder of Marilyn Williams. You were her traveling companion?"

"No." I didn't think Aunt Gladys could have heard him from her post in the hall, but I didn't want to take any chances.

"No?"

"I wasn't her traveling companion. We shared a table during the lunch rush in the dining car." I looked over my shoulder.

"Will you excuse me for just a minute?" I stepped back into the hall and smiled at

Aunt Gladys. "Okay, thanks, Aunt Gladys. I can handle it from here." She gave me a look that said I owed her an explanation. Then, she grudgingly returned to the kitchen.

"You were saying, Lieutenant?"

"She also came to your compartment for a drink the night she was killed."

"Yes."

"Exactly how did you two meet?" He had to have the report. This must have been the "will-he-tell-the-same-story game."

"I was hungry, and her table was the only one available. The waiter asked her if he could seat me there."

"I see." He made notes. I felt like I was being interviewed by one of those rag magazines. I know he had to ask, but I didn't have to tell him anything extra.

"And what did you talk about?"

"Oh, her job, and I told her about mine. You know, stuffs like that."

"That's right you're a private investigator, aren't you?"

"Part time, when I'm not going on auditions."

"What do you do with the rest of your time?"

"Go to auditions."

"Did she want to hire you?"

"She wasn't a producer. I think she was a model."

He forced a lot of air through his nose rapidly, like a bull warming up to gore a matador. "Did she hire you to investigate something?"

"No." It wasn't exactly a lie. We had decided to talk about her "case" after she'd had some sleep. She hadn't lived long enough to hire me. Somehow, telling him about the key seemed like a betrayal. She would have hired me in the morning, if she'd lived. So, my client confidentiality extended to the grave.

"What is your business out here, Mr. Ryan? I mean, are you working on a case?"

"No. My uncle just died. Here for the funeral." Also, not exactly true since Hobart had already been cremated, but stated baldly enough, funerals generally made people feel a bit nervous and guilty. Then usually went away.

"I'm sorry. I won't take up any more of your time. Let me know if and when you leave town. Will you be staying at this address while you're here?"

"Will do, Lieutenant, and yes, I'll be here."

He smiled, and I could see him checking me out with every agency from New York to Shreveport. "Thank you for your time."

"No problem. Good day." I shut the door behind him and went back to my breakfast. My coffee was cold. Before I could punch the button on the microwave, there was Aunt Gladys, standing in the doorway like a bouncer in a bar. She wasn't going to let me get by until I'd paid the cover.

"I thought you said it was an easy trip. No problems."

I hated getting caught in a lie, even just an evasion, with my aunt. She always made me feel like a wounded animal that just wanted to go off and die somewhere. "Yeah, well, I didn't want you to worry, that's all. How much of that did you hear?"

"Enough. So, what are we going to do about it?"

"Nothing, have a doughnut."

The ride to the lawyer's office was relatively quiet. I kept thinking about how hard this must be for Aunt Gladys. She'd survive; she was tough, but I hated to see anyone I loved go through it.

As we stepped out of the elevator, I saw an attractive receptionist, headset balanced gingerly over her upswept honey hair and typing away as though she had twenty pages of script revisions to get out.

She stopped and looked up. "Can I help you?"

"Yes. We have a ten o'clock appointment with Mr. Firth. My name is Sam Ryan, and this is my aunt, Mrs. Gladys Ryan."

She smiled. "I'll announce you."

As the receptionist led us into Mr. Firth's office, I saw a tidy man in his early to mid-thirties, tall, good-looking, wearing the usual three-piece suit, neatly tailored. "Won't you please have a seat?" he said.

After offers of coffee or tea from the receptionist and the usual polite (mine) and nervous (Aunt Gladys') refusals, he got right down to business.

Suddenly, my ears burned, and my mind did a half gainer. I sat up straighter in my chair and stared at Mr. Firth. It seemed that Uncle Hobart had left me eight hundred thousand dollars. For yours-damned-truly!

Just yesterday, I wasn't sure if I had enough to get back to New York. Now, I could apparently stay and spend as much time with Aunt Gladys as it took to make sure she was all right. Really set.

I hadn't expected Uncle Hobart to have left enough to keep my aunt from having to take a nickel-and-dime job clerking in some store, let alone anything like a fortune for us both, but there it was. Mr. Firth assured me that Gladys was a very wealthy woman, and with his firm's financial management, she was likely to become even wealthier. I shook myself like a dog coming out of a sprinkler and looked at my aunt.

She nodded. "That's the truth, Sam."

Mr. Firth, tactful to the toes of his supple Italian loafers, slipped from the room for a moment.

"Did—did you know about this? I mean hundreds of thousands of dollars?"

She shook her head. "I suspected only because of what Hobie was able to do for me, Sam."

I sat there in total shock. "You're really okay then, aren't you, Gladys?" I finally managed in a raspy voice that wouldn't have gotten me a part as a dying door mouse.

She nodded. "More than all right Sam. Hobie's portfolio was probably worth twice that a while back, and Mr. Firth wasn't joking about his astute financial management. Hobie was only sorry he couldn't get you around the death and inheritance revenues, but he left this for you in his desk."

She handed me an envelope, a large nine-by-eleven job, used, crinkled, with a fresh label pasted over the old one. My name had been written in Uncle Hobart's scrawl. It gave me a painful twinge. I hadn't seen that handwriting in over twenty years; Aunt Gladys had done the corresponding when we wrote each other.

"You have time to open it and go through it here, Sam. Mr. Firth won't be back unless I call him. He was kind enough to let us use his office for a bit." She gestured for me to get started.

My hands shook noticeably as I peeled back the flap.

Inside was a letter from my uncle, the same short-on-words uncle I had known since I was nine. He hoped I was over my 'spot of trouble' and that this would get me underway, tide me over while the feds sorted out his death and their taxes. He was sorry about the taxes.

I felt tears flood my cheeks. He'd signed it love, the word he could never use in daily life—not with me, at any rate. I felt so damn sorry. Survival after Margaret's death had been such a desperate and solitary pursuit. I never knew if it was something atavistic that made me seek out all the loneliest places of the human soul while I tried to deal with the pain, or if she and I had had such a short time together that I wanted to crawl off and hug those few years to me like a lost teddy. Whatever made me feel I had to keep it inside about her death had hurt people who loved me. And they had gone on loving me in spite of myself. I knew Margaret would have been furious with me.

She hadn't had family. She had looked forward to our having enough money and time to come out here, so she could meet mine. Then, she died, and I felt too guilty to cherish the support of the additional thing Margaret had been cheated of besides life, family.

Now, here was Uncle Hobart reaching out a comforting hand from beyond the grave in the only way he knew how, and my beloved Aunt Gladys sat waiting for me to cry out the last of my many regrets and honor her husband by plunging back into life with a real vengeance.

I knew I'd never shut myself off like that again. I got up and threw myself into Aunt Gladys's waiting arms. I blubbered a bit more, and we both said things we should have said long ago, and things I should have said to both of them all along. Then, she gripped my shoulders and insisted I get my "Irish" together and pull up my socks.

"Okay," I grinned at her and swabbed my cheeks dry with a handkerchief. "I've got a great idea, Aunt Gladys. Let's go celebrate, my treat. We can raise a glass to Uncle Hobie."

I could tell by her smile that she approved.

"Where do you want to go? I mean, if you could go to lunch anyplace in town, where would it be?"

I don't think I could have imagined the rosy tint that suddenly colored her cheeks with a girlish glow. "Well, in all the years I've lived out here, I've always wanted to go to the Polo Lounge on Sunset Boulevard. I never told your uncle; Hobie was never much for restaurant food. He loved my cooking, even though it was just plain fare."

"I can't fault him there, Aunt Gladys. You're the best, but I don't want you turning into a galley slave while I'm home." I took a quick count of the bills Uncle Hobart had left to 'tide me over' probate. With Uncle Hobart's idea of 'tiding over,' we could rent the Polo Lounge.

"Okay," I gave her a wink. "Let's stop at home and get dressed up for the occasion."

"I could have afforded to go anytime," she said. "But I always wanted to do that with someone I cared about. Now there's you." Aunt Gladys dimpled like a schoolgirl all the way to the house.

When we arrived at the Polo Lounge, we were seated right away. Aunt Gladys, trim in her navy suit, red silk blouse, and the solid gold door knocker earrings I'd sent her four years ago for her birthday, followed the waitress down the aisle to our table. Margaret had found those earrings and insisted we splurge on family, a magic word to Margaret. It felt just right that part of her was here with Gladys and me. It may have been that moment that I made an inner decision that would affect the rest of my life and change it forever.

As we browsed the menu, I saw just what I wanted, a juicy New York steak.

I looked across at my aunt. "Have you decided yet?"

She nodded firmly. "I decided when we were still back at the house. I'll have a broiled Maine lobster." She winked. "It's the one fancy thing I've been happy to grow accustomed to in recent years."

I reached for her hand across the table and was about to say something when I saw a brisk movement out of the corner of my eye; there stood a drop-dead beautiful cocktail waitress. Naturally, she wore a short dress to show off her long legs. Sometimes, I think restaurant owners push the legs harder than the food. I looked this pair up and down. I'd buy.

"Would you like to order a drink before the meal?" she asked.

After taking our orders for the bar, the waitress turned and left. I watched her walk away. "One of the things I most enjoy about restaurants." I sighed.

Aunt Gladys just shook her head, smiled, and said, "You men are all alike. You're always looking; one track minds."

"Well, I'll tell you something. When I stop looking, check for heart failure."

Aunt Gladys laughed. "Yes, and it will be the looking that causes it!"

I could forgive the raised eyebrow from our approaching waiter — after all I was clutching my heart and looking longingly after the girl with the great legs. I unrumpled the front of my lapel and ordered for us. Obviously, our waiter didn't appreciate good dinner theater.

"And how would you like the steak?"

"I'd like it so that with careful attention, it might survive."

The waiter smiled and said, "Very good, sir." I hadn't a clue as to whether he meant it as a compliment to my line, one of the drawbacks of a live audience. Of course, he could have been stuffed. It's wonderful what they do with automation these days. He turned and left.

"Say, after lunch, I could treat you to a movie."

Aunt Gladys looked at me as if she were deciding whether she could handle all this activity in one day.

"I don't think so. Besides, Mr. Firth said it would be at least a month before all of the paperwork would clear. Remember, you aren't wealthy yet."

Aunt Gladys always knew how to give me a little dose of reality when she thought I needed it. "Okay, you win. We'll enjoy lunch and go home." I had more than enough to get by, but who knew what looking into Marilyn's death would cost? Investigative work wasn't cheap, and I'd be footing the bill for this one myself. I owed Marilyn. At least I felt like I did. Maybe it was just a part of that decision I'd come to, the one I wasn't completely clear about just yet.

The food was almost as delightful as the cocktail waitress, if you believe in comparing apples and passion fruit.

As we were leaving the restaurant, I saw a man standing between two cars about sixty feet down the street from the restaurant entrance.

He was leaning against one of the vehicles. When he saw me looking at him, he busied himself with unlocking a car door. That seemed odd. If the jerk had just kept staring and not looked away so quickly, I might have thought nothing of him. Now, I was going to watch him.

Aunt Gladys hadn't noticed. She was already sliding behind the wheel and putting her purse in the backseat. Just before I climbed in, I turned and looked behind me. I saw the man start his car and wait to pull from the curb.

I didn't want to alarm Aunt Gladys. I watched through the right outside rear-view mirror while she drove. In the sunlight, as close as he occasionally tailed us, I got a better look at his features.

Thin upper lip, sallow skin, maybe Latino ancestry, black hair stuck greasily to his scalp, the length of it held at his nape in a ponytail. His forehead was shallow and his jaw soft. I had no idea about height or weight, but his build was on the slight side. My description wouldn't have got him picked up in an APB, but it would do for a police line-up. The car, a primer gray Nova, lacked a front plate. Probably had a back one obscured with mud or too bent to read, maybe both. It wouldn't fare too well in an all-points bulletin either.

When we pulled into the driveway and got out, Ponytail drove on by and disappeared around the corner before I could confirm any suspicions about the rear plate without making a big deal of it in front of my aunt. I didn't know what Ponytail was up to, but I was sure this wasn't the end of it.

FIVE

The next morning, while I was having my coffee, the same thought kept coming back to me. Why was Ponytail following us last night? I was sure it had to do with the murder or, more specifically, with the key Marilyn had been murdered for.

My first step had to be to find out what the key led to. Probably a locker, but what would be in the locker? While I was deep in thought, the front doorbell rang. Aunt Gladys had just left for the grocery store; maybe she'd forgotten something and didn't want to bother fumbling for the deadbolt key.

When I opened the door, a big hand hit me in the middle of the chest and thrust me back into the hallway. It hit me hard enough to cost me my wind and knock me on my ass.

I looked up to see who this nut case was and found myself looking at a very sharp knife. As my eyes slid down the blade to the handle, I could see the holder of this persuader. Or rather, I could see a ski mask where his face should have been.

The intruder was big and heavily muscled. He was wearing a worn-out pair of buttoned Levi's that looked a size too large and a seersucker jacket over a crewneck tee. If he hadn't been in a crouch, and I hadn't been flat out on the floor and gasping, I could have estimated his height.

"If you're after a lift ticket, you'll have to go down the street to the Sports Chalet," I said, running what I hoped was distraction enough while I collected myself. Through the gaping mouth hole of the mask, I saw the sort of leer that said my attacker was going to enjoy himself.

"We can do it hard or easy. Your choice." The voice was hoarse, that of a two-pack-a-day habit coupled with frequent hard liquor.

"What do you want?" I edged my hands under me for a fast push-off.

He smiled again, "I want whatever that bitch on the train gave you."

First, he barges in uninvited and pushes me on my ass; then he points a pig sticker in my face. Thank God for my Irish temper. I pushed up hard, kicked him in the groin, and laid a right hand against his face as he doubled up to lean into it. He fell back on the floor, dropping the knife.

I was about to reach for that mask, thinking I had time to make a choice between it and the knife. Big mistake, he heeled to his feet, and I began to see the wisdom of those baggy Levi's. As he scrambled for the knife, I kicked at his head the way Pele would a soccer ball. I connected.

The guy had a head like a rock. He went down on one knee, stayed only a moment, and came at me. I made my choice. I kicked the knife into the living room. As he straightened and swung at me, I got a glimpse of his build. He had me by a head, and he had the reach to go with it. I knew this was going to be round two. I didn't know it was going to be so short. He let go with a punch that sent me reeling across the hall and up against the stairs. I got my arms up into a defensive position, but it was like holding off a bull by the tail. He was all over me like pepper on a steak. I felt myself blacking out. Just before I lost consciousness, I heard somebody say, "Hey, what's going on here?" After that, the curtain came down on the scene.

I opened my eyes slowly. I felt like I had been run over by a herd of camels rushing to an oasis for the last of the water. I tried to move and was immediately stopped by a sharp pain in my ribs. I heard someone saying: "He'll be all right. He just needs some rest." I looked up and saw Aunt Gladys and Crazy Joe looking back at me.

I spoke, "Hi Auntie, what's up?" I'd have grinned at her, but that would have been painful with a fat lip.

"You tell me."

I winced. "Would you believe I didn't have change for the paper boy, and he took it out of my hide?" I heard Joe laughing. He had that maniacal laugh Richard Widmark had in the movie where he threw his old wheelchair-bound mother down the stairs.

"Sam, you haven't changed a bit. How are you, old buddy?"

"Not too good at the moment. I feel like a race car laid rubber on my chest."

Aunt Gladys just said, "Who did this?"

I did my best to ignore her. "What brings you around, Joe?"

"Heard, you were in town, so I thought I'd come over and say hello. When I got here, I saw some guy in a ski mask that looked like he played center for the Oakland Raiders using you as a tackling dummy. He took one look and ran past me out the door." He blew on his knuckles and rubbed them against his chest. "Guess I still got it."

"There you are with the ole' maniac look eh, Joe?"

"Whadda you know? You were lying on the stairs doing an imitation of a carpet."

"Yeah, well I felt like it. You didn't get a look at him?"

Joe shook his head. "He just tugged that sucker down harder over his face and took off like O.J. Simpson running through an airport." He squinted at my face.

"I haven't seen you look this bad since we took on the Delgado brothers after they egged Glady's car."

Aunt Gladys had enough of avoiding the issue. "Are you going to tell me what's going on, or do I have to hit you in your other eye?" She wasn't smiling, so I figured I'd tell her the whole story.

"Well, remember the girl I told you I met on the train?"

"Yes, but what does she have to do with all this?"

"Everything, I'm afraid. She was murdered." Aunt Gladys gasped and put a hand to her heart.

I would have to tell her. Tell them, because the visitor had seen Joe and had come to Aunt Gladys' home. It was their business and partly their decision. "The night before it happened, she gave me a key to hold for her and said she would explain everything in the morning."

"And before she could, she was killed?" Aunt Gladys was nothing if not astute.

"If you want me to," I said, watching my aunt intently, "I'll turn it all over to the police. But I feel I owe the woman something. She was going to hire me, and I respect client confidentiality."

Gladys looked at me for a long moment and nodded. "If you would have helped her when she was alive, you can do no less for her now, Sam."

"You got it. The man who was just here said he wanted whatever Marilyn gave me. I don't know if he's the one who murdered her, works for the one who murdered her, or is an independent." I rubbed my jaw. "But he punches like a mule kicks." Joe laughed.

Aunt Gladys spoke, "It looks as though we have ourselves quite a dilemma; what are we going to do?"

"We! No. No, we don't. I do. You two are not going to do anything."

Aunt Gladys gave me that look again. "What are you talking about? He broke into my house."

"Like I said, you're not going to do anything. End of story." She started fixing the bed around me as if I hadn't spoken.

"Okay, if that's the way you feel about it." Somehow, I don't think I got through to her.

"Yes, that's the way I feel about it. I want you to pack some things in a suitcase and go over to a friend's house. That lady you went on the cruise with. Stay there for a few days. I'll call you when it's safe."

"You need my help?" Joe looked like a retriever begging for something to fetch.

Maybe I could have used Joe's help, but I didn't want anyone else mixed up in the matter. These guys were playing for keeps, and it was about time I did too. "That's okay, Joe. I think I'll let the cops take that part of it."

"Oh, Mr. Ski Mask maybe left you a calling card? I mean besides that fat lip and the lump on your thick skull? A name and address you can give them?" Joe challenged.

"Joe, I'll find out who he is and turn him over."

"How you gonna do that? Ask him next time he punches you out?"

"Hey, Joey, I'm a professional investigator. We know how to do this stuff. I promise I'll call if I need you. For now, just stay with my aunt until I get a few winks." I thought about the knife I had kicked into the living room. My head swam when I tried to recall if Ski Mask wore gloves or not. I fingered the cut on my lip. Somehow, I didn't think so.

Joe gave me a mock punch on the shoulder and went off mumbling the way he always had when he didn't like my decisions. "Don't like it. Not one bit, no sir," came drifting back down the hall toward me. Then he was gone.

Aunt Gladys just looked at me as if I were a cop who'd told her she couldn't park in the only available space in the neighborhood. Without saying a word, she turned and walked out of the room.

I got out of bed with extreme difficulty and hobbled downstairs. Gladys was giving Joey coffee and the rest of the doughnuts in the kitchen. There was the knife, right where

I thought it would be. I picked it up in a handkerchief, carried it quietly back up to the bedroom, and tucked it into a dresser drawer. Maybe as good as a calling card Joey, I thought.

I must have dozed off. When I awoke, it was early afternoon. I decided to try to get up. It was worse now that sleep had given my body a chance to stiffen. I knew one thing: The people behind this would try again. What I didn't know was when. I started fumbling my way through my drawers and getting dressed. Joey came up to make sure I was up to defending my aunt and myself. He didn't agree with my affirmative answer, but he left. He and Karen had to take their girls shopping.

Thirty minutes later, I was standing in the middle of the room with my clothes on. I didn't really want to be upright, but with all this coming down I didn't want to be caught with my pants down sort-of-speak either.

I went downstairs to the kitchen. Aunt Gladys was all packed, sitting at the table with her suitcase by her side. She was drinking coffee.

"Any coffee left?"

"Sure, there's some on the stove. Sit down. I'll get it."

"No, that's okay. I'll stand up for a bit. Is everything all right with your lady friend?"

"Yes, I'm waiting for Beth to pick me up I figured you'd be needing the car." Her voice sounded tight, hurt.

"Yes, thanks. I appreciate the loan." I was beginning to feel like a heel, kicking her out of her home and telling her what to do, but I knew it was for her own good. "Look, I'm sorry for the way I talked to you earlier. It's just that this is getting nasty, and I don't want you to get hurt."

"I understand. I don't like it, but I understand. What are you going to do now?"

"Well, when I spoke to Marilyn on the train, she mentioned she worked for a modeling agency in Hollywood. I don't remember the name. Have you got a Hollywood phone directory?"

"Yes, over there in the drawer." She pointed across the room to the China cabinet. Before I could get it, the doorbell rang.

"Hold it, don't move. Let me get it." She sat back down in the chair. I hoped Ski Mask wasn't here for another lift ticket. My gun was assembled and in working order, but I didn't want to upset Aunt Gladys. I waited until I was out of her sight before I slipped it out of the small of my back.

I went to the side window and peeked out. There was a sweet looking lady in her sixties waiting for someone to answer. She was definitely not dressed for the slopes. I stowed the gun.

"It's okay. It's your friend. You are expecting a lady in her sixties, nice smile?"

"Of course, it's Beth." Aunt Gladys shook her head.

I stood through the introductions and watched them leave. Beth was a nice, solid lady. Not flighty. I had a feeling she'd do her best to follow my last-minute instructions. I warned them against opening the door to anyone they didn't know and told them to call the police immediately if anyone suspicious showed up and then call me-too. Cops sometimes take a rather laid-back view of elderly ladies with prowler reports. I wouldn't. I told them about checking under the car, in the back seat, and keeping an eye peeled if they went out and Beth told me they had covered all that in their self-defense class at a Neighborhood Watch meeting they'd attended.

"Maybe you should go to one, Sam."

I knew Gladys had an uppercut behind it, but I fell anyway. Maybe I thought I owed her. "Why?"

"Because you're the one, who opened the door, to that hooligan without looking out the spy hole first."

She pulled her smug look into position and glided out of her door with Beth like the QE2 with a tug in tow.

"Won't happen again, Aunt Gladys," I called after them, properly contrite.

Once they pulled away and I was sure no one had followed them, I flipped through the Hollywood phone directory. I kept trying to pull the name of the agency out of my bruised brain. The pages that listed the modeling agencies were more than a few. I began to leaf through.

As I searched, I remembered that Hollywood was also known as the city of broken dreams, and they mostly started right here under: Agency, Modeling. God, I couldn't believe there were so many other deluded idiots, like me, who would give up a normal life for vague promises of glitter and glamour that might never come true. And what did one put on the bite of the acting bug to relieve the itch? I'd been wondering for years.

After going through what seemed like hundreds of names, there it was in front of me, The Taylor Brown Agency. I could almost see Marilyn's pretty mouth forming the words. It gave me a rough moment but assured me that I was doing the right thing.

I pulled into the self-service aisle of a station and started filling the Mustang's tank. There was a funny little man running around on the full-service side cleaning the windows and checking the oil of the car next to me. I heard him talking to the driver in the other car. I couldn't understand a word he said. He had a thick Latino accent...

Just then, an African American biker pulled into the station behind me. He looked to be about six foot two or three with long black hair pulled into a ponytail. He wore scruffy jeans over motorcycle boots and a denim jacket that looked like it had been through a war. It also probably hadn't been washed since coming home from that war. The jacket had so many patches it looked like a package that had been shipped around the country. One belt loop sported a chain that leashed his wallet. Good thing, because it looked like it was about to fall out of his back pocket. He also had a hunting knife, about ten inches long, in a sheath on his belt. The horn handle ended in a metal wolf's head; teeth bared for business.

He was riding a Harley. I remember I once thought about getting one. There was always that mystique connected to the Harley Davidson machine. It wasn't a bike; It was an institution.

This was a 1982 shovel head, and I loved the color— candy apple red with ghost flames deep beneath the gloss. Some artists had given his all to the rendering. I walked over to it. The flames came and went as my angle on the tank changed. If this guy was from around here, I was sure he would know Hollywood.

"That's a nice-looking bike. It's a '82 shovel head, isn't it?" I said, hoping for a bit of a friendly chat. Maybe it would take that intimidating look off the guy's face. Finally, he spoke.

"Yeah! You have a bike?"

"No, when I was younger, I was a wanna be but never had the money for one."

"Well, they are expensive." His attitude had altered a bit after I'd complimented his bike. "What's your name?"

"Sam Ryan and yours?"

"Lone Wolf."

"You keep a clean bike. I'll bet she runs good."

He got that look fathers get when you say something nice about their children. "Yeah, not like those rice burner bikes. Drink out of it today, ride on it tomorrow."

I laughed. "Yeah, all aluminum I know what you mean." I grinned. "Hey, when I was a kid, I had one of those while I dreamed about one of these," I admitted, trying for just the right amount of mix between embarrassment (over my youth) and envy (over his bike).

"Well, Sam, everyone's entitled to one mistake. This is America, right?" He smiled. Nothing opened enough to show teeth, but it seemed to be a genuine smile. He whipped the gas nozzle from the tank and squinted at the finish to make sure he hadn't dripped. He swiped at the color with the hem of his T-shirt and looked up at me.

"You get a bike, we'll. ride, gotta run."

I felt sincerely complimented and returned the smile. "Hey, can you tell me how to get to Melrose in Hollywood?"

He looked at me like I was the one who was dressed funny. Now that I think about it, I probably was, compared to him. It seemed to take forever for him to decide to answer me. He looked as if he thought I was trying to put him on. "Are you lost, Where you from?"

"New York. I grew up out here, but it's been a long time."

"Well, man, you are gonna need a guide if you get a bike, whereabouts on Melrose?"

I reached into my pocket and drew out the paper with the address, but before I could read it to him, he leaned over and looked at the number. "Okay." He pointed down the street. "Just take the freeway south and get off at Highland. Head down Highland to Melrose and watch the numbers. That's it."

"Thanks."

"No prob."

"Nice talking to you. See you around; I'd like to buy you a drink for your trouble."

"I doubt it, unless you're at a bar called The Place on Pearl off Santa Monica."

"I'll keep that in mind."

"Yeah, do that." He never looked at me as he kick-started his bike and headed out of the station. If he thought he'd never see me again, he was wrong. The actor in me began to rear his head, and I paused for a moment to write Lone Wolf and that self-contained smile down in my notebook and jot the name of that bar. Hey, we Irish pay our debts, especially when we can drink them.

It was nearly three o'clock when I pulled up in front of a big gray building that looked like it was the set of an old movie. The outside was done in Art Deco.

Looking at the Taylor Brown Agency, I knew I was going to have a few props to put anything over on the ladies inside that building, a class act. Most of my props were stashed in my car, which was stashed in a garage in New York while a fellow actor sublet my apartment. No help.

I went over to a phone booth and looked up a print shop, the kind that does business cards in just a few days. I didn't have a few days, but I had an idea.

I strolled into Frogash Printing and inquired about business cards. Then, I made myself such a nuisance that everyone was glad to park me with some sample books in the lobby.

Eventually, I found a sample business card for a photographer that Frogash had done in the past. The problem was the name. I just didn't look like a Langhorn Dabney Lewis the third. Yet, it could work.

I pulled the card free from the mounting and tucked it into my pocket. Then, I lugged the sample books to the desk and thanked them for their help. They didn't shed any tears at my lack of an order, another advantage of starting out as a pest.

On my way back to the agency, I stopped at a camera supply shop and a men's shop. At the haberdashery, I bought a subtle ascot and matching handkerchief for show. I selected a patterned dress shirt just subtle enough to look a bit effete when matched with my jacket.

In the dressing room, I changed into the shirt and combed my hair with a low side part and some greasy kid stuff to slick it down and darken it. That was the look: slight curls subdued with gunk. I tweaked one free here and there.

I took the matching handkerchief and folded it into my breast pocket with a small packet of photographer's lens paper arranged to fall out at the first opportune flourishing, if necessary.

A Nikon lens cover went into my jacket pocket for the same reason, and I practiced several vocal affectations, settling on a slightly Southern, and upper-class, accent to go with the name.

I was sure that my acting coach would be proud of my ability to develop such a well fleshed-out character with such a limited amount of time, investment, and research. But I know he wouldn't have been pleased that the result of all his careful training was crass chicanery. Oh, well, you use what you've got.

In the parking lot, I added a very thin, slightly drooping moustache, carefully applied with spirit gum. Done right, the hairs look individual, and it's as if you just miraculously sprouted them from your upper lip in the blink of an eye. It was just enough Tennessee Williams to be convincing.

I parked in front of the agency and went inside. The secretary at the front desk looked up. "Can I help you?"

I presented my card. I had neatly penned in my aunt's telephone number and lined out the printed one. "My name is Langhorn Lewis. I'm a photographer, and I'm looking for a model for a shoot."

She stared at the card. There was always that moment when you hoped the card you'd used wasn't from some extremely prominent and recognizable professional, someone you obviously weren't. "Did you have anyone in particular in mind?" Apparently, I'd passed. Samples were almost never genuine.

"Yes," I said drawling slightly. "I'm looking for a Ms. Marilyn Williams."

The receptionist's face blenched until she reminded me of one of those actors I'd seen in Kabuki theatre during my duty tour in Japan. She spoke very slowly, "Have you worked with her before?" She looked as if she might be starting to doubt my identity.

I pulled the handkerchief free and waved it without using it for anything other than to fan my face a little. "So beastly out there today. What would we do without refrigerated air?" As planned, the packet of lens paper fell directly in her line of sight. I pretended not to notice and let her retrieve it for me. I wanted her to get a good look for my dollar.

"Mr. Lewis?" She handed me the packet.

"Thank you." I blotted, refolded, and pocketed both papers and the hanky, and then I fixed her with a hopeful and expectant stare.

She leaned over an intercom. "Mr. Brown? A Mister—" She checked the card and still said it wrong. "Mister Langhorn Dabney Lewis wants to see you. He's a photographer. He wants to use Marilyn Williams."

She obviously knew that Marilyn was dead. Why else would she look like Casper the friendly Ghost FG?

It wasn't long before Mr. Brown appeared, and she handed him my card. The man with her was dressed like a used car salesman. He stood about five ten and was the right weight for his size. He looked credible enough, but I wouldn't have bought a bicycle from him. Something about his expression gave him a nervous look when he smiled. Clothes may make the man, but it's the smile that gives him away.

"Mr. Brown." I leaned over as I shook his hand and pointed at the first name on my card. "That's Langen." I said, glancing compassionately at the receptionist without obscuring the condescension, a look I'd perfected for an audition as Oscar Wilde in the throes of his famous court trial.

"A family name. The 'horn' is silent."

He looked a bit taken aback. Good, I wanted him off balance. "Fine, Mr. Lewis. Won't you come into my office?"

The decor matched the outside, early Hollywood pictures of old movie stars on the wall, my favorite of Monroe almost holding her billowing white skirt down — a big leather swivel chair behind a wide dark oak table, and a pair of nouveau lamps that resembled leaping fish in frosted pink glass. Some, very nice Lalique renderings of ladies as metamorphosing dragonflies and wood nymphs. I do appreciate Lalique, thanks to Margaret, and I suddenly wondered, with a considerable pang, what had become of the little glass dish I had given her for our second anniversary: Lalique crystal with a repeat of sparrows or some such in relief around the boarder. The sort of thing I was only just beginning to be able to afford for her.

Mr. Brown wrenched me from my thoughts. "Please, have a seat, Mr. Lewis." He tucked my card in the desk blotter's leather corner. It gave me time to pull myself back into character. Real-life personal observations could be the swan song of character continuity.

I sat and watched as he walked around to the other side of the table.

"Now, how can I help you?"

It had been a while since I'd been in the photographer/model role. I hoped I would remember how. "I'm just in from New York. I've written a local number on my card, and I'm looking for a model that typifies Hollywood for one of my clients. They want to do a tourist-type layout for a new slick. It could be a possible back cover, maybe a foldout just inside the front cover. See Hollywood,' etcetera, you know, that sort of thing."

"Do you know Ms. Williams?" He looked at me for a moment as though he was deciding if I was legit or not.

"Not really. I met her recently in Chicago." He flinched. "She recommended your agency. I thought she'd be perfect for the job."

After a moment, he spoke. "Well, she's not available just now, out of town job."

"I'm sorry to hear that." The look on his face said he didn't expect I'd be able to wait for her to return.

I continued, "Well, she did mention that her roommate got her on with your agency. From the wallet photo Marilyn showed me of them, the roommate could be an alternate for this job." I tried a combination look: aggravated and distressed. "I just can't recall her name or enough to give you a good description." I looked apologetic. "I was concentrating on Marilyn. Such great bone structure. But I'm sure she said you handled them both." I gave him a smile, "Very happy with your representation. Thrilled, in fact, with the cover work you sent her way." Good, just the hint of the effete. He cringed off balance again.

Mr. Brown leaned over his intercom. "Get me a file on Marilyn Williams's roommate, will you Maureen?"

"Yes, right away Mr. Brown." I noticed he didn't have to use a name for Maureen to know who he meant. I guessed the roomie must have been thrown into the spotlight along with her murdered friend. It was more proof they all knew about it and was keeping it quiet.

"How long do you plan to be out here, Mr. Lewis?"

I pulled a pocket calendar from my breast pocket and consulted it while I pressed a frown into my forehead. "I'm only here until this coming Wednesday. Then, I catch a plane back to New York."

Mr. Brown smiled, a smile that told me not to take any bicycles from him. "How unfortunate, Miss Williams won't return in time."

He seemed so smug. I couldn't help myself. "When is she due in? Perhaps I can juggle my schedule?"

He looked a shade paler and two inches thinner, "I'm sure I recall that she was booked solid through the end of the month. She is one of our most popular girls."

I tried on an accommodating look. "I'd certainly prefer to stick with the agency Marilyn recommended so highly." There was no harm in appealing to his spirit of competition.

"Maureen, bring any files for similar types, will you?" He clicked off his intercom with something approaching irritation, and I knew the reluctant suggestion of my being forced out to another agency had touched a nerve.

The receptionist came in with a thick file and an office portfolio and put them on Mr. Brown's desk. She leaned close to him. If something wasn't going on between those two, I'd eat my new ascot.

"Mr. Brown, Ms. Pittman is back from her shoot, should I send her in?" she asked softly.

"Give us a few minutes, Maureen."

He showed me some stunning pictures of Marilyn's roommate, and after what seemed like an interminable amount of time, the door opened and a stunning, well-dressed woman about my height walked in. I stood up.

"Debbie Pittman, I would like you to meet Mr. Langhorn Lewis." I had to give him credit. He said it correctly…must have learned from poor Maureen's mistakes. "He's a New York photographer."

I walked up to her as she looked at me and held my hand out. I felt as if I was about to give an oral report, and she was the grammar schoolteacher. Of course, they didn't look like that when I was in school. They probably still don't. "How do you do? It's so nice to meet you." She flashed a picture-perfect smile and tilted her head to show off her cheekbones. She looked a little like those models that had their molars pulled to create appropriate hollows. I looked for spaces at the back of her smile, but there weren't any. Guess her "hollows" were the real thing.

Her hair was jet black and bobbed. She wore a black jumpsuit with thin little straps and a wide red belt. Dynamite, she arranged herself in the best light of the room.

She was non less than I would have expected. Actors were also trained to upstage everyone and grab the best position in any grouping-one that, preferably, displayed one's most photogenic side and to pose, pose, pose. Jobs could be anywhere, along with potential employers. Even candid or tabloid photos should be a marketable asset

"I believe I would like to use you for a shoot," I said, squinting at her and moving around in a half-circle. "We could probably do it in one day."

"You two can use my office. I'll have Maureen draw up the necessary papers when you're ready. Now if you will excuse me." He left.

Debbie walked over to the window and looked out, pausing in the nearly perfect light. Then, she turned and asked, "Why me, Mr. Lewis? I don't know you. Not many photographers ask for a model by name when they haven't worked with her before."

She was sharp, very sharp. Or else, the recent trouble with her roommate had honed her senses. "May I call you Debbie?" I dreaded this next move, but I couldn't see any other way. Her antennae were definitely up and twitching.

"If you wish."

"Debbie. I'm not really a photographer; I was a friend of Marilyn Williams. She gave me your name." I waited a minute and watched her expressions run from startled, to hurt, to angry, and back to control. She had an excellent non-verbal range. When I saw she wasn't going to bolt or yell for Mr. Brown, I continued. "I met her on the train the night she was killed. I'm a private detective."

She looked hurt and angry again, but I didn't think either emotion had anything to do with me. Shows how wrong I can be if I set my mind to it. "Mind if I smoke?" she asked.

"No, of course not." What nonsense. Of course, I cared if she committed slow suicide in front of me, but I had pushed it as far as I was going to. "My name's not Lewis."

She smiled. "Not Langhorn Dabney?" She pronounced it correctly and looked at me with a questionable look as she dug for a crumpled pack of something with "slim" in the brand name. "What a shame. It has a ring."

I smiled back. "Yes. But it's Sam. Sam Ryan."

"No ring." She'd meant it to hurt. She clicked a slender gold lighter to life and puffed.

"Not exactly 'tintinnabulation,' but I like it." I wasn't thin-skinned.

I could see her eyes were watering as she lit up, and I didn't think it was the smoke. "I told the police everything I know."

"When was the last time you saw Marilyn alive?" She started to pace back and forth, puffing on the cigarette like it was an oxygen mask.

"Look, I can't talk to you here, but if you come over to my apartment, say, around eight tonight."

"Of course, I understand."

"No, you don't, but you will. I'll just tell Mr. Brown I'm not really the type you had in mind for the shoot after all." As she spoke, she picked up a pen and piece of paper from Brown's desk and wrote her address and phone number. "I'll see you at eight." She closed the office door firmly behind her.

After about a minute, Mr. Brown returned. "I'm sorry Ms. Pittman isn't right for you. Perhaps one of our other models…" He gestured at photo book on the table and edged it toward me, fractionally.

"Let me think about it." I shook hands with him and looked at my watch and spoke, "Sorry, I don't have time to go through your book just now."

As I left his office and entered the lobby, I could see a throng of beautiful models waiting there. I hadn't seen so many attractive women in one room since my last audition for a romantic role, which I didn't get. I guess they were all waiting to be discovered. I felt a little cheap when they all gave me that dog-hoping-for-a-bone look, and I was more than a little sorry for them all. I'd been there. Occasionally, I was still there.

SIX

As I turned down Debbie's Street, I checked the time. It was a little before eight. In some areas, Burbank looked more residential than Glendale. The streets were lined with palm trees. It was going to take me awhile to get used to that.

There was a big difference between these streets and the ones in Brooklyn. I was used to seeing streets lined with uncollected garbage, dented cars, and scruffy kids leaning on the fenders or playing stickball. I was pretty good at stickball as a kid: choosing up sides, using the sewer covers for home and second, using car fenders for first and third. God, that solid feeling of success when you connected with the ball and watched it go Success was so much simpler then.

I found a parking place almost directly in front of Debbie's apartment. Something else to get used to in L.A.— being able to use a car and being able to park it most of the time, for free. I went inside, found her name, and pressed the button on the security system. Debbie inquired and then buzzed me in, her voice cut to ribbons by the tinny intercom.

As I walked through to the elevator, I noticed the lobby had wall-to-wall mirrors and fake flowers everywhere. There was music playing as I stepped onto the elevator and pushed the button for the floor.

I don't know why they go up so slowly. Maybe they don't want to give the more elderly tenants vertigo. I thought about how Debbie would have to take Marilyn's name off the mailbox. Someone would have to pull those little white plastic press-in letters out of the corrugations in the dark green register in the front hall.

I knocked at 2C.

"Come in, Mr. Ryan. I'll be with you in a minute," she called.

I entered and nearly collided with a huge statue of Buddha. The living room was all red, black, and gold. I sat down on a straight-backed lacquer chair.

Debbie came out of another room wearing a tank top and a pair of old jeans. As ratty as the jeans looked, it still seemed as if she were modeling them, something about the walk.

She looked great, but she wore a serious expression. I knew this wasn't going to be easy.

"What would you like to drink?" she asked. She stared at my much different costume and the lack of fuzz on my upper lip. "Oh, you're good, Mr. Ryan, Very good."

"I usually drink Irish whiskey, but a Scotch-and-water will do nicely." I hadn't thought it necessary to keep up the charade of the effete photographer, nor was an explanation in order. Coming clean with her in the office should have been enough.

She ran a nervous hand through her short black hair, and I saw her fingers shake a bit. "No Southern accent either." It wasn't a question. She smiled as she moved behind the bar, but the feeling I got from those bared teeth wasn't friendly. "Mr. Ryan, how did you meet Marilyn?"

The bar was built-in and had a bamboo front that almost went with the Oriental furnishings. She slopped Scotch into a glass.

"The waiter put us together in the dining car, because there were no empty tables." She handed me my drink without wiping the outside of the glass and sat on the couch across from me. I whipped out my handkerchief and continued: "We had dinner and talked about L.A.," I said, blotting the booze from my fingers and the hexagonal crystal.

"I see. Did you sleep with her?"

I was in the middle of swallowing when she said it, and I almost lost a full mouth of Scotch to the front of my jacket. "Why do you ask that?"

She gulped down her drink and made another. It looked like vodka, straight shots. "You wouldn't be the first." She was getting more upset by the minute. "She's done it before. She was nothing but a common whore. We were lovers, Marilyn and I. Did you know that?"

As opened-minded as I liked to think I was, some male-chauvinist part of me was thinking, "What a waste." I wasn't expecting it, but I tried not to show my surprise. "I didn't know. I'm sorry for your loss. And, for the record, I didn't sleep with her. She asked for my help."

"Shit." I couldn't tell if she meant it as a denial or an apology. Her body started to shake as she sloshed more liquor into her glass and downed it. Tears rolled over her cheeks, like water off a newly waxed car. I didn't come here to upset her, and I wasn't so sure that I'd triggered all this. I wanted a second Scotch, but Debbie looked less like a hostess by the minute.

As soon as I got up to help myself, I knew I was in trouble. Suddenly, I felt dizzy. When I looked at her again, the tears were still there, but she had this unforgiving smirk on her face. Like all of it was my fault.

I felt weak. I tried to walk to the door, but my knees felt like wet cement in a downpour. Next thing I knew, I was on the floor. My mind started failing.

The last thing I remember thinking was that the bitch had put something in my drink, and I was going on a trip without my luggage.

I was awakened by a familiar, rhythmic sound, and my body was vibrating all over. I wasn't sure what it was at first. It could have been Magic Fingers for all I knew; reality was lost in a drug-hazed oblivion. I opened my eyes. I could see the sun moving through the cracks of the ceiling. Somebody put in another quarter, and I lost some more of my life to oblivion before I finally pushed back the haze once and for all.

This time, when I looked around, I could see I was inside a boxcar. I wasn't alone. There were two other people with me. Let's just say they were a far cry from my last train companion. They eyed me with no more affection than I did them as I pushed myself to a sitting position and felt the car reel more than mere steel tracks could account for.

The train was slowing down, maybe getting ready to stop. I got up, and my head was pounding like the jackhammer under my window in New York.

I held my hand to my head, hoping the pounding would ease, hoping to hold the damn thing in place. I went to the door and tried to open it. It was stuck on its tracks.

Then I finally managed to slide it back a bit, the noise and vibration almost derailed my head from my shoulders. The train was slowing but showed no signs of stopping as it edged on through a small town. The two other people in the boxcar just sat there watching me. They were professional riders, Hoboes. "Anyone see who put me aboard?"

One man shrugged. The other played with the loose flap of his sole and ignored me.

"You here when I came on?" I had to try. The one who'd shrugged shook his head.

"Did he come on with you?" I gestured at the sole-slapper.

A nod so much for clues. As subtly as possible, I checked my pocket. If they came on after me and thought I was just asleep, that must be why I still had my wallet. They were old and battered and hadn't known my drug-induced sleep would have given them all the physical edge they'd have needed.

"Does this train stop soon?" Another shrug.

I looked out the door as a sign thanking me for visiting Los Osos slid past. The whistle sounded like fingernails on the chalkboard of my soul. Maybe it would start to pick up speed soon. I took a deep breath and jumped.

I'm getting too old for this, I thought, as the force of the train still moving forward slammed me into the ground. I hadn't had that kind of fall since I played football in high school. It was falls like this that made me quit long before I got into college ball. I did remember my training and rolled with it, which prevented me from breaking anything, but not by much.

I stayed still for a moment and waited for everything to stop throbbing. Once I knew there was absolutely no likelihood of that happening, I got up slowly and dusted myself off. At least now, my body matched my head: they both hurt. This was not my idea of travel. The service was lousy, my head was killing me, and they didn't even change the linen. Somebody was going to pay for this trip. Speaking of which, I checked my wallet more carefully now.

Why hadn't Debbie rolled me? Maybe she hoped I was dead and wanted someone to be able to identify my body for burial, such a considerate girl.

Somehow, I couldn't see Debbie endangering a nail to haul heft me out of her building herself, so she would have had a partner. Of course, I hadn't pegged her for being likely to dope me either, so maybe I was wrong again. Maybe she was a weightlifter and tossing my body around like a sack of meal was no big thing to her. She certainly had been in shape. God, the questions alone could make my head throb, and it needed no help.

As I looked around, I could see some buildings up ahead. I started walking toward them, and every step brought a vibration to a different part of me. All I could think about was getting a cup of coffee and shaking out some cobwebs.

The restaurant was almost empty. I sat on a stool at the counter. There were a few people sitting in the back booth, laughing and talking. My head wished they would stop.

"Can I help you?"

The waitress was standing there ready to write. She looked to be in her mid-thirties. She had on one of those ugly uniforms that most waitresses hate to wear, because macho bosses picked them out. The skirt was about mid-thigh length, the kind she had to keep pulling down because it rode up whenever she did any reaching or bent over. It had food stains on it.

There was a little seedy-looking man standing behind the register. He was probably the boss, and I'd have bet he was just waiting for her to reach or bend. "Yes, please. I'll have a cup of coffee and some toast." She smiled. It would have been a pretty smile, but her teeth were chipped badly in the front. Despite that, she was probably a pretty good-looking woman when she set her mind to it. A smidgen overweight, but all the excess was in the right places.

She poured me some coffee as she spoke, "Toast will be up in minute."

"Thanks. Is there a bus station around?"

"Sure, right down the street on your left." She pointed.

"Do you have a pay phone?"

"Yes, in the back." She pointed again and walked away.

I called Aunt Gladys at Beth's house. She picked it up on the first ring.

"Hello? Aunt Gladys?

"Where in the Sam Hill are you? I've been worried sick."

"I'm fine. I'm in a town called Los Osos."

"What the heck are you doing up there?"

"I'm not quite sure. Look, I'm going to catch a bus back, and I should be home late this afternoon. I'll answer all of your questions then."

"Where is my Mustang?"

"Parked in Burbank, it's okay. I'll see you later, don't worry." I hung up before she could throw a tantrum and went back to my toast.

A tall slim gentleman came in the front door wearing a uniform that advertised a lean gray dog. He removed his hat and walked up to the counter, leaned across it, and gave the waitress's butt a friendly slap.

"Hiya, Sadie. How are things going?"

She never moved. She reacted as if he had done it many times before.

"Mac, you know I don't like that."

I got up from my end of the counter and walked over to the driver. "There a bus going to Burbank?"

"Sure thing, and I'm driving her. We're leaving in about thirty minutes. I can take your money on the bus."

"Great." I sat back down and finished my coffee and toast. I was still hungry, so I asked the driver the fare and figured I had enough on me for a hamburger and a shake. I ordered and sat back to wait.

When the bus pulled out, the buildings blurred past by my window, and the town disappeared. I wasn't sorry to see it go.

I tried putting the pieces together again. Debbie had some answers, and I wanted them. My head felt better, and I had half a chance at a thought pattern. Why did Debbie do this? What was she hiding? I kept seeing those tears, than her sadistic smile as I took that nose-dive to the carpet.

My thoughts wandered; I watched the scene outside my window change as trees and part of the Pacific Ocean passed by. I didn't know what was going on, but I was going to find out.

SEVEN

W hen I reached the place where I'd left Aunt Gladys's car, I found the building swarming with police. I started to get into the Mustang, but I had the troublesome feeling that this was my business. I walked up to the cop standing by one of the patrol cars. "Can you tell me who's in charge here?"

"That tall man, over there with the shades. The one talking to the uniforms. That's Lieutenant Terrana from homicide."

Oh, yes, Terrana. I walked toward him. Jesus, my troubles were just starting. If the victim in the body bag was, as I suspected, Debbie Pittman, I knew that unless her killer had given her time to do the dishes, my fingerprints were on at the least one of the glasses in her sink.

I couldn't help but notice that one of the two uniforms was a woman. I can be swift when I have to. Besides, the closer I got, the better she looked. The two medics wheeled the gurney past me as I gawked at her. I turned my attention to the body I hoped was not Ms. Pittman. I had to know for sure. I spoke to one of the medics, "Hold up there!" I tried to sound officious enough to merit compliance. As I reached for the zipper, I heard a familiar voice.

"Can I help you, Mr. Ryan?"

Damn Terrana's shades didn't dim his powers of recognition.

I turned and saw him glaring right at me. The glasses were in one hand, and he was swinging them by the stem. "Possibly," I said, trying to come off as casual as he was. "But maybe I can be of more help to you."

"You know something about this?" The look on his face told me that despite the "I'm cool" attitude, he wasn't in any mood to hear flippant dialogue. Besides, the glasses hung motionless now.

"Well, to tell you the truth, I came by to pick up my aunt's car." Hoping he didn't want to know why my car just happened to be parked here without me, I continued. "Do you mind if I look?" I gestured at the bag.

"Why? You have a passion for dead bodies?" His smile was ugly, and it wasn't from a lack of orthodontia in his youth.

"No. If my hunch is right, this is Marilyn's roommate."

He nodded at the paramedics. "Maintenance man found the body when he came to fix the toilet this morning. It seems she called him for an appointment last week to fix the toilet."

"Building maintenance is more efficient out here, eh?" He gave me a look that told me he'd never been in a pleading quarrel with a New York building super. "What time was that?"

"Eight thirty a.m. Time of death about nine thirty last night."

I pulled down the zipper and she had unsaw the icy stare that told the living the dead had crossed over. It was Debbie all right. She had a knife wound in her chest, just one. Her killer hadn't fumbled around, nor had he been in a rage. It was a neat, cold kill, nothing like what Marilyn's must have been. Maybe she'd convinced them she didn't know anything. Maybe they hadn't cared if she did or not.

"Did you know her too?" He slid the "too" in like a blade. I ignored it. "No. I met her yesterday for the first time. Like I told you, I encountered Marilyn briefly. I came over to talk to Debbie about her roommate."

"What for? It's an open police case, Mr. Ryan. L.A.P.D. is on it courtesy of,", he checked his notebook, "Lieutenant Callahan." I was fairly sure he hadn't really had to check that notebook. More window dressing, the shades hung by one stem from his breast pocket.

I smiled and said, "Ah yes, Colorado's answer to Mr. Holmes." "I get the idea that you don't like him."

I knew that smile. I'd run into it before. Just then, I thought Lieutenant Callahan had loaned it to him. I didn't like it on either one of them. "Let's just say I wouldn't pal around with him and leave it at that."

He relaxed a bit. "Okay, take her away. So, tell me, Mr. Ryan, what did you find out last night?"

"She makes a terrible drink." I hadn't noticed it before (probably the lack of good lighting on my aunt's front porch), but his eyes were this pond-scum brown-green color. I half expected to see slime drip from the corner of his eyes.

"What do you mean by that?"

"Nothing." Just then, the pretty, uniformed policewoman came over to us.

"Lieutenant, everything's just about wrapped up here. The lab boys are still upstairs."

"Oh, by the way, Ryan, you said you were picking up your aunt's car?" I saw a ripple beneath his eyes. Those fish were in there somewhere. I should have known.

"I left it here last night."

He had a grin on his face. "Run out of gas, Sam?

I just looked at him. He'd borrowed Callahan's sense of humor, all right. "No, she got fresh, and I walked home."

The pond iced over. "Give your statement to Officer Kelly. You can sign it later." Turning to the pretty brunette, he said, "Take down the info on Mr. Ryan. I'll want to talk to him again." He started to walk away. "I'm not going to have to remind you about working on anything related to an ongoing police investigation, am I, Mr. Ryan?" He didn't wait for my answer. He just kept walking.

I've seen a lot of pretty women, but never in L.A.P.D. navy. Officer Kelly looked out of place. The chauvinistic that I was, she looked as though she should be on television or out surfing someplace, not involved in a murder. "So, what do I call you, Miss?"

She looked at me straight-faced. "You can call me Officer Kelly, Mr. Ryan." Her pen was poised over her notebook. "Now, phone number and address?"

"Do we have to be so business like? Don't you have a first name?" She looked up. Her eyes were the shade of emerald. There was no pond water in them, just spring leaves, rainforests, and everything hopeful.

"I'm sorry, Mr. Ryan, but this is business. It's a murder case, not a cocktail party."

I wondered if she was as serious off duty. I clutched my hope, which was beginning to swirl in steadily decreasing circles like disappearing dishwater and tried again. "Are there any cocktail parties coming up that we could attend? There's gotta be one going on somewhere in this town." She took in a deep breath, "Church social?" I stammered on.

Finally, I gave her my best side and my best smile. She seemed to relax a little and said, "Maybe, but not today. Your number and address?"

I gave her the information and my slightly abridged version of the story. She jotted notes in the neat, square printing of someone who'd studied drafting in high school. She looked up sharply when I got to the part about hitting the floor and waking up in a boxcar.

"I hear Los Osos is lovely this time of year," she said, fighting to keep from laughing.

"And me without my tennis racquet."

She laughed. "Do you play?"

I shook my head. "Not tennis. You?"

"My father and I used to volley a bit, but these days, I don't have much free time."

She went back to more serious questions, and long before we were finished, I knew I had to see her again. She was too interesting to let go, and far too beautiful. "Will you have dinner with me tonight?"

She looked at me for a while, and I saw a hint of a smile as she spoke. "I don't know; are you safe? I mean, will I have to call for back up?"

I grinned. "Probably not, I'm new in town. I'm not familiar with all the good mugging spots."

She laughed openly at that, pulling out all the stops and filling the air with the sound of fun. "I really don't know you, Mr. Ryan."

"What better way for a Ryan and a Kelly to get acquainted than over a lovely dinner?" I said pouring on the brogue and trying to cut her off before her refusal could work up any ring of finality.

She stopped printing in her notebook and stared at me for a long quiet moment. "I could start by pulling your rap sheet."

"Actors don't have rap sheets. They have credits. I'll tell you mine over dinner."

Her eyes searched mine, probably for any hint of degeneracy. "I thought you were a private detective."

"That's what I do. What I am is an actor."

"You mean you're adept at handing out a line?" She smiled as she said it, but I was sure it was a case of kidding on the square. I get that a lot. Women think if you're in theater, you must not be capable of an honest emotion.

"When it's just a line, I get paid to say it. No one's hiring me to ask you out, Officer Kelly." I didn't have to be an actor to look hurt and a little offended. There was an edge to my words I didn't have to put there. Like I say, I get that a lot.

She softened. "That was uncalled for. I'm sorry. Sometimes my sensitivity is completely overridden by my love of a great comeback." She smiled, and I melted.

"Apology accepted, if you'll let me take you to dinner."

"Is the brogue real?"

I nodded. "Took years with a dialogue coach to smother it and it didn't quite get it all."

She flipped to a clean page and printed her address and phone number in that brisk, unfeminine hand. She was wearing a gun on her hip, cuffs on her belt, a night stick, a radio, and God only knew what else. I know I spied mace as she turned away. I made a mental note probably for our date.

"Pick me up at eight thirty, Mr. Ryan." She walked away. "I share a house with my father. He's L.A.P.D., retired."

The words drifted back over her shoulder and pushed it into my brain. I understood that wink. I'd have to pass more than her muster. "Eight thirty Officer Kelly."

"Kathy." She didn't even turn to look longingly at me. When I got back to the house, I heard a noise coming from the kitchen. I thought maybe Ski Mask had come back for seconds. Just what I needed after a damaging ride in a boxcar— more bruises. I crept quietly upstairs to get my gun and came back down the hallway with it in hand. I peeked around the jamb.

There was Aunt Gladys, standing by the stove. I was relieved but angry that she hadn't stayed at Beth's. "What are you doing here?" I said, sliding the gun into my waistband.

At my first word, in one motion, faster than I would have believed in a woman of her years, she simultaneously grabbed a knife from the stove top, screamed with karate-like vigor, and turned on me. She stopped just short of my stomach, knife out in front of her like a samurai.

"Sam!" she said, relaxing her stance. "What are you trying to do? Scare the bejesus out of me?"

I took the knife from her hand and set it back on the counter. As a woman living alone, she had acquired an unusual set of survival skills. While she might have fended off the casual intruder, Ski Mask would have laughed and killed her with her own kitchen tool.

"I told you to stay clear of this place for a while. I don't want you to get hurt."

"I was worried about you, Sam. Los Osos? What if you needed a doctor or a ride to the hospital?"

"I don't, and you're outta' here. Come on." I grabbed her arm and marched her to the car. "Where does Beth live? I'm driving you."

"It's just a few blocks. I can walk."

I started the car. "Tell me where to turn." Aunt Gladys sat there with a hurt look on her face while I took enough extra turns to assure me, we weren't being followed. I hadn't meant to be so hard on her. "I'm sorry, I didn't mean to yell. It's just that things could get worse around here, and I don't want you in the middle of it all."

"I just want to help."

"Well, if you really want to help, stay put this time. I'll let you know when it's safe to come home." I gave her a kiss on the cheek and helped her out of the car. "I love you." It was way overdue, that phrase. Somewhere around my late teens, I'd quit using it until I'd met my wife.

She reached up and hugged me hard. "I know, Sam." I watched until she was safe inside and waving from Beth's front window.

The house seemed dead without Aunt Gladys bustling around in it. Better a dead house… I thought, remembering what a close call it had been with Ski Mask. What if it had been Aunt Gladys who had walked in on that fight instead of Joe? I poured myself some coffee. Just thinking of it made me shake like a tambourine in the hands of a gypsy. Eyeing what was left in the fridge, I heard a cheer from my midsection. Nope.

I'd been eating too much on this trip. Pretty women of all ages and the lure of good restaurants always did it to me. I thought fondly of the New York steak I'd had with Aunt Gladys and wondered about tonight's dinner plans. From what I could see of Kathy in uniform, unless she made this dinner an official meeting and kept to her blues, I'd probably never notice what was on my plate.

I needed to do some thinking, and about more than just Kathy in street clothes. My thinking was always much clearer when I was running.

I changed into a pair of shorts and a sweatshirt. I had a few hours before I had to spruce up for my date, so I went to my old stomping grounds in Venice.

I've always liked to run somewhere interesting because I really hate almost all forms of exercise. Fortunately, the sights in Venice are so totally engrossing that they take my mind off of the fact that I'm doing something good for me.

In New York, running north along Central Park East made exercise more palatable. The horse-drawn carriages and the wilderness look of the park on one side contrasted so sharply with the traffic noise and the elegant residences on the other, that it kept me just off-balance enough to forget the repetitive ache as the soles of my Nike's slapped the cement, an ache that transferred all too quickly to my forty-four-year-old knees. It was particularly hard on the knee I torqued sliding through the wet Louisiana streets while chasing after the car that hit Margaret so many years ago. Usually it would take something outrageous— a purple-clad velour and satin pimp jaunting past the Guggenheim— to take my mind off that.

Within half an hour, I was following the winding path that paralleled the Venice scene. It was one place that hadn't changed much since the last time I'd been in L.A. I could hear the raucous battle of differing music whipping by on shouldered ghetto blasters cranked to deafening decibels-a fortune teller in a swirl of colors was crooning to some tourist that she was going to meet someone on her vacation.

The barkers pushed their wares as I jogged along trying to ignore the starting stitch in my side telling me I had been lazy for too long. I breathed deeply and stretched into the pain.

The stitch was finally fading, and my stride was settling into a comfortable length and pace. I had just passed by the Sidewalk Cafe and the Old World Book Store when I saw three rough looking characters, who quite obviously were not shopping for the latest best seller. They were watching me. I jogged on, hoping they were just impressed with my discipline and fine form. Maybe, I postulated, I was one of the interesting sights that had brought them to Venice.

They started walking along the bike path that paralleled the beach. They kept up with me. Not a good sign. They talked and stared. They moved closer. I picked up my pace. They did too. I began to feel like Henry Fonda in the Last of the Mohicans. This was feeling like forever already. Curly, Moe, and Larry were definitely gaining. I pushed for some more speed and turned to see how the Stooges were doing. Unfortunately, there were only two. That was worrisome, but not as worrisome as finding out what had happened to number three.

As I tried to scan the beachfront crowd for the missing stooge and still keep an eye on one and two, my position left me painfully vulnerable from the front on the ocean side. Number three had circled widely and come up from the breakers. I fell heavily over the foot he stuck out in front of me. By the time I got back up, Curly and Moe were on me. They took turns hitting me. It was polite, but still not much fun. I blocked Moe's attempt to hit me with a left hook. At the same time, I brought my left elbow up hard and caught sneaky Larry on the chin before his foot went into my ribs. He went down. If I was to stay in this little confrontation, I was just going to have to be more aggressive, and a quick too. I hit Curly right on the button, and he went down. I had to hustle to duck a swing from stooge number two, and as I came around, I popped him with a right cross. He went down, and the third one came at me. My instincts told me to turn around; when I did Moe was coming at me. I stopped him by stepping on his front foot, and at the same time I decked him with an uppercut. This was starting to look like one of those brawls out of a John Wayne movie.

Closing in against me, Broken-nosed-Moe muttered a promise of worse things to come.

"Hand over what you got on the train." Unfortunately, he had a painful way of punctuating his sentences.

Some of the people from the beachfront were watching like it was a Friday night fight. The tourists were probably enjoying it. Now they had something to tell Aunt Edna back in Ohio.

As hurt as I was, I knew I had to do something, or I would be history. I grabbed Curly in the sleeper hold just long enough to put him down for the count. Then Larry turned and took off running like there was a sale at Sears. That left Moe, and he wasn't having any of this since he was now alone, so he too headed off in the other direction.

I heard shouting in the distance. There were two cops on bicycles pedaling toward me. Curly got up, his mouth and nose spurting blood onto the sand. He pointed his finger at me and said, "I'll be back. Then, you'll be dead whether you give us what we want or not." With that, Curly helped Moe to his feet and beat feet with Larry in the lead. The two bicycles were in ready pursuit.

One of the cops dropping his bike near the walkway high-stepped it through the sand and asked if I was alright. I nodded, and he started to help his partner who was wheeling after Curly, Moe, and Larry. Un- fortunately, the Stooges made it to their car, a dark blue sedan with a cracked rear window, and skidded away at a speed that took the heart out of the cop on the bicycle. He spoke into his radio and headed back toward us.

I didn't want to make a big deal about it. I gave them my name and address and said I would press charges if they brought them in. I said I could probably identify them. I thanked them for their help and went to my car.

I was in no shape to run anymore. If they kept it up, Curly and his friends would demolish what little discipline I still had for working out. It was certainly time to take that knife into Terrana's boys and see if they could find a print.

By the time I drove back to Aunt Gladys's, I felt a lot better. I was willing to consider that maybe I didn't have any cracked ribs after all, though I couldn't get past the split lip with any amount of positive thinking. Every once in a while, a good old donnybrook was actually fun. Only, these guys weren't foolin' around. Next time, the Stooges would see to it that there would be no rematch.

I hauled my aching body into the shower and turned the water on as hot as I could stand it. Aunt Gladys had one of those pulsating shower massage attachments. I turned it to the equivalent of a small fire hose and stood under it for a long time.

Bruises were purpling all over my torso, and the split in my lip was tender enough to burn like fire when the water hit it.

When I stepped out and toweled off, I thought I just might have a lovely reproduction of Curly's ring in tones of blue and black over my sternum. All I could recall was a flash of gold and red. Now it seemed as if I might have enough of a mark to identify it more clearly. Except for the lip, my face didn't look too bad. It was mostly the body.

I laid down on the bed and tried to catch a few winks before getting ready for my date. I'd have to leave fairly early if I wanted to first take Ski Mask's knife into the station and make a report.

EIGHT

I was standing in front of Kathy's house. She lived with her father. The clean paint job around the wooden paneling on the doors and windows attested to a person who had retired and liked to keep busy. I rang the doorbell.

When the door opened, I was taken back by the figure that stood before me. He must have been at least six foot four inches of whipcord muscle under iron-gray hair; he filled the whole door opening. He definitely was not a leprechaun; though he spoke with the thickest brogue I've heard this side of the Atlantic.

"Can I help you, lad?"

"Yes. I'm here to see Kathy."

"Aye? Are you now? Will you come in then?"

I said, "Thank you," and stepped through the entry into the hall.

He showed me into the living room and asked me if I would like a beer.

"No, thank you. I'm not much of a beer drinker. Beer is a bit weak for my taste."

He laughed and said, "What might your name be?"

"Sam Ryan."

"A name like Ryan, and you'd turn down a Guinness? You should be ashamed of yourself."

I really wanted a Scotch on the rocks, but I didn't think it was the time to ask for it. So, instead I said, "I'll take some Irish whiskey with a touch of water, if you have it." Just being around that accent was sure to make my own brogue infect my speech soon. I took a deep breath and thought of my dialog coach. God forbid Mr. Kelly should think I was imitating him.

"That's more like it." He spoke as he poured me the drink, "Kathy will be ready in a minute. Have you known her long?"

"We only met today." Fathers never like to hear that. It's like they expect their daughters to be exclusively theirs forever, and when they do go with anyone else, they should somehow have known them for a century or two before accepting so much as a soda pop. I guess I can't blame them. I know I'd be the same with my own daughter, if I'd had one. I cringe as I remembered that Margaret had been pregnant when she was hit. I shook off those thoughts and tuned back into life in the little green and white house in Studio City.

"Here y'are, lad."

I knocked back the stuff, not wanting him to think I was a sipper. It had been a while since I had Irish whiskey. I had acquired a taste for Scotch, and that stuff went down hard. I heard a hearty laugh as the drink hit bottom with the flavor of iodine.

"What's the matter, lad? Too strong for you?"

He reminded me of my old sergeant when I was in the Air Force. He used to like to bellow like that too, but once you got to know him, he was an okay guy. Underneath that Neanderthal exterior, he was probably a warm-hearted person. "Actually, I was thinking it was a little weak, but then again, I usually drink later in the evening."

He gave another hearty laugh and said, "I like you lad. You've got spirit."

Spirit, now there's word you don't hear too often. At least not today. Before I could come back with an adequate quip, I heard Kathy say, "Are you ready, Sam?"

"Yes. Sure. It was nice meeting you, Mr. Kelly."

I turned and saw Kathy standing in the doorway. I definitely liked her social attire better than her work apparel. She had on a white silky dress that clung to her just enough for me to want to do the same. The front closure crossed between her breasts in a daring collection of soft little pleats and left her tanned arms bare. The flared skirt was smooth over her hips and ran out of material just in time to bare her knees and show well-shaped calves which tapered neatly into slender ankles. All of it was accentuated by three-inch heels.

It made her just about an inch taller, but who cared? Her smile spot-lighted her beautifully smooth complexion and reached deep into her vivid green eyes. Out of the business-like French twist, her hair was long, and she allowed the curly black mane to be wild and full. I felt like I had just won my dream date.

When we got outside, Kathy said, "You'll have to excuse my father, he's a little…"

"Like a father?" I said, knowing she felt awkward about the apology.

She smiled and then asked, "What happened to you?" I knew she meant my little run-in with the Three Stooges.

"Oh, you mean my lip?"

"Did someone hit you?"

"Yeah, well, I had a little too much exercise."

"Care to explain that one? I think I missed something."

"There are much better topics, like how nice you look. This morning, I thought you were fantastic in uniform. Now I see you in silk, and words fail me."

"Words? Fail an actor?" But she was smiling as she said it and looked quite pleased.

"Thank you. Seriously, that dress is a knock-out! And so is the lady in it."

She laughed. "It's a favorite of mine, but it's only a copy. I could never have afforded the original."

I tried to look interested in her words, but I was too busy staring at her swan-like neck rising gracefully from those delicate white pleats.

She caught me staring (or maybe I was salivating) and smiled. "Thank you, again," she said graciously.

I blushed and asked her where she wanted to eat. I couldn't help but notice the blue eyes and her black-haired Irish coloring that made her so attractive.

"That depends. Do you like steak or seafood?"

"To tell you the truth, I'm a meat and potato man."

"Good, then you'll like this place. It's called, Jack's Steak House. They have a great prime rib, they make their own bread, and the dessert tray is to die for."

"Sounds like you won't have any trouble deciding what to order."

She smiled and shook her head. "Nope."

"You got it." As we headed down the street, I had a good feeling about the evening.

Dinner was fine. What came afterward was even better. Kathy suggested we go for a walk by the beach, saving me the trouble of figuring out how to ask her.

We went to the Santa Monica Pier and walked down to the end of the boardwalk. I motioned to one of the benches, and she sat close to me in the moonlight.

It was a beautiful clear night. There was a half-moon, and you could count every star, that is, if you had a few years to kill.

"So, Sam Ryan, are you ever going to tell me about your lip?"

"That depends on whether you're asking as a friend or a policewoman."

"A friend, of course. As you can clearly see, I'm not in uniform."

"I've been meaning to talk to you about that." A smile scampered across her gamine face. It allowed the girl within the woman to show herself for a moment. There was no doubt one enhanced the other. "You look beautiful." The words fell out of my mouth, which was already hanging open in admiration. I couldn't have stopped them if I'd wanted to, and I didn't want to.

Even by the half-moon's light, I could see a faint blush darken her cheeks. "Thank you, but you're straying from the question."

"I am, but you're sidetracking me, in a nice sort of way."

She smiled. "I think you've kissed the Blarney stone a few times too many." She stole a quick kiss from my cheek to let me know she meant no harm with her words. "I'm still waiting for an answer."

"Ah yes, my lip. Well, I was running on the beach this afternoon, and I met these three guys, let's call 'em Curly, Moe, and Larry, and to make an otherwise long story short, my lip got in the way of a fist a few times."

"Does it have to do with the dead girl we saw this afternoon?"

"Debbie? No." I wasn't lying. I had been forcefully convinced it had to do with Marilyn's death on the train, or more specifically, the key she had given me. Of course, I was splitting hairs, but for now, I just wanted to get to know Kathy personally, no business.

"Do you want to tell me more?"

"I don't want you involved. These guys aren't playing games." She gave me a look that told me I had been both inappropriate and insulting.

"Oh, how kind. After all, they never taught us about self-defense at the academy."

"I'm sorry. That was condescending and chauvinistic. I just don't want to talk about it tonight. Conflict of interest, you understand."

Kathy smiled. Her expression held a tinge of triumph or maybe expectancy. "Yes, work does tend to conflict with lots of interests." She moved closer and slid her arms around my neck.

I could have stopped it right there, but Aunt Gladys didn't raise a total fool. Kathy's lips were soft and warm. I felt the heat in her kiss, and it fueled my own passion. The way her body fit against mine was something that I hadn't felt since Margaret. Then it was over.

She looked at me and said, "I don't swallow that excuse for a minute, but if you change your mind, I'd like to help."

I thanked her. What else could I do? It was hard to concentrate when I had a gorgeous woman staring at me. We talked for a while about everything and nothing before I took her home. It was late when I dropped Kathy off and headed back to Gladys's house. I kept thinking about how the evening had gone. She made me feel as if we were the only two people in the world, even when we were in a crowd. I was remembering what she had said about why she joined the force. It was strange for me to hear all those noble reasons for becoming a cop after what had happened with Margaret. I felt a little better knowing there was at least one person out there who was committed to the law, even if she was ten years too late and in the wrong city.

She wanted to be a cop for all the right reasons and was working to be a really good detective. I thought she'd do it too. She wanted to be like her father.

The next morning was what I expected from southern California weather. Hot and smoggy. They say the smog is worse here than anywhere else. I believe them. Los Angeles reminds me of a pool room with a hundred versions of Minnesota Fats all puffing foul cigars and flailing at life with pool cues. Even the Los Angeles sky was the tawny brown of well-cured tobacco.

I pulled on a pair of jeans and the lightest shirt I had as I glared back at a brutal summer sky. The heat was already building inside the house, and my morning coffee made me feel sticky. I dropped about six ice cubes into a glass and poured the java over it, complete with milk and sugar. Better. I carried my iced coffee to the car and headed for Glendale.

By the time I arrived at Debbie's apartment, it was going on ten. I parked and took a stroll down her block to check for cops. I didn't see any, so I ambled into the building and rode that unenthusiastic elevator up to the second floor.

Sure enough, the door was all bandaged with yellow police tape and warnings, but no boys in blue, or ladies in blue for that matter. I carefully picked the lock and ducked under the tape.

The apartment looked like I remembered, except this time Debbie wasn't going to come walking out of her bedroom.

I started with the kitchen. You can tell a lot about someone by looking around her kitchen. I knew that Marilyn hadn't been here for a while that left Debbie as housekeeper.

From what I could see, she was either messy or she had collected a lot of bruises on those svelte hips from the corners of open drawers. I didn't really know what I was after, just something that would give me a starting place. I was sure the police had done a thorough job, but sometimes you get lucky.

So far, luck wasn't my middle name. I checked the bedrooms. The first one turned out to be Marilyn's. Somebody was definitely looking for something the night Debbie was killed. Even if an entire police department had been in here, they couldn't have wreaked this havoc.

I went to the desk and started looking through the drawers. Nothing unusual about them, except a few was still on the floor. Note paper, pencils and pens, some candy in one drawer, envelopes and stationery in another and more candy. Off the top of my head, I'd say that Marilyn had a sweet tooth. I recalled her figure. If so, only Marilyn and her dentist knew for sure.

I went through the closet; not an inexpensive wardrobe and every stitch in shreds. Somebody was desperate for that key. I needed to find out what it opened. Maybe it would be in today's mail. I started to leave when I spotted an end table I hadn't checked. I opened the drawer, and there it was, the one drawer everyone has, the junk drawer. It had everything from a beer opener to a hairpin. I found a receipt in an envelope marked 'deductions.' Marilyn had scribbled 'continuing education' across the front. It had some receipts from a dancewear shop. I put it back.

I thought about my first visit to Debbie's. I had arrived there at about eight. I couldn't have been there longer than fifteen minutes before Debbie's Los Osos Special took effect. Terrana had said the maintenance man discovered the body at eight in the morning. That had been twelve hours later. He also said they figured she was killed about nine thirty. I'm not a large man, by any means, but Debbie sure didn't lug me off to the train station by herself.

I couldn't see her murderer doing anything but leaving me there on the rug to take the rap for him—or her. So how in hell did I get to Los Osos? Who had helped her dispose of me, and so rapidly? Had her accomplice been waiting in the closet?

I went into Debbie's room. In contrast to Marilyn's, this one was nice and neat dark, but tidy. Marilyn's room caught the morning sun. Debbie must have done a great job of convincing them she had no idea what they were after; the only thing broken was the bedside lamp. They must have killed her because she'd seen them, rather than for what she wouldn't say. Maybe she came in on them when she got back from dumping me, poor sorry, bitch. No luck with Marilyn or Mickey Finn.

After looking around for about fifteen minutes, I went to her nightstand and opened the drawer. Something was stuck down in the side at the back.

I worked it free. It was a picture of Debbie and some man. I turned it over. On the back it read, The Weasel and me—4th of July. Who was the Weasel? The picture had a piece missing. The top left corner. The shot showed Debbie and whoever standing in front of a building. I turned it so that it caught more light. Looked like a restaurant or something.

The corner of the picture that was missing had probably contained the name of whatever they were standing in front of. One thing about this job, it's never boring. All I could read was an S and the word Place. That narrowed it down. There were probably only about a million joints in town that were named 's Place. That final S could have been a possessive tacked onto almost anything! Jeeze! I put the picture in my pocket. The police had either missed the picture or they didn't think it was important. In any case, I had my starting place. As I passed the door to Marilyn's room, I squinted at the hot sunlight that streamed in the window. That squint was a sort of break after all. High on the sun-struck wall was the faint triangle of a paint shadow, one that would have fit a school pennant perfectly.

I was sure about the key now. I also knew what I was looking for: 'continuing education.' I hurried to the living room and searched the bookcases. No school yearbooks.

I was on my way out when I saw a stack of magazines and newspapers in one of those racks you put next to an easy chair. I knelt down and went through them.

There it was: The Sundial, a campus paper for California State University at Northridge.

Being careful to lock the door and avoid tearing the police tape, I left the apartment and headed back to the house to see if my envelope had come in the mail yet.

Good ole' Uncle Sam came through. There was my not-too-legible handwriting scrawled across an envelope on the carpet of Gladys's front hall. God Bless the U.S.P.S.

I ripped off the end and dumped the key into my palm. C.S.U.N. What with her saving receipts for dancewear. I was willing to bet the key was to a gym locker' the W on the tag for women's gym, of course.

I grabbed the map and then headed for the university in Northridge to see what I could turn up.

I turned onto Zelzah Street and headed north, then west onto Plummer. All around me were the clues to the acres of citrus orchards that used to flourish here. I drove until I came to one of the many entrances to the campus. There was a guard shack there with a stop sign. A young black man was looking out the window. He saw me and came to the car window.

"Can I help you, sir?"

"Yes. My daughter attends classes here." I looked at a notebook as if checking her class schedule. "Can you point me toward the gym?"

"How long will you be, sir?"

"No more than an hour."

"Okay, if you'll just wait a minute, I'll get you a pass."

"Fine." Now, if I could just get in and out of the gymnasium without any trouble, I'd be happy.

"Here you go, sir. I also gave you a map of the campus. You can park right over there." He said pointing to a lot with a machine that collected quarters at the entrance and tire-sized Cuisinart's embedded at the exits.

"Thank you very much."

After looking over the map, I headed for the women's gym. It was a three-story building, light yellow and pale white in color. I could tell it was a fairly new building.

Next to it was an outdoor pool with a high dive tower. There was a swimmer on the high board getting ready to jump. I remembered when I use to dive in high school. It had ended with the state meet where I nearly decapitated myself doing a half-gainer layout. I came too close to the board and tucked to keep from hitting my head. It disqualified me. With that thought, I wished the diver more luck than I had had and headed inside the building.

The dark interior after the bright sunlight outside temporarily blinded me. My eyes finally adjusted, and I could see a long hallway leading to the other side of the building. The hallway was lined with doorways on either side. I passed a caged counter on my left with a male attendant. A sign on a door to the right said, 'Women's Lockers.'

A girl opened that door, and I could see inside. It was only for a moment, but that was enough. I saw a caged counter like the one up ahead only with a female attendant, so much for sneaking in. I'd have to come up with a different approach.

I saw a young woman moving along the hall toward me and decided to take a chance.

"Excuse me," I said. She was a petite girl with long brown hair, maybe all of eighteen.

"Yes sir?"

I winced. You know you're getting old when they refer to you as sir. I put on one of those fatherly looks. "My daughter had to drop out of school after a car accident. She asked me to come and get her things out of her gym locker, but—ah—I just realized I can't get in there." I tried to look pathetic, helpless, and embarrassed by turns. "She gave me her key." I held up the one Marilyn had given me. "I was wondering if you could get her things for me."

"Sure, sir, no problem. What was her name? Maybe I knew her."

"Marilyn Williams."

She thought for a moment and said, "No, the name doesn't ring a bell."

I gave her the key and told her I would wait there. "I hope I'm not keeping you from your class."

She laughed, "Oh no. I have a free hour. I was just going to work out a little. I'll be right back."

I watched her walk away. In a few minutes, she was back. She had a puzzled look on her face. I hoped she hadn't had any problems.

"Well, here's everything that was in there. There wasn't much." She handed me a gym bag. "There was also this." She held out a pendant with the initials G.D. on it. The initials were not those of Marilyn Williams.

"Hope your daughter will be back soon."

"Thanks." I held up the pendant and smiled. "I'm sure Marilyn's cousin will be glad to get her necklace back. She's probably the one who was really in a hurry for this stuff." I grinned and tried to look like a beleaguered father. "Kids always in a hurry."

We both laughed and she walked away leaving me to my family problems, as it were.

I checked the gym bag. One rumpled leotard: black with metallic blue side-panels. One pair of tights: same sparkly blue. One pair of leg warmers: deeper royal. For a moment, I got this sick feeling in my stomach as I thought of Marilyn and how great she would have looked in this dancewear.

In the bottom of the bag, I found a business card: Pacific Yacht Club… Sondra Chase, owner. I tucked the card in my wallet and headed for my car. What else? I felt around in the bottom of the bag and came up with a packet. It was the sort of envelope you get from a photo store. I dumped the contents into my hand.

About fifteen pictures of beautiful girls, some in various stages of undress. Well, Debbie had said she and Marilyn were lovers. I kept thumbing through the pictures. They weren't exactly titillating. I mean the girls were pretty, but not posing. All I could guess was that they were some candid shots of her modeling friends back in a changing room. Off hand, I'd say Marilyn certainly belonged in front of a camera. She sure didn't belong behind one.

That's when I saw two men standing by a water fountain about twenty yards from the gym. They looked too old to be students and too tough to be professors. Unfortunately, they were standing between me and the most direct route to my car. Even more unfortunately, they saw me. There was no way I could beat them to my car or either of the buildings to the right or left of the gymnasium.

It seemed I was going to have an unpleasant conversation with these goons, whether I wanted to or not. They started toward me. Just then, classes let out. Somebody up there liked me. Students materialized by the hundreds. I didn't have to make much of an effort to get lost in the crowd.

I hurried back inside with no idea where I was going—just that if I could hide in the crush of students long enough to slip out another exit, perhaps I could make it to my car.

Suddenly, a door opened and about thirty guys with play books stormed the hall. The football team was evidently having skull practice. I looked for tackles and guards, the biggest guys on the team, and followed them in my effort to stay "lost." Good thing. I glimpsed the two goons coming in the gym doors.

I hurried down the hall, darted into a side passage, and saw a door that said: Coach's Office. I ducked inside and waited.

I heard a bell and lots of footsteps outside in the hall; then, it got quiet. I let out the breath I had been holding. Just then, someone tapped me on the shoulder.

"Aren't you a little old for hide-and-seek?"

I jerked around and saw this older gentleman dressed in a sweat suit. He looked like something out of an old Pat O'Brien movie.

"Who are you?"

"I'm the head coach. Who are you?"

I had to give myself enough time to be sure those two guys were gone. "Ah, I'm a journalism student." What the hell? Students came in all ages nowadays. "And I was thinking of doing a story on the summer activities of the football team."

"Be a pretty skimpy story."

"Oh? I thought I just saw a bunch of guys with play books out in the hall."

"Skull practice is considered a pain in the ass to do, let alone write about."

I checked my watch. "Well, maybe a rousing article about how important it is to a well-played game…?"

He shook his head. "I'm willing, but I don't think you have a winner there."

"Well, I guess I'll bow to your superior judgment, sir." I thought enough time had passed. "Thank you very much."

"Sure. Come back anytime. Maybe you can do a story about us when we're winning. We're gonna win big this year."

"I know we are. I'll do that." I smiled at him and turned to the door. "What's your name, mister?"

"Ryan. And yours?"

"Coach Thorpe." I thought to myself, that's too much.

"Good day, sir." I stepped into the hall and looked around carefully. No goons.

Outside, I did another quick check.

I walked to my car. They had left a note on the door: 'No more snooping. No cops. Give us what Marilyn gave you or the old lady is history.'

The bottom dropped out of my stomach for a moment. They had to mean Aunt Gladys, but the only time I knew I had been tailed when I was with her was on the way back from the Polo Lounge. These two guys must have been working with Ponytail. Now, I was really glad I had sent Aunt Gladys to Beth's. But, if they had followed me here, maybe they had been following me all along.

If so, they had to be good or at least worlds better than Ponytail, because I'm a pretty fair hand at spotting that sort of thing.

I went to one of the many pay phones on the campus and dialed Beth's number. I waited through three rings. "Hello, Aunt Gladys? Is everything all right?"

I heard her familiar laugh and then, "Of course, what do you think?"

I didn't want to let her know about the note, so I just said, "I was concerned about the two of you. Listen; don't open the door to any strangers."

She must have picked up something in my tone. "Is there a problem, Sam?"

"Not yet. But there may be trouble. Be careful."

"Well, we'll be on the lookout. Don't worry, Sam. Everything's fine on our end."

I headed back to the house to think things over.

While I was thinking, I fixed myself a sandwich and took my gun out of the small of my back. Lt. Terrana wouldn't approve, but since my last beating, I'd decided to start carrying. I'd put the automatic on the sink and was downing my second beer when I heard a knock on the front door.

Easing my .38 off the counter, I went quietly down the hall and though of my aunt as I looked out the spy hole. Relieved to see Kathy standing there, I pulled the door open. "What are you doing here?"

That smile I'd grown to love wavered a bit. She diverted the muzzle of the gun further toward the floor with her index finger. "Well, that's a nice way to greet me after I decided to share my day off with you."

"I'm sorry." I put the gun on the hall table. "I didn't mean this the way it looks. I'm glad you're here." I leaned over and touched those beautiful lips with mine. They seemed to go so well together that they touched a second time without even trying. "Mmm, did I remember to thank you for last night?"

"Uh-huh why?" She leaned back a bit and looked at me.

"Too bad."

"What?"

"If I hadn't already done so," I said, taking aim at her mouth with mine, "I could do it now." I kissed her with even more zeal.

Kathy's body snuggled harder into my arms, and she murmured in my ear. "You know what they say about a good thing, Sam?"

I nodded against her mouth. "Well, gratitude can be fantastic." We finally came up for air.

"C'mon in." I reset the lock on the door as I closed it.

She was wearing white shorts that were rolled to a cuff at mid-thigh. I let my gaze linger again on the tan expanse of great legs. The shorts seemed to have been made from a former pair of extremely snug jeans, so the fit showed off a winsome curve of cheek as well. I was a happy man. And that was before I noticed that her lime tank top was cropped short enough to bare her trim waist each time she moved.

She walked past me and went on into the living room. I could tell she had something on her mind other than a pleasant visit.

I waited.

She paced the room.

Finally, I stepped in front of her, put my hands on her shoulders, and looked into those shamrock eyes. "Okay, what's wrong?"

She replied, "I have good news and bad news."

I smiled. "Okay, give me the bad first." I thought she was about to give me one of those speeches that starts with, 'You're a great guy,' and ends with a 'but.'

"No. The good news is I'm going to get my first break out of uniform." Her eyes sparkled as she told me, and she looked as if she'd just been handed the whole world on a platter. "I'm officially plain-clothes for a trial period."

"That's great, Kathy!" I was happy for her, and happy for me. She'd be less likely to get shot at as a detective than working in the streets. I hugged her and collected a sweet kiss into the bargain.

"The bad news?" I prompted, holding her away from me a little.

"My trial case is the Pittman case." She paused and looked at the floor, then up at me. Her eyes were pleading, slightly sorrowful, like they'd be if she had an old dog, she knew she had to put out of its misery. I hoped I wasn't the dog.

"Sam, I just read all the reports on the Debbie Pittman case. They found a kilo of heroin in her apartment."

"So, why are you worried? I didn't put it there."

"Sam, this case is going to be big. I feel it. When we dig into her death, we'll be digging into someone's pockets. That someone is going to go down. It could be the collar that gets me into detective work full-time."

"Well, that's just great, Kathy. But remember that when you cut into someone's pocket, they can get very nasty about it. You be careful. Especially if you think its drug related." I hugged her. "What's the bad news?"

She pulled away. "Sam, I have to be sure that I won't run into you on this case."

"Hey, I know the rules. It's an open police case right?" I felt like a real shmuck looking at her with all this sincerity and holding back. I thought of the recent threat to Aunt Gladys. Then, I thought about how the cops had botched things when Margaret got killed. The one thing I could not do was look Kathy in the eye and make a promise I wouldn't be able to keep.

She wouldn't let go. "So, you'll stay out of it?"

"Don't worry."

She smiled. "Remember, no one's hired you; you're not getting paid."

"That's right," I said as soothingly as I could.

"Don't patronize me, Sam. If you stay in it, I'm the one who'll have to arrest you." I could tell that was hard for her to say.

"You're not going to have to arrest me," I said. I could promise that much. If anything happened to Aunt Gladys, I'd get vengeance or die trying. Then, there'd be nothing left of me for her to arrest.

She nodded, but her eyes had that extra glint that could preface grateful tears. "Arresting someone you care about is so hard on a relationship." She was trying to diffuse the intensity with a flip remark, but she was slightly shy about admitting to the caring.

Nothing could have made me feel more like a heel. "I care too," I said, taking her in my arms. I kissed her, but it felt like some cheap consolation prize I was offering instead of the truth.

What did she know? She leaned into that kiss with all she had, leaned into it until it changed and became everything I could ever want of passion and promise. She pressed against me, and I hugged every curve. It was a long time before we both came up breathless.

I backed off a little, and when I looked at her, I knew. I just knew this could be the woman I'd been waiting for. At that instant, I knew I could love her. Those eyes: If I fell into them, I could fall forever and not hit bottom. Right now, that's just what I wanted to do.

We settled back against the cushions, and I began to think about the two of us doing those things that men and women do so well together. I thought about it until we went upstairs and made it reality.

Later, as we lay snuggled beneath the rumpled sheets, I thought about how right this felt, how right I wanted it to feel for a long, long time to come.

Suddenly, there was a God-awful pounding at my door. I looked at the receiver I had taken off the hook and grudgingly slid out of bed. "Stay here, sweetheart. I'll be right back."

TEN

Pulling on my swim trunks as I hop-stumbled toward the stairs, I yelled at the unidentified visitor to hold on a minute. At the landing, I slid my feet into my sneakers. Any needed action was the pits if you were barefoot. Shoes or boots always trump bare arches. I took the rest of the stairs trying not to trip on my laces.

By the time I reached the door, I had given each set of shoestrings a healthy yank and tucked the streamers in at the sides. One quick peek while my hand hovered over the gun I'd left on the hall table earlier and I jerked the door open. Beth practically threw herself at me.

"You were so right, Sam! Something did happen."

"Beth, calm down. Is Aunt Gladys all right?"

"Yes. But a couple of nasty-looking men followed us from the supermarket. It's getting so warm, and we had the windows down instead of the air—cold air bothers my arthritis—anyway, we came to that long stoplight near my place, and this man threw something in my car.

I felt sick to my stomach and so angry that I began to shake, but I let her spill and get it all out.

"Gladys screamed, and I stomped back on the brakes. Then, the car started to fill with this hideous smoky stuff. It was awful! I could hardly see. Gladdy was choking, and tears were streaming down her face. Mine too. While we were gagging in the intersection, they just squealed off and got away."

I patted her shoulder. "Easy Beth, where's Aunt Gladys now?"

"At the house, I made her stay there and bathe her eyes and take her asthma medication."

"Did she lock all the doors?" Christ! My aunt's asthma, she and Uncle Hobart had moved to Southern California because of her lungs. Something like this could put her in the hospital.

"Oh, yes, and I checked the windows upstairs and down before I left her. She's fine except for that gas or whatever it was. I made sure her medication was starting to work before I left to get you." She paused. "What's wrong with the phone, Sam?" Suddenly, she got that stunned mullet look people get when they go into shock: "D'you think they cut the wires?" Her lips trembled and she clapped one shaking hand to her mouth.

I smiled and shook my head. "Too much television Beth." I put an arm around her shoulders and improvised. After all, I was an actor. Impromptu scenes were my stock and trade. I felt shitty about it, but I couldn't shock this sweet lady back three generations by telling her I'd been upstairs bouncing bedsprings with a woman I'd dated once, even if I already knew I could fall hard and permanently for Ms. Kathy Kelly over the long haul. "I was taking a nap, and I guess I must have knocked it off the hook or something."

I could see Beth's eyes were still very red and it wasn't from crying. "Oh, my Arnold used to do that sort of thing. He'd even answer it in his sleep and just drop the receiver back in the cradle without saying a word." She waited a beat. "I moved the phone to the dresser across from the bed so he had to get up before he could reach it." She beamed at me as if sure a hint to the wise would be sufficient. "Fixed that problem right away, quick."

I nodded contritely. "I'll be sure and do that as soon as I go back upstairs to change." I took her shoulders in my hands and questioned her seriously for a moment. "Did they say something? Yell at you as they passed? Anything?"

Beth looked confused for an instant and then sure of herself: "Not really. They just yelled, 'Yo!' and threw that awful thing in my car and sped off. Should we call the police, Sam?" She looked uncertain. "Maybe it was a prank… school kids, not related to your trouble at all." Even she didn't sound convinced.

"Beth, one'!' does not a preppie college stunt make. Did they look like young college boys?"

Defeated, she shook her head. "No, Sam. They looked like just what they were: hoodlums!" She said it with such emphasis I almost smiled.

It was a word you didn't hear much nowadays, like spirit.

"So, should we call the police?" Beth was saying when I tuned back into her.

Her question yanked me to the upstairs bedroom where my own favorite cop was still—I hoped resting quietly. Very quietly, I hadn't been this nervous about a date since I'd lived here in my teens! "What do you remember about their car?"

She thought a moment. "Well, it was sort of a gray, or maybe it was blue." She suddenly looked as though she were about to cry. "I guess I didn't take a very good look. I mean, what's with that smoke filling the car and all and…" She wound down and I handed her a tissue from the box on the hall table.

"Listen, Beth, you go back and take care of Aunt Gladys, and I'll see what I can do about all this."

"Oh! The back window!"

"Back window?"

"Of their car. I remember now. It was broken. Not out, you know, just all… like a spider's web. Does that help?"

"Absolutely; good work." I flashed on the car from the beach. Maybe blue. Broken back window. "All right, Beth. You go home and stay there. Call the police station and see if they will come out and take a report. Tell them you can't drive your car, or you're afraid to, anything. If they won't come out, I'll drive you both to the station. I'm going to see you home and then jog back here and dress."

"No. That's silly, Sam. I can manage three blocks by myself in broad daylight. I'll be alright Now that I'm on the lookout." I saw fierce determination in her ace.

"You'll be all right?"

"I got here, didn't I?"

She had a point. "Okay. I'll wait for you to call me." I stepped outside with her and checked the street. It was empty for as far as I could see.

Just some kids biking down the block. A skateboarder, coming around the corner, on the sidewalk.

I watched a station wagon pull into a drive, but a young woman got out and began to unload grocery bags from the back. She'd had the street to herself, all clear.

I told Beth she'd been a great help and walked her to her car, reminding her to make sure she wasn't followed and to drive past her house and straight to the fire station if that should happen.

"I took my safety classes, Sam. You put the phone back on the hook. I'll call you as soon as I know if I need you to drive us."

"All right." I was anxious for her to get back to Aunt Gladys; it didn't seem wise to have either of them alone for any longer than necessary. They'd probably be okay as long as I did what I was told. I was pretty sure this had been a warning to yours truly, but the smoke bomb and the accident it might have caused angered me more than I cared to admit; never mind my aunt's asthma! I walked back inside.

If the car Beth saw was the same one Curly, Moe, and Larry used at the beach, then maybe they had been taking turns following me all along. But where did Ponytail come in? He hadn't been at the beach.

Of course, one of the stooges could have worn that ski mask and come to Gladys's, but somehow, I didn't think so. The general build and shoulders of the man who had attacked me in the front hall seemed burlier than any of those three at the beach. That would make a total of five men—all after the same thing: me—and that key Marilyn gave me.

Who was working with whom, or for whom? I knew the three at the beach were a team, but what about Ponytail? He sure didn't look like the brains of anyone's outfit. How did Ski Mask fit in if he wasn't one of the beach trio?

Well, all I knew was that I was quitting, giving it up. It wasn't my case. It wasn't going to endanger what little family I had left. I was going to make a certain police officer a very happy lady. As Kathy said, no one had hired me, and my idle curiosity over the murder of a woman I had met briefly on a train was exacting too high a price.

I took the stairs two at a time. Kathy was still curled in bed like a kitten in a basket. She reached out her arms to me, and I sat on the edge of the mattress.

"Who was at the door?"

"Aunt Gladdy's, friend Beth."

"Something wrong?" She said.

I smiled. "No, I might have to help her with an errand. She'll let me know." I struck a noble pose: "No rest for the wicked and all that."

She laughed and pulled me down into the pillows. "Then come be wicked, again, first."

I cuddled her a moment, inhaling her sweet scent, and then sat up. "While I wait for her call, you can catch a few winks, rest up for the really nice lunch I want to buy you, and then who knows?" I leered at her.

She stretched and yawned. I stuck my finger into her open mouth, and she looked pleasantly startled when she closed her jaws on its tip. She laughed, grabbed my hand, and drew my finger suggestively into her mouth, her tongue circling the knuckle, wet and warm.

"Promise me you won't let it ruin our day together if I have to help Beth and Aunt Gladys. It won't take me long."

The phone rang. It was Beth telling me to relax. She was home. Aunt Gladys was fine, and a policeman would be over soon to take a look at what had been pitched into her car. He'd take a report. "Okay, Beth. Thanks. You call me if you need anything at all." I spoke with my aunt for a minute, but it wasn't easy to keep my side of the conversation neutral and mostly directed at her asthma symptoms, which—thank God— were fading. I had a feeling she must have known I had someone here with me, but she didn't make an issue of it. Bless her.

I hung up and lay down on the bed with Kathy. "They're fine. When would you like to go for that lunch?"

In response, she dragged me down on the bed next to her and pulled the sheet up over us like a kid building a tent in the backyard. I heard a noise from downstairs. Kathy was out of bed like a shot. I followed.

She dashed downstairs in her beautiful altogether and dove on her handbag. Nothing jiggled that wasn't supposed to. Perfection, I'd always loved performance art. I wasn't going to miss a single curtain call. I admired the firm curve of her buttocks as she leaned over the couch, the line of her backbone from cleft to narrow waist… I sighed.

She pulled a telephone beeper from her bag and read a number off the LED. "It's work. I need to call in, Sam."

She went to the phone, dialed, and turned dead serious. No remnant of the fun we'd been having was left in her eyes. She cradled the receiver and darted up the stairs, with me following, again. Following this particular nude lady through the house could get to be a nice habit real nice.

"I've got to get to the station ASAP. There's been another murder. Some guy they connected with a latent fingerprint they found in Debbie's place." She threw on her top and worked her shorts up those tawny legs. Within all too few a number of minutes, Kathy was ready to go.

"Be careful, sweetheart. I guess lunch is off. Let me know if you can make dinner."

She had the grace to look a little disappointed. "I will call if I can make it, Sam, but—"

"I won't expect you. Hey, this is your big break, go get 'em." I hugged her hard, and she ran downstairs and out the door to her car. "They'll love the shorts!" I teased.

She tossed me an unladylike gesture. "I've got street clothes in my locker."

I caught my last view of her as her white Honda Accord barreled down the street with one of those plastic police bubbles revolving on its roof.

Now I was the one left waiting. Since I was voluntarily out of a detecting job, and not so voluntarily abandoned, maybe I would use the afternoon to try to see about some acting auditions while I was here. I pulled out my address book and phoned the Hollywood branch of my New York agency.

I gave them my credentials and made an appointment to drop by some glossies and composites later. Actors carry their portfolios everywhere, especially if that everywhere is an impromptu trip to the movie capital of the world.

I jumped into the shower and stood there with the hot water hammering my skin like a hard tropical rain. I thought about my morning and Kathy and turned the tap over to cold. That would help me get through the day maybe.

I toweled off, pulled my go-to-meeting suit out of the closet, and began to dress for my appointment. "Clock" pecked on the window, and I went down and got him some crumbs from the kitchen, along with a cup of coffee for myself. It had been a nice morning. The best I'd had in a long time.

I scattered the crumbs on the sill and put a double Windsor knot in my tie while I waited for Clock to come back.

I heard a fluttering and then pecking. Good old bird. I dragged a chair over to the window. As I sat watching the sparrow, I became aware of a car that had parked about a block and a half down and across the street. It looked vaguely familiar. It was gray.

I got Aunt Gladys's binoculars from the hall closet and trained them on the car. Primer gray. The magnification flattened the hood of the car, putting it in almost the same plane as the driver. There was that thin body hunched behind the wheel, the droopy moustache.

It was Ponytail. Just seeing him there made me glad I had decided to give all this up. Soon, they would realize I was out of it, and Aunt Gladys could come home.

I picked up the phone and dialed Beth's. "Beth, keep a sharp eye out. I think someone's watching this place. They weren't here when you left but keep an eye out."

"Shall I send the police over when they get here?"

"No, don't do that." The warning about "no cops" blinked like neon in my head. I had to get out of here. The last thing I needed was for Ponytail to see me consorting—let alone fraternizing with the police.

"All right, Sam."

"I'm going out for a while. I should be back before too long. You just lock up good after the cops leave."

I thought about the things I had found in Marilyn's locker. I would have to turn them over to the police now. No doubt about it. I put the business card and the pendant in my portfolio, along with the packet of candid photographs. I could take it all in on my way back from dropping off the composites. And before the end of the day, I wanted to get someone to help me guard Aunt Gladys and Beth.

I looked at my watch. I'd have to hustle.

I carted everything downstairs and headed for the car.

Just as I climbed in the Mustang, a black-and-white pulled up and blocked my driveway. Two cops got out and came toward me. I took a quick look. Ponytail cranked up his car and pulled away from the curb.

As he vanished into the distance, the cops loomed larger than life. There wasn't a doubt in my mind that he had seen the cops coming to talk to me. No doubt at all.

"Mr. Ryan?" The officer said.

I nodded. I felt a wild helpless panic that had nothing to do with the duty-bound officers approaching me. Ponytail would report the cops at my house, and Gladys would be in deep oatmeal. Had Beth sent them over after all? How had they arrived so quickly?

The cops explained that something had turned up with regard to the knife I had brought them; they needed me at the station. That explained it. Different cops. Different topic.

I followed them to the North Hollywood station on Tiara off Lanker-shim. My escorts took me right inside the red brick single-story building and past the front desk.

Kathy was waiting in one of the offices. I'd have cheered, but Terrana was with her.

"Ah, Mr. Ryan. Nice of you to come in I understand you had a little trouble the other day with a knife." He didn't pause long enough for me to say anything, but Kathy gave me a look I could have died from. "You brought it in to this division and made a report about the attack?"

"I did."

He pulled a file from his desk. Kathy looked anxious. That was nothing compared to what I was feeling. "What's this about, Lieutenant? You find the guy?"

"Well, let's just say we found a match to the partial print on the knife. I'd like you to look at some pictures."

"Lieutenant, I never saw the man's face. He wore a ski mask."

"I read your statement." Terrana smiled. "Humor me, Mr. Ryan." He pulled some Polaroid's from his desk and spread them on the table. "You ever see any of these men?"

I looked at the pictures. Then I looked again. There he was the guy from the train. Baldy with his handlebar moustache, Daddy Warbucks himself. The moustache was in its adolescence, the handles only starting to look as imposing as they had on the train, but it was the same guy. His head wasn't as cleanly shaved in the photo either, but it was him.

I picked up the photo and handed it to Terrana. "This man I saw him on the train. He was in the dining car when I had lunch with Marilyn Williams. What's going on? That knife was his?"

Terrana smiled. He looked like a lion that'd just swallowed a Christian. "Well, all I can say is that there's a body in our morgue whose fingerprints match what we found on that knife and a partial we lifted off Debbie's skin. You just picked that body's picture out of my little lineup here." He scooped the Polaroid's back into the drawer and shoved it closed.

"It looks like he's our killer. He saw you with Marilyn. He was on the train. Marilyn died on that train. Then, this man apparently donned a ski mask and came after you in your aunt's hallway." He leaned forward.

"Why would he think you needed coming after, Mr. Ryan? And why didn't he kill you like he did Ms. Pittman?"

I hoped I didn't look as nervous as I suddenly felt. If I volunteered all the information now, I'd be off the hook with Terrana, but on the spot with Kathy. She'd be furious at me for holding out on her. But that was small potatoes compared to how badly I might need that evidence if Ponytail were stirring up trouble for my aunt. The contents of that locker could be my only bargaining power.

"Nice to know you're so concerned about me, Lieutenant. I guess I'm just an inconsiderate big city slob who prefers not to get killed in his own front hall even if it means more work for you in the long run." I had to get out of there and check Beth's place. I was desperate to find some help in that department. I'd stay with them as much as I could, but I had to sleep, and I definitely needed some time to straighten things out with Kathy. If she'd let me try.

Terrana nodded. "And that cozy little meeting over drinks in your compartment the night Marilyn was killed? Did the waiter arrange that, too?" He wore the smile of an assassin. Kathy's expression proved he was. My love life had just crawled off into the corner to die.

There went all I had been hoping to build with this lovely lady. I just prayed she'd give me a chance to explain. "Marilyn had too much to drink when she came to visit. I told her to go back to her compartment until she sobered up."

"How noble. I wonder if most men would respond that way to a beautiful blonde who's a little out of control. A little overly willing?"

"I'm not most men."

"Officer Kelly, get him out of here. And remind him not to leave town." Kathy came toward me, and we left Terrana's office.

"Dammit, Sam, the least you could have done is told me about that knife fight. I read the report; you turned that evidence in the night you took me to dinner! I asked you about your lip, so don't say you had no opportunity to tell me about it." We were nearly to my car.

"Different fight."

"What? Sam, are we trying to start a relationship?

"I thought so."

"Some start lying to me."

"What lying? We agreed it was an unofficial evening, dinner, not business."

"An omission is as good as a lie. Besides, I said I'd listen as a friend."

"Kathy, okay, I was wrong. Have dinner with me tonight as planned and I'll explain." I opened the door of the Mustang.

She looked hard at me. "You really sent that girl back to her cabin?" I nodded.

"The autopsy reports should confirm that at least."

She seemed to ignore that statement; "Two different fights in twenty-four hours?"

I nodded again. "I want to explain."

"And I want to hear it. More importantly, I want to believe it." She looked a little desperate and a lot confused. "I can't believe I'm saying this." She turned away in agitation. "I should just give you a one-way ticket out of my life. Why don't I? What is it about you?" I put an arm around her and tried to turn her toward me. She pulled away. "Don't push your luck. I think that sort of thing can wait until after the explanation."

"Tough lady." I smiled at her.

"I have to be. I'm a cop." She started back into the station. "I'll call as soon as I go off duty."

As I pulled out of the lot, I wondered where I could get some help protecting Beth and Gladys for a while just until things settled. I stopped at a 7-Eleven and called directory assistance to ask for the number of The Place on Pearl in Santa Monica. I dialed and waited anxiously for the bartender to pick up.

"You have a guy there named Lone Wolf?" I asked.

"Who is this?" The voice sounded aggressive, and I wasn't sure I'd get anywhere with my request.

"Sam Ryan, I need to talk with him."

"Hang on." He was less than enthusiastic.

Lone Wolf came on the line. "Hey, Sam, how's Mr. Wannabe? You get a bike yet?"

I laughed. "No, I have a problem I think you might be able to help me with. Or you'll know someone who can."

"Lay it on me." "Rather talk in person. Are you going to be there a while?"

"Yeah, a couple of hours anyway." I said.

"I'll see you there. I can buy you that beer I owe you."

I called Beth's just to be sure they were still all right. The police were there taking down the report.

By the time I arrived at The Place, it was close to one thirty. When I went into the dimly lit bar, I saw that it was done up like something out of an old Marlon Brando movie. The smell of stale smoke and spilled liquor was overpowering.

It was hard to see even in broad daylight. Most of the windows were painted black or covered with blinking beer signs, the kind with falling water or trumpeting elk flashing across a painted plastic surface. A flap of thick black curtain hung over the doorway as if the place was a rental darkroom where they thought amateur photographers might just come in fast and screw up developing film.

A bar coated in one of those gloss resin jobs with curios embedded stretched into the gloom. There was a brass foot rail and any number of mismatched stools, mostly empty from what I could see. There was, however, one thing I could see quite clearly. The bartender, a blind man in a pea soup fog could have seen the bartender.

The guy behind the counter looked like a farmhouse with a face. He would have made Santa Claus look clean-shaven. A puckered scar ran from about an inch above one eyebrow, through the lid, which puckered and drooped a bit, and down into the tufts of black hair that sprung from his right cheek. A tattoo of a flying eagle decorated his left forearm. A cobra was on the other.

From the look of him, I would say it had been a long time since he'd said hello to a bar of soap, but it wasn't my place to make introductions. I asked for Lone Wolf. Without saying a word, he pointed.

"Thanks."

Lone Wolf was apparently at the other end of the bar in the corner. I couldn't see him yet.

"What's up, Wannabe?" His voice reached out to me.

"I need a favor." I moved toward the voice, following the line of the bar and trying not to bruise myself on the smoke. Ebony-skinned and hard-muscled, Lone Wolf seemed to sprout from the wood and take shape as I watched. It was an eerie sensation.

He looked at me for a long moment before he spoke: "Why should I do you a favor?"

He was right, why should he? I thought I had a reason. I pulled a picture from my wallet and handed it to him.

A few months before I got the call from Aunt Gladys, I'd been involved with some bikers from a Harley club in New York. We got close, and they gave me a picture of all of us together, said if I ever needed help, the picture might open a few doors. It was having the desired effect.

"Yeah, I know this guy." He pointed to a beefy redneck looking biker with a skull tattooed on his bare chest. "Psycho Man. Rode with him down to Florida for the Daytona run."

I smiled. "I always wanted to do that."

Lone Wolf grinned. "Okay, Wannabe, how can I help?"

"I need a bodyguard for a couple of days." The grin widened. "Not for myself," I added. I explained the trouble.

"You mean you need me to babysit two little old ladies?"

I shrugged; "If you want to put it that way."

"Shit. What would Psycho Man say?" He grinned as he said it. "Sure. Ought t' be a hoot."

"Let me buy you that beer and we'll go."

For an answer, he held one finger up in the direction of the bearded house. The bartender reached under the counter and pulled out a can.

I didn't recognize the label until he slid it down the counter. It was black, with the family Harley Davidson Emblem on it. "I didn't know Harley had their own beer."

Lone Wolf flexed a sizeable biceps and gripped the can. Without that denim jacket for camouflage, I could see his T-shirt sleeve strain as he bent his elbow. There wasn't an ounce of fat on this guy. For a moment, I thought he was going to tear the top off that can with his teeth. "You can only buy it down Daytona way," he said. "Maybe a few other places. Cherry, here, orders it special for me. Don't you, Cherry?" He grinned at the bartender.

The house smiled through his beard, and I noticed he had one tooth in the middle of his mouth. I wondered briefly if he had lost the rest over that name and who had been big enough and dumb enough. He moved back down the bar, wiping it with a dingy rag.

Lone Wolf took a long pull from the Harley can. "Let's ride." I grinned, gave him the address, and followed him to Beth's.

ELEVEN

If I had thought Beth and Gladys would be a little alarmed when I brought in Lone Wolf, I was wrong. As soon as he pulled into the driveway, Beth was out the door and ogling the Harley. She bent her head close to the machine and had Lone Wolf rev the engine for her. Then, she fixed him with a gimlet eye.

"That needs a little something, young man. You work on it yourself?" Lone Wolf shook his head.

"I usually take it in. I've got this guy who takes care of it for me."

"Well, you see where that gets you. You just bring it on into the garage."

Before I could even introduce everyone, Beth was firing up her old Indian bike and showing my friend what a really finely tuned engine should sound like. By the time she had laid out all her "mechanics credentials" (that bike and the tools and handbooks), no introductions were necessary.

Beth took Lone Wolf over to a workbench and showed him what he should do by way of adjustments, demonstrating on the carburetor of an old Harley she was repairing for a friend. Then, she placed her cherished tools in his hands and pointed.

Lone Wolf, looking only slightly bewildered (I had to hand it to him), did as she instructed and listened to his engine problems smooth out before his very ears.

"Well, I'll be dipped in dog—"

"Sam!" my aunt interrupted, before I could embarrass myself in front of her lady friend. And I would have, too.

I inhaled exhaust fumes, cringed at the noise, and looked from a happy Lone Wolf to his bike, to the Indian, and on around the shop again. "What is all this, Beth?" I asked, reluctant to trust my senses.

"Well," she said, placing a fond hand on the bike, "this is the nineteen forty-nine Indian I'm restoring, Sam," she said, calmly. "And this," she waved around us, "is where I'm restoring it."

I shook my head. "You're restoring?"

"Why, yes." She nodded with a fierce pride. "My Arnold and I had this as a project for our 'golden years,' only he turned out to have a slightly more tarnished set of them than we had thought." Her eyes sparkled momentarily with unshed tears. "Now, I'll finish it for the both of us." She gestured to the carburetor she had used to demonstrate to Lone Wolf. "To afford extras for the Indian, I take in piece-work repair and tune-ups for friends in the motorcycle club Arnie and I used to ride with."

"We went all over the United States with those folks. And when the Indian's finished, I'll go again!"

I shook my head. "I've no doubt you will."

"Sam, it's not very different from when I used to work on the Mustang," Aunt Gladys said, elbowing me firmly. "Except Beth's a much better mechanic than I'd ever be. And it beats getting seasick!"

Beth took a deep bow and I had to laugh, remembering what my aunt had said about her abortive cruise to Mexico. It had, in fact, been Aunt Gladys who had put the first wrench in my hands, not my uncle.

"Well, it certainly all makes sense." I grinned at Lone Wolf and continued. "If you think about it."

He shrugged and leaned back over the Harley with Beth. In no time, she had told him the secret to keeping his maintenance problems at bay, as well as given him some of her special wax to use on his tank and fenders.

He seemed to take it all in stride. Even complimenting Beth's choice of colors—a bright metallic orange, so deep you could dive into it—for the newly restored Indian gas tank.

"Then, I'm going to get all this chromed, as soon as I save up," Beth said, pointing to the wheel rims, the exhaust pipes, and some other miscellany.

The two of them went on like that for a while, and then, the ladies went inside to put together some refreshments.

"They are great," Lone Wolf said, his eyes following Beth into the house. "Yeah, they are. I wouldn't want anything to happen to them."

"No prob. This is personal now."

"I'm getting out of the case tonight anyway. Then the heat should be off Aunt Gladys for good."

Lone Wolf gave me a look. "Tell me why you don't sound sincere?"

I shook my head. "Long story."

"I'm not goin' anywhere."

I guess it was the first time I had ever felt comfortable talking about it in detail. Maybe it was because I didn't know Lone Wolf very well. Or maybe it was because he had this knack for seeming like an old friend from the beginning. Or maybe it was just time to get it all off my chest; I don't know. But I told him about Margaret, and about how the cops had done nothing to catch her killers, zip, big zero, and about how I'd felt and what I'd done, all of it.

Lone Wolf didn't say much. He just nodded and listened.

I even told him about how I'd gone back to Shreveport after I got my P.I. license to try to solve it at last. How ironic it was, that after I'd acquired all the skills to do everything the cops had failed to do at the time, it had been far too late to achieve any success.

I mentioned that I'd never wanted to trust anything important to the cops ever again if I could help it. Lone Wolf was silent for a long time after I'd stopped talking. Then, he just sighed and clapped a hand the size of a rump roast on my shoulder. "Can't fault you for that, friend."

"Come and get it!" Beth called from the back porch and the moment was gone.

We spent the rest of the afternoon drinking beer and eating the chicken Beth and Aunt Gladys fried up in an old cast iron pan in the kitchen.

Around five, I left Lone Wolf to his protective vigil and went home to get ready to meet Kathy.

It felt good to be looking forward to that date with some of Margaret's ghosts laid to rest.

At eight, I was still waiting for Kathy's call. By the time we got through with dinner, it was after ten, and I had long since been grateful for Beth's late lunch of fried chicken.

The only good thing about the lateness of the hour was that I got to delay telling Kathy the truth about the knife fight and the altercation at the beach. She'd said she didn't want to hear shop talk until after she'd eaten and had a hot shower. I was just as glad to leave it until we were cuddling in bed together. That and the fact that with Gladys and Beth under Lone Wolf's protection, I'd be free to give her all my primo evidence from the locker, an act that I thought should square things between us.

Back at the house, I lay listening to the hot water of Kathy's shower. I was on my way to join her when the phone rang. I was halfway back through the bathroom door when I heard Lone Wolf's voice on the answering machine. I dove for the nightstand and picked up the receiver.

"Sam?"

"What's the matter?"

"They got 'em, Sam."

"Who?"

"I don't know who they were. But they got Beth and Gladys. I'm sorry."

I squeezed the receiver so hard I felt my fingers go numb. "I'll be right there."

I threw on clothes and dashed into the bathroom. "Kathy!"

I pulled open the shower door. "An emergency with Aunt Gladys. I gotta run."

Kathy squeezed soap out of her eyes and stared at me. "What?"

"An emergency, I'll explain later, sweetheart." I planted a kiss on her wet cheek and hurried to the door.

"Sam!" Kathy stepped wet and dripping from the shower and followed me to the top of the stairs, a towel clutched to her chest.

"I'll be back as soon as I can," I said, and I ran for the Mustang. Kathy would be angry, but that couldn't be helped. The bad guys had just changed all my plans. There was no way I was going to trust the cops with a kidnapping.

TWELVE

eth's front door was gaping open and Lone Wolf was standing by the garage. I ran over to him.

"Jesus! What the hell happened?" He looked like Shane after the bar-room brawl scene. His jacket was torn, and he sported a five-inch gash on his forearm. He held a bloody tea towel wrapped around it. An ugly bruise was darkening near his temple. At his feet lay the remains of his shovelhead. Neither of them looked like they'd live through the night.

"I'm sorry, Sam. I couldn't stop them."

"Back up and tell me what happened." I led him into the house and sat him in a kitchen chair. He told me about it while I fixed an ice pack for his head. Some blood had trickled down the back of his neck and was staining the ribbed edge of his T-shirt. Apparently, it had taken a lot to knock him out—more than the blow to the temple, anyway.

"They showed up about…" he looked at his watch. "Thirty, thirty-five minutes ago. We were doing fine until they attacked the Harley. Then Beth roared out the back door with her broom handle and things got away from me."

"How many of them?"

"Three, I think."

"You get a look at them?"

He nodded carefully, as if he thought his head might come loose from his shoulders. "Sort of. The one with the knife," he held up his arm, "was a skinny Latino with a ponytail. One had a flat face with a broken-looking nose. The third one, I never saw. He came up behind and cold-cocked me." He flinched as I put more ice against his head. "You know 'em?"

I nodded. "Two of them. Ponytail's been following me and sort of staking out the house. Broken Nose and two others filled my dance card at the beach the other day."

"You see their car?"

He stood up slowly. "Yeah. Beat up gray Nova with a cracked back window. No plates on the front. Never saw the back end. I was out when they left." The thought sent a shudder through me.

"They're long gone."

"Cops could put out an all points?"

I shook my head. "Been gone thirty or forty minutes now. This time of night, you can be anywhere in this city in that much time." I looked at him. "Besides, I told you how I feel about cops when there's something big at stake. Kidnapping is about as big as it gets."

I rinsed out the tea towel and took a closer look at the forearm cut. "This should have a few stitches."

Lone Wolf made a face that pushed deep furrows between his brows and made his supraorbital ridge look almost Neanderthal. "Piss on that!" he said. "Let them doctors get at you and put in a half-dozen bits of thread or staples, and pretty soon you can't move it, get it wet—nothin'! You just got to sit around and baby the damn thing. It'll heal." He took the box of Band-Aids away from me and trimmed himself some butterfly bandages out of the sticky ends, tossing out the gauze pad sections.

When he had about seven of the tape butterflies laid out on the edge of the table, he motioned for me to help him hold the edges of the cut together. Then, he slapped the tape across the wound as neatly as any physician and grinned at me. "Got an Ace bandage?"

I laughed. "You've done this before," I said and rooted in Aunt Gladys's bathroom cabinet until I found one of the elastic rolls of pink-beige bandaging. My aunt was terrific; there were the two little metal clips right where they should be. I tossed the roll to Lone Wolf, and he one-handed it out of the air and began to wrap. In a moment, he was flexing to check the tension and nearly as good as new.

"So? What are we going to do?" Lone Wolf got up and headed out to the garage.

"I wish to hell I knew more than I do," I said, following him. "Holy shit!" I said, looking at the mess on the drive-in front of the garage. "Sorry about your bike," I said, feeling the inadequacy of the words as I spoke them. I promised myself right then that as soon as I got my inheritance, I'd replace it for him.

"Hell with the bike. It's a goner. We gotta make sure Beth and your aunt don't end up in the same condition."

"Yeah, and quick." As my mind catalogued the little bits and pieces from my investigation, I looked down at the wreck that had been his beautiful Harley. Gas dribbled from a crack in the tank and pooled on the drive. A few blows had knocked the carburetors free of the engine. One was lying at least a foot from the bike. I figured he was right. It was a goner. I didn't see how it could possibly be fixed.

Then I saw it. Something that was no part of Lone Wolf's bike, I hunkered down and picked it up.

"What you got there?"

I held it up. "Looks like a shark's tooth." I tossed it to him, and he plucked it like fruit off a tree.

"Damn. Too bad it doesn't have a return address," he said, trying to find humor where there was none.

"Hang on. Maybe it does." I hurried to the Mustang and dug in the portfolio I had never gotten around to showing Kathy or delivering to my agent. I fished out the business card.

Lone Wolf came loping gently across the front lawn. "What'cha got?" The way he moved; I would have bet his head hurt like a rupturing appendix.

I handed him the card.

He focused for a moment then looked at me. "You think?"

"I think we've got to give it a try."

"Guess you couldn't get a better address for a shark's tooth than a yacht club." He grinned and started to climb into the passenger's side of the Mustang.

"You know how to get there?" He nodded. "You're sure you don't want to get your head injury looked at first?"

He threw me his scowl-growl combo, and I shut up about getting him help. "I hurt I'll mend." He motioned me around to the driver's side. "Besides, if we find those guys, I don't want any bandages in my way." He clenched those huge fists in his lap, and I already felt sorry for whoever would be on the receiving end.

The Pacific Yacht Club dozed along with the rest of the waterfront at the marina in Newport Beach.

I parked on the street about a hundred yards down from the sign for the club. Lone Wolf was out almost before I set my brake. I wasn't far behind him.

We flattened into some shadows when a security car drove past, and then hurried to the building to look for a way in.

"Weren't for bad luck, as the saying goes," Lone Wolf muttered as he tried the last set of sliding doors on the harbor side of the club.

"No problem," it was my turn to tell him I pulled some lock picks from my coat pocket and looked over the situation. Illegal as hell, but a gift from a B & E man I'd helped in Shreveport. I looked into a few things for him while I was working on Margaret's case. I was luckier on his behalf than my own, and he was very grateful. "Not exactly Fort Knox. Can you take care of the alarm?"

Lone Wolf nodded and began tracking down the hookup.

When he gave me the okay, I went to work on the door. The small lock box for the sliding bolt was mounted at the top of the frame. It was a little awkward picking a lock that was higher than my head, but it's the sort of thing that's done mostly by feel, anyway. If you're good at it, and you have enough practice, your arms don't even get tired before you're finished. I hadn't had a lot of recent practice, but at least we were inside before the guard made his next pass.

In a quick but thorough search that only depressed me, I learned my aunt was nowhere on the premises.

"Any bright ideas?" I frowned at Lone Wolf. "What was that you said about bad luck?" I stared out at the harbor. "The boats," I said, with the dawn taking a long time getting here. "They had to have stashed them on one of their boats."

"Great," said Lone Wolf looking out at all the hulls bobbing on the night swells. "That ought to take about a million hours of legwork."

"There has to be a record here of who's registered as being in a PYC slip," I said, yanking open a file drawer marked S. "Nothing under renters or slips." I looked for Lone Wolf and noticed a greenish light off to my far left.

He was seated at a computer terminal and accessing records like crazy. "I think they'll be in here," he said, apparently warming to his work.

I watched in awe as Lone Wolf typed some unidentifiable combinations of letters and symbols. After a few different attempts, he swore softly and rested the heels of his hands against the edge of the keyboard for a moment.

"Where the hell did you learn to do all that?" I asked, stunned at this startling side of my Harley-riding friend.

"All what?" Lone Wolf didn't even look up from the terminal as he tapped keys. "This high-tech shit?"

"Yeah. This high-tech shit," I confirmed.

"Oh. I'm a systems analyst for a bank."

I felt my jaw sag and fought to pull it back under my control. "Guess you can never go by appearances," I said, more to myself than my friend.

He looked up with a grin, "Sure can't." He looked me up and down and stared meaningfully at my set of lock-picks. "I never would have guessed you for an actor."

I laughed. "Yeah, you and everybody hiring in L.A." I looked over his shoulder. "So, what's a systems analyst?"

"A trouble-shooter somebody who gets rid of the bug's people put in the computer system when they're unhappy about being fired or when they're bored on the job and ready to quit anyway. And there's the routine stuff. We test old programs and do upgrades to new ones." He fell silent and adopted a serious look for a moment. "Besides, it's my favorite hobby after bikes." He scowled.

"What's wrong?"

He shook his head. "Damn passwords. Computers fall into the hands of amateurs and right away, everyone's James Bond."

I watched screen after screen come up and demand a password. "Can you get around it?"

"Maybe, but it all takes time. Lemme' make a call first." I listened while he dialed and sent out the alert. Before too many more hours passed, every biker in Los Angeles would be looking for a gray Nova with a cracked rear window and no front plate. If Beth and my aunt were still being driven around in that car, their kidnappers were as good as busted.

He cradled the receiver and looked at me. "Okay, now I got time." He leaned over the keyboard again.

It wasn't looking hopeful, to me anyway. Lone Wolf didn't seem worried. In fact, he seemed delighted.

Suddenly, the screen went blank and then came on again clicking and whirring into its start-up. He slammed two keys down simultaneously and answered a typed question in the affirmative. Then he typed some more.

The slip rental records scrolled onto the screen.

"System sure needs to be upgraded to something faster." He set up the commands to print out a hard copy of the slips and renters.

As soon as the printer stopped running, Lone Wolf tore off the sheet and we stepped outside. "Jesus, thirty-two boats." He looked at his watch. "It's nearly four. We haven't got much time."

I nodded. "Thank God the club only owns four. Let's check them first."

Working separately, we searched as rapidly as we could. It was about time and just our luck that, some gung-ho fisherman would show up to catch the early tide or some damn thing.

I was checking out the fourth and last club-owned boat and finding no sign of Gladys, but I guess it was lucky that it was getting a little light or I might never have seen it. I was crossing the deck of a large motor-sailor when I caught a glint of something against the dark teak. When I reached down for it, I found it to be one of the earrings I had given Aunt Gladys for her birthday almost a year ago. It wasn't as distinctive as those Margaret had picked out—the gold doorknockers—but this one was either my aunt's, or it was the most monumental coincidence in the world that someone had been on this ship and had lost one that looked so much like it.

"Hey, Lone Wolf!" I said in the whispering shout of an overtired man trying to get attention without drawing any.

His head appeared over the gun whale of the blue Bay liner in the adjacent slip. "We just got luckier," I said, and he grinned. I held up the earring. "Gladys has been here. All we have to do is find out more about this boat. I'm going to check the log. Keep watch."

I hurried to the helm. Sure enough, the log was in plain view. I flipped through it for the last month. I looked at the most recent entry, logged in for today's date. There it was: Harbor Cruise. Swell. That told me exactly nothing except that he'd had the boat out for an hour and twenty minutes. That told me even less. I wondered where in Newport harbor area he could have gone for that amount of time. I mean it was a large harbor, and the speed limit was only five knots or no wake, so it would take a while to get anywhere. It didn't take much mathematical ability to figure that they had brought the ladies here and shipped them out immediately. But to where?

There was one entry that came up repeatedly: Departure: Newport Beach, Destination: Long Beach, Barrington Docks. Each entry was initialed R.R.H. Now, if I could match a captain to those initials, I'd have someone else to question.

I was about to leave when I saw a stiff white card stuck between the unused pages at the back of the log. I pulled it free and looked at it. It was a formal invitation to a party aboard a Barrington Lines Cruise ship. Black tie, I tucked the invitation in my shirt.

Lone Wolf was waiting for me at the bottom of the gangplank. We started walking down the dock when a familiar figure came from the PYC building and headed toward us. I squinted through the early morning light, and we managed to recognize each other at roughly the same moment.

Broken nose saw me, then Lone Wolf, and took off. After our episode at the beach and his bout at Beth's when he'd helped the others wreck the Harley, fear must have flowered vividly in his mind.

I saw his eyes go wide and heard a whistling sound. Something flashed through the field of my peripheral vision, and I heard a solid thunk an instant later. Lone Wolf's knife quivered in the wall just about one inch from where Broken-nose had been standing. Fortunately for him—and maybe for Lone Wolf—he wasn't there anymore. That knife would have no doubt skewered him through a vital part and had Lone Wolf dealing with some sort of murder charge.

Faster than a man with a head wound and a slashed forearm should be able to move, Lone Wolf jerked his blade free of the wood and bolted after Broken-nose.

THIRTEEN

We chased him in and out of the docks and boats for a bit, but it soon became obvious that we'd never catch him on his own complex turf. When he hit the murky water in a running dive and vanished behind the sleek silhouette of a forty-two-foot Grand Banks, we had no way of guessing where he might come up again.

I glanced around to see if it was still clear, and we combed the docks for about thirty more minutes trying to see if we could spot the sneaky little shit. Lone Wolf, rigid with unspent revenge, stared into the dark water and waited. I stood with him and thought equally dark thoughts about my Aunt Gladys.

I hated the feeling that in losing Broken-nose, I had lost one of my best chances to find her before something worse happened. Broken-nose had done a disappearing act, so we finally beat it back to the Mustang. Again, our timing in leaving PYC private property skirted the security guard's drive by. We headed home.

Lone Wolf and I got back to the house around six a.m. The morning traffic was just getting heavy. I was glad not to be on the freeway at the height of rush hour. It becomes a parking lot between six and ten, especially on the Ventura. Heck, the Ventura was a parking lot anytime, except maybe between two and four a.m. unless there was the added bonus of road repairs.

I went into the kitchen and put on some coffee. Lone Wolf wanted to make another call to see if anything turned up about the Nova. While he dialed, I gathered my clues. From the scowl on his face, I assumed that none of his buddies had spotted the kidnapper's car.

I brought the portfolio in from the Mustang and spread everything out nice and neat on the kitchen table. As soon as he was off the phone, I showed him the key and the locker contents and told him all that had happened.

He leafed through the pictures of the girls. "What do you think?" I asked, as soon as he'd returned to the first shot.

"Great ass," he said, pointing to one girl who was pulling a dress over her head.

"What else?"

"Whoever took 'em should've waited until they took more off." He shot me a wicked grin.

"Yeah," I said, leaning to look again. "They really aren't very good shots, are they?" He shook his head.

"Well, she was a model, so her friends—these girls—were probably models, and what do they know about the backside of a camera? Eh?"

He shrugged and dumped the negatives from the glassine packet and held them up to the light, squinting fiercely. At last, he put into words what had been bothering me about the pictures: "So, if she wanted great shots, she couldn't do better than to rip 'em out of magazines or get their publicity photos, could she?"

"But she didn't. This must have been an event of some importance to her anyway." Lone Wolf agreed.

I took it a step further. "So, if these are just candid shots, what were they doing in a locker—a locker someone was willing to kill to get into?

"Beats the shit out of me, maybe they have nothing to do with it. You ever think of that, Wannabe?"

That struck me hard. "Run with that."

"Well, her gym clothes were in the bag, and they don't mean anything to your case, do they?"

Maybe the photos were incidental? I looked hard at Lone Wolf. "Just some shots of friends, like the ones I take at cast parties and nothing more?" My gut said no.

Lone Wolf didn't answer. He picked up the envelope and methodically slid the packet of photos inside. He had a look on his face somewhere between puzzlement and anger. He looked at the negatives again, returned them to the glassine sleeves, and put the sleeves in the photo envelope.

"What you thinkin'?" I asked him.

"You know, they used to take down everything but your mother's maiden name when you turned in your film. Now when I drop some off, I worry I'll never see them again." He winked at me. "If they're real hot, I worry someone else will."

I laughed, but my eyes were glued on the virtually unmarked envelope from one of those one-hour developing shops. "Son of a gun!" I had assumed the photos were Marilyn's, but they could have belonged to someone else. I reached for the phone.

"What are you doing?"

I held up a hand in mute request for patience while I dialed the number on the envelope and got one of those disconnects messages with no forwarding. While I listened to it, I took Debbie Pittman's number from my wallet. It wasn't her number that I had dialed, which meant it wasn't Marilyn's either. "I think we just got a break."

Lone Wolf looked like a hound on a scent. He was smiling. "Broke the first rule, huh?"

"Yeah. Never assume." He grinned.

I called a phone company friend in New York, asked and promised favors. He agreed to call me as soon as he had something worthwhile. I hoped he would be able to talk some L.A. phone supervisor into looking up the name that went with the disconnected number.

As I hung up, the phone it rang. Talk about timing. I picked it up and heard this Latino-sounding voice at the other end. "Stop snooping where you don't belong and keep away from the cops if you want to see your auntie and her friend alive again."

I hung up and stared at Lone Wolf. "That was Ponytail."

Lone Wolf replied, "The one who staked out your house and helped break up my bike?"

I nodded. "The same. It wasn't good. He warned me about snooping and again about involving the cops. I don't like it. These guys are serious, and now that they have Aunt Gladys and Beth, there's no telling what they'll do."

"Then you and I better figure this all out before they decide to take action."

"You bet. See what you make of this one." I showed him the picture of Debbie and Weasel, hoping that we had more meaningful clues here than I had thought.

He took the photograph and studied it a moment, turned it over, and read the back. "He does sort of look like a Weasel, especially with that nose."

"Never mind the nose. Do you know where it was taken?"

He held it closer and stared. "I'd almost bet that's Maxx's Place on Yucca in Hollywood."

"Great. When's it open?"

Lone Wolf checked the clock. "Maybe nine, it's a neighborhood place. They suit the needs of the locals."

I nodded. "How long would it take you to see if this Weasel is over there?"

Lone Wolf thought a moment. "With my Trans-am, forty minutes or so, only the car is in the shop. I blew the engine. It won't be ready for a few days yet. Damn! I was countin' on that bike," he added angrily.

I handed him the keys to the Mustang. "Hang on a second." I looked at the business card again and wondered about Sondra Chase.

I dialed the private number of one of the heads of the William Hamill Agency. While it rang, I doodled, ivy leaves and vines across the kitchen note pad.

I hoped Tom Hamill remembered the great time I'd showed him when he visited his brother, Willie, in New York. And the work I'd done for him on a private matter that had nothing to do with his capacity as one of my agents. "Hey, Tom, Sam Ryan, here," I said when he answered, and then gave it a long count.

The nickel dropped. "Hey. Sammy! You in L.A.?"

"Yeah." I was relieved to hear the note of recognition behind that nasal twang. Tom's voice sounded like a cross between a mouth harp and a rusty hinge. So did his brother. "I need to collect on that favor, Tom."

"Anything; anything. You need a little work, maybe?"

"Always, I just made an appointment to drop my portfolio off at the agency."

"Hey, you're okay! If we get a call for your type, you got it."

"Thanks, but that's not the favor."

"Oh? Speak." Fortunately, that voice wasn't the only thing that ran in the family, so did loyalty.

"You know anything about the Sondra Chase Agency?"

"Sondra Chase?" He muttered the last name several more times, and then I could almost hear the smile in his voice. "Yeah, a modeling agency, right?"

I praised his acumen and pressed on. "I need to know about the owner. Who can I ask?"

"You could ask me, maybe? Some of my clients used to work for her, just 'til things started happening for them, you know?"

"Okay. What can you tell me?"

"Listen, why don't I meet you at Jerry's Deli? I got some time before I have to be at the agency. You know the place?"

"No but give me the address."

"Numbers," he muttered a note of disgust evident in his voice.

"Ya' can't miss it. It's Ventura Boulevard, next to a bowling alley in Studio City. Right down from the Sportsman's Lodge. It's famous."

"Okay, what time?" If I needed an address, I'd look it up myself. Everyone in this town seemed to work on a sort of radar for the "in" places. Between that and the "landmarks" method, it was hard to get an actual address out of them.

"Let's see, meet you there at—" There was a pause while he checked something, maybe his watch, maybe that fat appointment calendar he was famous for. "—eight thirty?"

"Sounds good, thanks." I jotted "Jerry's" and "8:30" in an ivy thicket at the edge of the note pad and hung up.

I looked up the phone and address of Jerry's Deli. Since this was Hollywood, I tried the cutesy spelling: J-E-R-I first. Nothing, just some hair and nail salons. Cute, it was Jerry's Famous Deli and there were several of them, two, on Ventura Boulevard alone. I took the address of the one in Studio City/North Hollywood.

I copied the address for myself and handed Lone Wolf the phone number.

"You see Weasel at Maxx's; you can call me here. I'll come right down and question him."

Lone Wolf moved past, gave me a high five, and took off.

I made sure to take the Thomas Guide map book, turned to the right page for Hollywood, and grabbed the keys to Beth's station wagon off the hook near the back door. If Lone Wolf did see Weasel, I needed to know how to get there from Jerry's.

I was at the deli in plenty of time to order a good breakfast before Tom arrived.

As I munched bagels and sipped hot coffee, I looked around at the Spartan decor. Old movie posters were showcased here and there, and they covered the entire length and height of the wall that led to the restrooms, but the furniture was plain hardwood tables and chairs to match the plank flooring. A few of the walls were bowed out into mullioned alcoves and these held lots of hanging plants. Other than that, I wouldn't have said a fortune was spent on interior design.

The ambiance, however, hummed.

Casually dressed wheeler-dealers hurried in and out with much glad-handing and name-dropping. Women met and kissed the air over each other's shoulders. Customers walked to tables in earnest groups of two and three and sometimes with an eagerness, so hearty it had to be phony, as they hailed more to join them.

I was half finished with my steak before I saw Tom press through the crowd waiting to be seated. His idea of eight thirty did not mesh with mine. Mine depended on the mundane, namely a clock.

I waved and saw him maneuver his bulky body between the packed tables. The buzz of

Hollywood, making deals in voices that got substantially louder when mentioning either money or famous names, nearly drowned out Tom's greeting.

His apple-round face creased in a smile around the chunky unlit cigar he held gripped in his teeth. I'd never seen him light one, just clench it endlessly between slightly yellowed champers. Tobacco stains notwithstanding, his wide smile was still his stock-in-trade. He leaned across the table and gripped my hand as if I were saving him from a shipwreck.

Fitting, since that was very nearly the job, I had done for him over a year ago. I had bailed him out of a real mess with a management agent who had scammed him out of a few grand and vanished with the commissions, as well as the salaries of several of Tom's irate clients.

"Sammy! It's been too damn long!"

I agreed and motioned him into the booth. The waitress brought him a menu, smiled at him, and chatted for a moment. Tom was a regular. Naturally, he introduced the waitress as—what else—an aspiring actress. In the half-an-instant introduction, Tom Hamill had managed to give the girl a rundown of my acting resume and impress her with my degree of sought-after ness. I was impressed that he had looked up my data before meeting me. Either that or he had a memory so long it extended into his brother's head.

Skill like that made Tom and his brother two of the best agents in the business. Back in the sixties, a folk singer named Rod Mckuen had done a version of Madame Butterfly in a fast-talking half-minute or some such ridiculous time frame. I always thought of that when I heard either of the Hamill's launches a spiel.

She took Tom's order for an omelets and toasted onion bagel and bustled out of sight, a slightly dazed look of admiration still turned my way.

"So, what do you want to know about this modeling agency?" Tom asked after he'd slathered his bagel with cream cheese.

I told him it was Sondra I was most interested in, and Tom talked his way through the omelet, a second order of bagels, and three cups of coffee before he ran out of scandalous tales.

"Tom, you ever think of going into the tabloid business? Bet you could give the National Enquirer a run for its money."

He sat there like the Hollywood potentate he was, not so much entertaining me as holding court. Tom laughed and gestured for the waitress. "What do I need with more? Between here and the New York office, my agencies do enough business to keep me and Willie real nice."

"Good to know you're not greedy," I said, snaking the check out from under his meaty paw. "I like that in an agent." I pulled out my wallet. "I'll get this. You're doing me the favor."

"By the way, who can I see about a makeover? A real professional job, face fur, toupee, and the works."

He dug through his appointment book and scribbled a name and number on one of his business cards. "You tell George you're the guy who solved that mess last year. He'll do right by you. His sister, Nancy, was one of the actresses whose salary you saved."

I nodded. "Thanks."

Our actress came over to tell me I had a phone call. "Excuse me for a moment, Tom. I'll be right back."

I spoke to Lone Wolf and hung up, paid the check, and tipped the girl before returning to the table.

"Gotta go Tommy, thanks for your help." I nodded at the front register. "It's all taken care of."

As I left Jerry's, I could see Tom chatting and laughing with the actress/waitress. She was smiling and refilling his coffee, leaning forward—low enough to display her potential.

I planned to drop by and relieve Lone Wolf for a while so he could grab a meal. Then, I'd go over and see if a decent make-up job and costuming could get me into the Pacific Yacht Club without anyone recognizing me. If not, it wasn't worth it to go and be made and maybe get Beth and Gladys into more trouble.

FOURTEEN

As soon as Lone Wolf was ready to resume his stake out, I gave him George's number and went off to see if the makeup artist could do anything for me. I purposely didn't tell Lone Wolf what I was going to try. He could be one of my first test cases. If I could fool him, maybe I could get away with crashing the party unrecognized.

Tom's friend, George, really did a job. I studied the way the iron-gray toupee blended with my natural hairline while the fullness subtlety altered the shape of my face. There was no time to build an orthodontic appliance like the one Brando wore around his teeth in The Godfather, but the illusion worked well with the help of the tidy beard he practically implanted in the pores of my face. I gave the beard and moustache an experimental smoothing with one hand and then the other, definitely a right-hand gesture for me. It paid to work these things out ahead of time.

I leaned over George's sink and slipped in the soft brown contact lenses I sometimes used when I worked. My natural eye color was such a distinctive blue that these lenses had come in handy in both my jobs more often than I could count, the real me was fading fast.

I dressed in the snappy gray western-cut jacket and ostrich-hide cowboy boots I had brought from Gladys's. Kenny Rogers had nothing on me. Now all I needed was a voice like his and even half his fans. I paid George and thanked him for taking me on such short notice. Then I drove Beth's station wagon back to her house.

I made a call and rented a Cadillac—white with red leather interior. A guy from the rental agency brought it right to the door. I left Beth's wagon parked in the driveway. It would help give the appearance that someone was home. Of course, the most valued things had already been taken, Beth and Aunt Gladys. I felt a sick twinge and hurried to the Caddy.

Although there is something exhilarating about being in character, the good feelings were marred by the steadily sickening dread that with every minute that passed, I was letting Aunt Gladys down. Progress was minimal. It was all taking time too damn much time.

I decided to use the accent I'd adopted for a play I'd done a few years ago called 'Send Me No Flowers.' It had been made into a movie with Rock Hudson, Doris Day, and Tony Randall. Clint Walker played the part I had had on stage, that of a Texan who was an old friend to Doris Day. Why they cast me for the role, I don't know. Clint Walker was a bear of a man who looked like an apartment building on the move. I'm nowhere near his size, but I guess my Texas accent was on the money; I'd have to depend on it again today.

I had one stop to make before I checked in on Lone Wolf. I tipped my hat back on my head and went inside. Every time I adjust the angle of a western hat, I think of that great bit of dialogue James Garner had in 'Murphy's Romance.' He told Sally Field's son all about what each nuance of hat-angle-lingo meant. Mine was tipped back in that way he'd described as being indicative of good digestion and an inherently friendly nature.

I approached the front counter. The blonde at the desk was typing away on the computer that Lone Wolf and I had just accessed about five hours earlier. She looked up and smiled.

The sight of me startled her a bit. I guess I had succeeded in my desire to be conspicuous, while being so unlike myself, that the real me would fade into the woodwork by comparison.

George had a great idea when he'd suggested the rich oil baron from Texas image. As Tom had predicted, George was ready to bend over backward to help the man who had saved his little sister's job.

The ostrich boots were killing my feet, and the mustache and beard tickled, but the costume gave me that beloved and familiar rush of playing a part to the hilt in front of an audience, even an audience of one.

"Good afternoon, sir."

Clint had played it suave. So did I, but with more humility. I removed my hat and fondled the brim with a studied nervousness. "Howdy, ma'am."

The blonde was obviously impressed, and I could tell my self-conscious act had triggered her nurturing instincts already. She smiled one of those comforting smiles that nurse's use when they want to prep you for surgery. "How may I help you, sir?"

I played with the brim of my hat again.

"Well, I believe I'd like some information about your club."

"No problem, sir, I'll call our membership coordinator." She looked a question at me.

"John Calder, ma'am."

"Glad to have you aboard, Mr. Calder." She flashed me a hundred-watt smile and made her request over the intercom.

I saw a beautiful Strawberry Blonde approaching us from one of the back offices. She had Strawberry blonde hair down past her shoulders and that rare treasure granted so very few blondes in this world—flawless skin with nary a freckle in sight.

"Leslie, this is Mr. John Calder. He'd like some information about the club and membership. Will you take care of him, please?"

Leslie made me a gift of a welcoming smile and her readily extended hand. "How nice to meet you Mr. Calder," she said and put her other hand over mine when I took the one she offered. I felt almost as if she were comforting me in a time of bereavement.

"Why not let me take you through while I tell you the basics? Would you like something to drink?"

"Oh, no thank you, ma'am. It's a bit early for me." I turned my hat in my hands. The flash of the prop diamond pinky ring George had insisted upon looked real enough to fool me.

She smiled. "Soda? Fresh squeezed orange juice?"

I tried to look properly sheepish, but I don't think there's an actor alive who can muster a blush on command. "Thank you kindly, ma'am. Nothing just now, but don't you let me stop you."

She turned and walked directly away from me, secure enough to know I'd follow, willingly. I watched her rear suspension at work with pleasure. It was covered in a nautical blue miniskirt and left a lot of neatly turned leg showing all the way down to red heels. "The club was founded five years ago by Ms. Sondra Chase and Tom Barrington. Mr. Barrington owns a cruise ship line and some freighters that go back and forth from here to the Orient.

"We have forty slips with thirty-two currently filled. We can handle boats up to sixty feet. Of course, since some of the larger boats are owned by more than one person, and because members of the immediate family receive complimentary membership cards, we have more than a hundred people on our roster, one hundred and four to be exact." She flashed me another perfect smile, and I mumbled something and tried to sound suitably impressed as I jerked my eyes from the stiletto heels and the pretty curve, they leant her calves.

She moved outside onto the docks and waved a hand in the direction of some empty slips. "Some of our members are in the process of buying new boats, and some are out for the day." She kept me walking while she pointed out this luxury accommodation and that special member facility, agilely avoiding getting those heels caught between the planking. God only knew how; certainly, I didn't.

At last, she set the hook—none too gracefully, I thought. "Are you interested in becoming a member?"

"Well, it's like this." I spoke slowly and deliberately. "My boat, a little fifty-footer called the Yellow Rose, is back in Galveston. But, if I could find a right nice spot for her, I'd have her shipped out. I have to be in this area for about a year, and I miss my Rosie already." I smiled soulfully and fought the urge to place my Stetson over my heart. "I'm planning to live aboard if I bring her out. Don't cotton much to city living where the buildings are slap up against one another. Used to the wide open. You understand."

Leslie nodded, sympathy already flowing, an encouraging smile at the ready. Either the genes were great in this part of town or the orthodontists were living well. "I like space around me, too, Mr. Calder unless I'm down here at the water. That makes all the difference, doesn't it?"

"Oh, yes, ma'am," I said, giving her my own genetically good smile.

"But maybe you could tell me about signing up?"

"Certainly, we have two plans." She rambled quickly through a lot of numbers and time spans that all sounded exorbitant and fairly foolish to me, but I tried to hide my plebian tastes and pocketbook and look calmly happy with it all.

"Now, that sounds right reasonable. You have a slip for my Rosie? She's a fifty-footer. I'd prefer a slip at the end of a dock, especially until I get my captain up from Galveston." I tried a self-effacing grin. She looked like she was buying. "I'm not all that good at the helm myself and the end slots are easier."

She laughed, a sound like a kitten running across a keyboard, and said that she was sure I was a better sailor than that and was just being modest.

Then we chatted some more, and I asked her to have coffee with me at the place I could see across the dock.

She looked hesitant. "Well, I don't know if I'm due for my break just yet, Mr. Calder."

"Let me ask your boss if you can take an early coffee. I am all alone in a new city, and we could talk about my membership while you keep me company."

"I guess I could ask," she said and vanished into the back office.

She came out smiling, so I guessed she'd gotten permission. We walked across to the cafe. I waited until we were settled with coffee and a couple of fresh muffins and then began to question her gently.

"How long did you say this club's been here?"

"Ms. Chase founded it five years ago. She bought in with Mr. Barrington." She looked over to see if I'd remember the earlier reference.

"Since that time, the club has more than tripled its net worth."

"Are there any other shareholders?"

"Why would you ask?" Her look became guarded.

"Well, if I'm going to invest in a club…"

"There are no shares available, Mr. Calder, only memberships." She tore off a bit of her muffin, dropped it on her plate, and then rubbed the crumbs from her fingertips. I was making her nervous. I'd have to couch my questions more subtlety. I gave her my most ingratiating grin and tried to look like a harmless version of Richie Brockelman supplicating James Rockford. She didn't completely buy it.

Television has ruined it for us normal folks, I thought. Actors on camera have it all over us when it comes to facial expressions, must have something to do with camera angles. I pressed on. "You spoke of Ms. Chase. Is she somebody in the boating world? The name sounds familiar."

She smiled. "Ms. Chase founded the Sondra Chase Modeling Agency and was a top model herself for many years."

She spoke with pride and, I would have bet, not a little case of hero worship. I had more than a suspicion that Leslie was a wannabe.

"You one of her models?" Flattery couldn't hurt.

She dazzled me with her very white teeth. "I hope to be, just as soon as I save enough for my portfolio. Sondra says I still need some eight by ten glossies and a composite sheet."

"I'm sure you'll be quite an asset to Ms. Chase's stable."

"Thank you. I hope to start working in that field by the end of summer. Ms. Chase was nice enough to let me do office work here at the club for her so that I could make my rent and start paying photographer fees."

"She must have a lot of faith in you, Leslie. Does she often help young models get a start?"

She beamed at me a moment. "Well, I think she's helping me out because she knows I don't have anyone else to give me a boost. My folks passed away, and my brother is a career man in the service." Suddenly, she seemed to recall that we were not here to talk about her future career in front of the lens.

I learned no more except a few details beyond what Tom had told me: that Sondra Chase had a fight with Taylor Brown ages back and that led her to found her own agency. That topic came up because Leslie was discussing the short-lived career of a model. That was apparently what had frosted Ms. Chase. Taylor Brown had told her she was over the hill at thirty something and she'd taken offense.

Apparently, it was still a hot battle on the rare occasions when they met. Having met Mr. Brown, I could easily see him being just that cut-and-dried about someone else's life.

"Can I ask you a question?" Leslie said, looking at me over the edge of her cup.

"It's only fair. I've been asking you questions."

"Are you married?"

"No."

"Is there someone special?"

I had to think about that question. There really hadn't been someone special since Margaret, but Kathy had come into my life.

"Yes."

By the look on her face, I could tell she was disappointed with my answer. "It figures. All the cute ones are taken."

I paid the check and walked Leslie back to the club. As we were making arrangements for me to sign membership papers, I knew I had to come up with an out. "Oh, Leslie, I almost clean forgot about Blue."

"Blue?" She looked confused.

"My dog whereabouts, do you walk the pets for their—ah, well, you know? Their dailies?"

She gave me an icy stare. "We don't permit animals on our docks. No facilities for their 'dailies' as you call it."

"I thought I saw a black cat on that blue Bay liner over yonder." I nodded toward the window that looked out on the slips.

"Well, that's a cat. People have litter boxes for them. They don't cause problems where people want to walk."

"Well, now, I may have to rethink this whole thing. I don't know as I could possibly put Blue in a kennel. I might just have to find myself a little ranch to rent."

Leslie looked stricken. Maybe she worked on commission. "Perhaps your dog would be just as happy on your Texas spread while you work in the city, Mr. Calder."

"I imagine he would, but we've always been together, and I don't know how I could abandon him after all these years." I pushed the papers back across the desk. "I reckon I'll just think on it some more." I almost got downright tearful over the future happiness of my fictitious dog. Well, that's what good acting was all about.

As I watched the docks over her shoulder, I saw the motor-sailor I had searched only a few hours ago pulling away from the slip.

Then the bottom dropped out of my stomach as I noticed that the deckhand coiling a line and stepping easily along the side deck and out onto the bow was Ponytail.

I forced a smile onto my lips. "Now that's a pretty little thing," I said, pointing at the gliding boat, which sometime earlier had held my Aunt Gladys captive. "Is that a club member?" I asked, already knowing part of the answer.

Leslie smiled. "Oh, that's the Free Sea. The club owns her, but only Ms. Chase takes her out. I mean she's not available for regular charters. Ms. Chase uses her to wine and dine our potential members." She gave me a grin. "If you'll tell me when you'll be back to sign up, I can schedule you for a complimentary champagne cruise."

I smiled. "Well, that's right nice of you, Leslie, but I have to check with my secretary and then think on old Blue. I'll call you."

We parted company on just such unpredictable terms, me thanking her for the offer of a free cruise and leaving a return visit open as to date and purpose.

By now, my feet were screaming louder than the original ostrich probably had. I hurried to the Cadillac and pulled my boots off as soon as I had the door closed and the air conditioning on.

I used the Caddy and its air to check on Lone Wolf. It was already ninety degrees in the shade that day.

When I turned onto Yucca, I saw Aunt Gladys's Mustang parked about a half a block down from Maxx's Place. A parrot in cream-colored neon flashed on and off high above the roof. If only that had been in the picture, it would have been a snap to identify. It must have cost the owner a nice bit of change. Some of the galleries in New York that specialized in modern art actually had neon sculptures like that for sale.

I saw Lone Wolf lounging against the side of Maxx's with a can of Coke in one hand and a burger in the other. I parked the Caddy and pulled on my boots again. Despite the worry that left an icy spot in the pit of my stomach, I couldn't resist staying in character for a few more minutes.

"Say, fella, you all know where that theater is where you can stand in John Wayne's boot prints?"

Lone Wolf looked over his shoulder and gave me one of the most disgusted looks I have ever seen on a living human being. I pushed a little harder.

"I sure would love to see if I could fill his boots. And the Missus would like to see the cement for Fred Astaire and Ginger." I took a deep breath as if I'd been on this treasure hunt forever. "I am just purely lost, boy, and the wife, she's gettin' a little edgy. Thinks I won't ever find what she wants to see, don't ya' know. Startin' to get mouthy about it."

"I don't answer anyone anything who calls me boy. Now get lost before I boot you clear back to your dirt farm."

"Well, now that's downright un-neighborly," I said and gave him a big smile. I dropped the accent cold and gave him the rest in my own voice. "And just when I was going to ask you if you've seen anything of Weasel?"

My stomach clenched and my palms felt sweaty as I waited for his reaction. It was worth the pinching in my toes and the itchy fatigue of skin beneath false hair just to see the look on his face.

He was flummoxed. I could see the look in his eyes go from the confidence of knowing my voice to the disbelief and confusion when he didn't recognize the face and get-up that went with it.

What a rush. My heart rate accelerated, and I felt as if I were breathing pure oxygen instead of the customary twenty percent air and eighty percent Los Angeles smog.

Lone Wolf looked hard at me for about a ten count and then grinned, a hesitant searching sort of grin. "Sam?"

I smiled then and nodded. Relief flooded his face. I wish I'd have known then that it was the first and last time I'd ever see Lone Wolf that far out of control. Something that rare, I'd have tried to bottle it.

"Son of a bitch!" he said, shaking his head and walking around me like a dog circling an intruder, all senses bristling. "That is fantastic!" He stared into my face. "How'd you lose the baby blues?"

"Soft contacts."

He shook his head, "Amazing. If you hadn't asked me about Weasel, I'd never have known it was you."

"I dropped the Texas accent just for you, buddy. And because I figured you were ready to hit me." I grinned at him, and he punched lightly at my shoulder in response. "Weasel shows up?" I asked, making that unwilling return to a worry-fraught reality.

"Naw, but I showed the photo to a regular and he's due in any time now."

"Keep a lookout. I gotta get rid of this beard and these damn boots."

I left the boots and the jacket in the Caddy and retrieved my solvent for the spirit gum and my contact lens case.

In the men's room, I carefully removed the face fur, tucking the bits into the container Bill had given me. Then, I used cold cream to remove the light pancake we had used to darken my skin a bit. Without making a concentrated effort, I don't get much of a tan in New York City, but a good Texan would.

Reaching into my eye with thumb and forefinger, I carefully pinched out the brown lenses and flushed my eyes with saline solution. Then, I recombed my hair and went back out to meet with Lone Wolf. Except for the western cut pants and shirt, I was me again.

No sooner had I hit the sidewalk than Lone Wolf nodded toward the side door of the bar. I walked with him and saw the stooped shoulders of a scrawny little man preceding us inside.

He turned as we came up behind him. One look at me and he wheeled from the entrance, pushed past us, and set off at a run across the parking lot.

"Damn!" Lone Wolf muttered and took off after him.

FIFTEEN

I left him to the chase and went on inside and took a seat at a table. I ordered three beers, and by the time they were on the table, I saw Lone Wolf returning with our merchandise.

Even in the dim interior, there was no mistaking the narrow head and sharp nose of Weasel. He had about two days' gray stubble on his thin jaws and scrawny neck. His hair was untidy and stuck up in greasy tufts. They moved between the tables toward me.

Suddenly, Weasel's face took on the feral look of an animal in a trap. He was jabbering even before Lone Wolf thrust him into a seat.

"I didn't mean you any harm, mister," he whined softly. "Honest. Man don't help his little girl, he ain't worth a shit." He blubbered some more, "Ain't worth shit."

I shoved one of the beers in front of him, and he stuck his thin nose into it with an air of desperation.

When he looked up at me, I felt a mild shock. They were identical to the eyes that had held a look of spiteful triumph when I had slumped into that carpet after my first Scotch, "Debbie your only daughter, Mr. Pittman?"

When he nodded, I realized I felt relief that there were no more at home like her. "Why'd you run?"

"Didn't take nothin' off you, Debbie neither. Why'd you have to do my little girl like you did?" He began to blubber in earnest, now, shredding the paper cocktail napkin with trembling, gnarled fingers. He tried for a swallow of beer but spilled at least two swallows' worth on the table.

It hit me full force. He thought I must have come back from my train ride to kill Debbie and get even. He probably ran because he was afraid, I'd come to do the same to him. "Look, Mr. Pittman, I didn't kill your daughter."

He gave me that look I've seen when trying to help an injured horse; the one that says they hope against all evidence that you aren't going to make them hurt worse, but they don't believe it for a moment. "I'm not going to harm you. I just need some information."

He dragged a shaky fingertip through the puddle of slopped beer. I signaled to the waitress for another. Lone Wolf and I had hardly touched ours. "Why don't you tell me how you happened to dump me in that boxcar," I said as gently as I could.

"Didn't mean you any harm, just had to help my little girl. She thought you were dead. Thought she'd killed you. Told me you killed her roommate, Marilyn." He pronounced it Mary Lynn, as if it were two names, "On that train."

The waitress brought our drinks, and I paid her, waiting for her to leave before we went on talking. "So, she thought she'd get even?" I said, hardly able to believe he'd admit such a thing, even about a dead woman.

He shook his head violently. "No, never she just thought she'd knock you out and call the cops. Then she got scared she'd killed you. She was hysterical when I got there."

"Why didn't you call them?"

"And tell 'em my own little girl drugged some guy with a P.I. license in his wallet?"

"You saw my I.D.?"

He nodded, "Could've rolled you. Didn't," he said, almost proudly.

"You just took me out to the train station?" He must be stronger than he looked. I reassessed his wiry arms and stooped shoulders and saw Lone Wolf doing the same.

"She helped me." He gave me a glance up and down. "We got you to my car. I did the rest. Then I called to let her know it was all right. She was so grateful, she was my little girl again, like we used to be… Now she's—" He started to tear up again and choked out a sob.

"You thought if you helped her out, she'd start listening to you again, maybe give up her way of life," I said with as much understanding as I could muster for a man who had hurried over, ostensibly to help his daughter dispose of my dead body.

He pounded a fist on the table. "Damn straight I did! Then the next morning the police rousted me out and accused me of killing her." His voice broke and he cried into his fresh beer.

"You touch anything in her apartment?"

"No, like I said, we just took your body out to the car. I never did go back to the apartment that night."

"Before that night, had you seen very much of Debbie?"

"No."

"Why?"

"We—Debbie and me, we didn't get on too well. Not since she started with Marilyn. Thought she'd give that life up. Then here comes Marilyn and Deb's all screwed up again."

"You fought over her being a lesbian." I didn't make it a question.

He looked around, angry, defensive. "She wasn't one of them. Not my Debbie. She just had some bad luck with her ex and this Marilyn woman led her down the garden path. That's all. Bad timing just bad damn timing." He blubbered harder and chugged half his beer.

"I still don't understand why you didn't call the police."

"Got a record, and then Marilyn, she got a restraining order against me few months back."

"You thought the police would suspect you?"

He nodded, "Questioned the shit outta me. We'd had some fights, Debbie and me, over at her place. Cops came out once, with that Marilyn, too. Good thing I had an alibi for when she was on that train."

"I'm sorry, Mr. Pittman. Sorry about Debbie, too. You think of anything might help me find who killed her, call me first thing." I handed him my number at Aunt Gladys's.

Lone Wolf and I got up and left the bar, Weasel fell heir to our untouched beers. I don't think he minded, and it was the least I could do.

"Well, that was no damn help at all," Lone Wolf said, heading for the Mustang.

"Oh, I don't know. I found out how the hell I got on that train. I also know why, and it had next to nothing to do with this case. In this game, what doesn't apply is just as important as what does."

"Profound man! Profound." Lone Wolf said, mocking me a little "Makes me feel ashamed to mention that it doesn't help us find Beth and your aunt."

I nodded. "Yeah, but that boat we found the earring on is Sondra's. And guess who works on it when it's out?"

Lone Wolf just looked at me. "Ponytail."

Lone Wolf yawned and rubbed his eyes. "Well, now that we know where to find him, what say we catch a nap and then go get him?"

I shook my head. "You know how bad I feel napping when they're still missing."

"Yeah, and I know how damned clumsy and stupid a zombie is." He stalked off and got into the Mustang. He was right, of course, and if I had any notion of crashing that party, I would need a little sleep. So, I followed him back to Aunt Gladys's, taking a swing past Beth's just to make sure the place was locked and still undisturbed. Her driveway was empty, and I presumed Lone Wolf's friend had come to collect the wreckage for him as he'd arranged.

I pulled the Caddy into Aunt Gladys's driveway. It took up almost the whole length. Lone Wolf parked the Mustang in the street.

Sleep and change of clothes wasn't all I wanted from the house. We'd had a call on that Nova. Good news, a biker had found it. Bad news, it was abandoned. We delayed the nap and drove over to check it out, but it had been pretty well stripped. As we drove home again, I was really beginning to feel depressed. Every time I thought I was getting close to finding something that would help me get Aunt Gladys back, it practically evaporated from between my fingers. I looked at my watch. Gladys and Beth had been missing for almost thirteen hours.

I don't think I'd been asleep very long when Lone Wolf shook my shoulder. I woke up with a cottony feeling filling my head. No surprise. That was usual for me when I didn't get the rest I needed. "What's happening?"

"Someone's coming up the front walk, a chick. Good looking."

I leaped from the bed and pulled the curtain aside.

Kathy's car was parked at the curb, the rotating flasher clearly visible on the dash. Unfortunately, I could also see a strange car parked down the block, and I would have bet money that Ponytail or one of his buddies was sitting behind the wheel with his eyes glued to my front door. I didn't need a cop at my door now—not even a pretty one. Dammit!

I threw on a robe and hurried down the stairs.

I pulled open the door and saw Kathy's fist in mid-knock. "Sam!" she said, taking in my state of midday undress in one suspicious glance. "Did I interrupt something?" Her voice had taken on a honed edge. Wilkinson had nothing on her.

"Kathy, I can't explain everything just now, but you have to leave, right now."

The hurt in her eyes tore at me. "It's not what you think. I just need you to leave. Pretend to sell me a ticket to the Policeman's Ball and get out of here."

"Sam Ryan, if you expect me to help you with your charade in addition to humiliating me, you can go straight to hell." Moving as stiffly as a junkyard dog, Kathy edged off the porch and then picked up speed as she neared her Honda. Within moments, she was squealing away from the curb.

I thought about how I would ever make it up to her, but I was more worried about that strange car down the street. The idea that I had persisted in talking to cops was surely what they would believe.

"Lone Wolf, you want to try to cruise off and then circle around and check out that Pontiac down the block?"

"Think its surveillance?" I nodded.

"You got it." He grabbed the keys to the Mustang, then put them down and headed out the door on foot. "Lower profile. See you in a few."

"I'll be in the shower."

I never made it to the bathroom. Lone Wolf hadn't been gone but five minutes when there was another knock.

I looked out the spy hole and nearly broke an arm getting the door open and pulling my visitor in off the porch.

"Beth how in the name of God?"

She gripped my arm, and her story came tumbling out as she hurried inside, "Oh, Sam! You've got to hurry. We've got to get Gladdy. She helped me escape, but I don't know if that horrible man will move her now that I've gotten away."

"Take it easy. Start at the beginning."

"Those men that snatched us, they took us on a boat and then to a small cave somewhere near the Corona Del Mar Beach. They left one man to watch us and Gladdy distracted him while I got away and climbed over the rocks to the highway.

Gladdy decided I would make better time without her. Her asthma, you know. So, I got away. I was afraid to stop at a house because those men kept saying that they wouldn't hurt us as long as you didn't talk to the police. So, I hitched a ride to an area my club used to frequent and got a friend to bring me here on her bike."

"Wait. You lost me, Beth. Gladys is in a cave on the beach?" Scenes from 'Captain Blood, The Crimson Pirate', and Errol Flynn taking on Burt Lancaster with a broadsword coalesced in my head.

"Right near the channel where all the boat traffic went in and out to the sea, there is a narrow beach and a cave. That's where they've been keeping Gladys and me. I hope she's still there."

"Not too likely that they wouldn't have moved her since you got away. Sit tight."

I hurried upstairs and scrambled into my clothes. Beth was making a bad habit of catching me in my robe in mid-afternoon. Lord only knew what she thought about that.

"You want to get something to take along, Beth?" I gestured toward the kitchen when I came back down.

"I couldn't eat anything, Sam. Not with Gladdy still in the clutches of those horrid men."

Clutches? It was sounding more like a Saturday morning western at the movies. I only wished it was. The bad guys always got what they deserved. The hero always rescued the lady in distress.

Beth and I were almost out the door when Lone Wolf came back from his reconnaissance. He didn't look pleased. "What'd you find out?"

"Well, it was someone connected with this mess. He stuck his hand out the passenger side window and handed me an envelope marked 'Sam.' He was gone before I could grab his hand. The driver took off down the street and disappeared around the corner. The license plate had mud all over it I couldn't make it out. I ran after him, but I couldn't keep up. Getting old, I guess.

He looked quickly at Beth and spoke, "Sorry."

Then looking at Lone Wolf, "Special delivery, huh?"

Lone Wolf nodded. Then he walked over and hugged Beth. "Glad to see you back, friend."

"Doesn't look good," I said reading the note. "He must have been planning to drop this in the door slot and couldn't when we beat him back here. Then Kathy showed up, then Beth. He must have been almost glad to see you coming."

"So, you gonna share that or just put it under your pillow?"

I handed it to Lone Wolf. Beth read over his shoulder. I felt as if the words were burned in my brain.

Bring what Marilyn gave you to the exchange. Ten thirty tomorrow morning. Then there was a map of the area near the new Equestrian Center. The name of a local stable was given, and the instructions said to rent a horse and ride along the trail they marked until I came to a tunnel. On the far side, we would make the exchange, my evidence for Aunt Gladys. Only the note said: "the old ladies." It made me feel a little bit better to think they never expected Beth to have escaped them even before the note was delivered.

Lone Wolf looked at me. "You gonna do it?"

"If I have to, I'll try anything."

"What other choice you got?"

"That party. Maybe I'll find out enough to get her back before I have to take that ten thirty ride."

Lone Wolf looked at Beth. "You have someone you can stay with out of the area?"

"My daughter lives in Chatsworth. I could stay with her."

"You think it would be safe?"

"Oh, yes. She and her husband have a little ranch with horses and several big guard dogs."

"Fine, you want to give her a call?" I asked.

Beth nodded. "I won't tell her anything about Gladdy and the kidnapping. My son-in-law would call the police right away. I could never stop him. He's a real straight arrow."

"I can drive her," Lone Wolf offered. "I have to be at work in about two hours, still got a week and half of vacation, and the boss calls me in for six hours of O.T. Can you believe it?"

I smiled. "Good money, Six to midnight?"

He nodded. "Yeah, beats the hell out of working for a living nine to five." He grinned. "My regular is a three by twelve. That beats it, too."

"How are you getting to work from Beth's daughter's house?" I asked.

Beth chimed right in. "He'll use my wagon. I don't intend to go anywhere until I hear from Sam that Gladdy's all right." She wrote her daughter's number on the chalkboard Aunt Gladys had above the microwave. Then she dialed that number and let her daughter know she'd be over soon.

"You need me, man, you call me at work." Lone Wolf added his work and his home number to the chalkboard.

"Thanks. I'll call you if I find out enough to make tomorrow morning unnecessary."

He nodded. "Otherwise, I'll just meet you at that stable, okay?"

I agreed and saw them off. Then I went up to get ready. Reclaiming my Texas persona would take a little time and a lot of doing.

I stood under the hard hot spray and willed my neck muscles to loosen. Their going had made the house feel suspiciously like a tomb.

Could Kathy's brief visit possibly have been enough to constitute a killing offense? I shook away that thought and hoped it wasn't in the process of becoming reality.

SIXTEEN

By the time I applied all my makeup and the face fur, I had time for a short nap in Gladys's recliner before I put in my brown lenses and slipped into the rented tuxedo. I didn't dare lie down with my number two pancake on and beard in place. One wrong turn and my pillow would be wearing more of my disguise than I would.

I set the alarm. Then, I set a second one across the room, my little wind-up Big Ben clock that would get a dead man out of a grave.

I thought I'd be too worried to do more than just lie in the chair with my eyes shut, but I actually went under like I'd been anesthetized. Well, it had been some time since I'd gotten any, much less, a full night's sleep. I certainly needed it. If nothing else, it would make my contacts easier to bear. When I woke up, I finished getting dressed, put in the lenses, and topped it all off with the black Stetson. Of course, I had to wear the black ostrich cowboy boots. Sure enough, they pinched in exactly the same spot. I winced and decided I would just as soon not fill my dance card that night. I looked in the mirror and failed to recognize myself. Swell. I was fairly sure no one else would either. I got into the Caddy and headed back through the light Sunday traffic to Newport and the Pacific Yacht Club. Barrie's Babe was tied up right where the directions on the invitation indicated. I eased through the crowd in the club lounge and headed out the back door.

A steady stream of party guests was trailing back and forth from a sleek yacht that was lit up like Christmas. I nodded and smiled my way up the gangway and on board.

Barrie's Babe took my breath away. The custom salon was carpeted in beige Berber wool. The wood I could see was whitewashed oak. The walls and ceiling liners were neutral Ultra suede. Mirrors added dimension, and the furniture was covered in the richest leathers, accented by gold and burgundy pillows of the finest silk. In one corner near the wet bar, there was a magnificent floral display in a copper urn that glowed as if lit from within. Subdued track lighting was aided by a few tasteful lamps.

The environment was striking enough, but the scenery was even more beautiful; I could have swung a cat and knocked out at least a dozen or more gorgeous ladies. Sondra Chase obviously owned half this setup, and the half she provided consisted of these lovely ladies—each one model perfect. I spotted Leslie in a striking emerald green cocktail dress that contrasted brilliantly with her Strawberry blonde hair and ivory skin. I was about to walk over to her when I saw her take an older gentleman by the arm and walk with him from the salon.

He didn't look like her type. Since she'd made that pass at me earlier, I was in a position to know. I wandered over to the bar and asked for a Scotch. It appeared instantly, as if by magic. Apparently, no expense had been spared—and certainly not on the bartenders.

A knockout in a French maid's outfit sidled up with a silver tray of fancy little hot pastry puffs and caviar on toast points. I drifted around checking out that fantastic boat and generally enjoying myself. It wasn't long before another lovely lady walked after with a gentleman, and Leslie was back and soon flirting with someone else. I sighed. That was apparently how deals were made. I wondered how many of her aspiring models. Sondra could strong arm into whoring for her.

I stood talking to a fellow about the joys of being a yacht club member, but soon, the conversation got beyond the minimal knowledge I had gleaned from magazines on boating and yachts and the limited experience I'd had in the Navy.

He wandered off, and I spotted the captain in his dress whites. I edged closer and tried to see if his uniform included a nametag. It didn't. I dreamed up two or three flattering questions for him and approached.

"Nice boat, Diesel?"

He nodded, "Twin Cummins, sir."

I smiled and tried to look impressed. Given that those were the best diesels going, it wasn't hard. "How many staterooms does she have?"

"Just two, Mr. Barrington had her customized to make the salon larger. He uses it mostly for these functions."

"Well, she's certainly a beauty."

"Yes sir. That she is." He allowed himself a half smile.

"How long you've been her captain?"

"It's been ten years now."

"Did you ever captain one of his cruise ships?"

He nodded. "Nearly five years. Then Mr. Barrington got 'Barrie's Babe' and needed me here."

"Are you on call all the time?"

"No sir. I have a beeper, but I live aboard. I have the office and stateroom, forward. The owner's stateroom is aft."

I wondered if the two staterooms were the destinations of the ladies and their gentlemen. I hoped not—for two reasons. First, I would have hated to think that the captain had to suffer such an invasion of privacy, and second, I had designs of invading that privacy myself. If Barrington kept any records aboard, they were sure to be there.

I had another drink, with soda and ice this time, and left most of it in the glass. Then I waited for my chance to slip into the forward quarters. I was inches from a clean getaway when Leslie trotted over and bubbled at me until she made it clear she wanted to introduce me to her idol and role model. Sondra Chase was the last person I wanted casting a curious eye upon me. It took some fancy footwork, verbal and otherwise, to convince her to turn me loose.

Unfortunately, as I headed forward, intent on reaching the office, I saw good old Leslie wending her way through the attendees and right up to Sondra. I knew my time would be limited before she started looking for me again. I thought of Aunt Gladys and had to chance it.

I edged through the door to the cabin and gently closed it behind me. The oak file cabinet, honeyed not whitewashed in here, stood near an elegant antique roll top desk and captain's chair. I slid the top drawer open. No luck. I pulled the next one open. A guest book was stashed at the front of the folders. I flipped it open and saw what I expected lots of names, some celebrities, as familiar to an actor as the credits of a major motion picture. There were numerous names of the feminine persuasion and lots of Japanese corporation titles and addresses.

I put it back and thumbed quickly through some of the file folders. Most were headed with business names. It didn't look hopeful. Then, at the very back, I saw some folders non-alphabetized that carried only a woman's name on the tab. One was marked 'Leslie Norton.'

I pulled it out and saw a listing of Japan-based companies. I started to read the list. That was as far as I got. There was a blinding pain at the base of my skull, and the room spun out of reach.

I felt nauseated, my head pounded, and I had one royal bitch of a thirst. My tongue felt glued to my teeth, and my teeth hurt as if I'd done an hour with a sadistic hygienist.

I braced my hands against the floor and pushed. The stabbing pain in my left palm made me give that up for a moment. I rolled my head cautiously to one side and looked at the rug next to me. My gun lay beneath my hand. Odd I knew I hadn't had it with me when I'd dressed up as a Texas bigwig.

I pushed it away and tried again. The room didn't hold still for that, but I fought the desire to lie down and give in to physical discomfort. I knew better than to shake my head to try to clear it, but the temptation was almost irresistible.

Gradually, I raised myself to a sitting position my head still slumped forward on my chest, my breath harsh with the effort. My vision cleared. I was in my own living room.

I saw a hand to my right, and I could make out part of a floral print. I got even more nauseated as I lifted my head and took in the full picture.

Gladys lay with her eyes wide and staring, blood making a rusty track from the corner of her mouth to her softly rounded chin. A dense stiff patch of long-dried blood obscured the daisy print on the front of her blouse.

"Oh, Jesus!" I felt a staggering sense of defeat. I sank back onto the floor. I tried to control my gaze, but it had more will than I did.

I stared at the tidy hole in Aunt Gladys's unlined forehead and vomited down the front of my rented tux and onto the carpet.

SEVENTEEN

I don't recall making it to the downstairs bath, but I do remember hanging over the porcelain bowl and wishing I would just die and get it all over with.

What the hell business did I have playing Philip Marlowe? I made a fine mess of things I did. A glance in the mirror at the stranger I had become for the party gave me a double shock. Not only did I look like someone I didn't know, but a bad someone I didn't know. Part of my beard had already been yanked free of my face. I didn't know how they found out the Texan they'd slugged in the office of 'Barrie's Babe' was the P.I. whose aunt they held hostage, but apparently someone had looked close—skin close. I peeled the remaining chunks of beard and moustache off my chin and jaw. My eyes looked like two black olives floating in a Bloody Mary. I'd had the brown lenses in when they'd knocked me out. Catching a short nap in soft lenses wasn't too bad, but all that down time—unconscious on the living room rug— had about fried my corneas.

I grabbed a bottle of saline solution and flooded first one eye then the other. I made a tentative try at a lens. Still rather dry and stuck to the eyeball. I flooded a few more times and finally pried them out and set them in their case. Now the blue, the red, and what little showed of the whites lent me a patriotism I certainly didn't feel. Especially in this land of quick tempers and quicker murder.

I was in the middle of my second cussing out and third swabbing of spirit gum from my face when a fist pounded mercilessly at the front door. I glanced at my watch. Seven thirty. I'd have to call Lone Wolf. We had no need to go to the stables in Griffith Park.

I wiped the vomit from my tux shirt as best as I could with a damp cloth and staggered to the front door, holding my head. It took a second or two for my eyes to focus on the doorknob. Lieutenant Terrana and two uniformed cops were standing on the porch.

"Excuse the intrusion, Mr. Ryan, but we received a call down at the station. The caller said there were shots fired. May we come in and look around?"

Whoever had framed me hadn't wasted any time. As I nodded and stood aside, the sick feeling was coming back. I was going to throw up again. "Excuse me." I ran to the bathroom.

I heard the front door close and turned around to see Lieutenant Terrana standing at the bathroom door. Kathy was close behind him. Jesus, talk about no end to humiliation. I fought to pull myself together.

"My men are looking around. Is there anything you want to tell me?" Kathy looked shocked and embarrassed as her boss questioned me.

The words I wanted to say were hard to get out. I still couldn't believe my aunt was dead. "My aunt is dead, but I didn't kill her."

"Come on, Mr. Ryan. We'll take a look together."

One of the two uniformed cops walked in from the kitchen. "Lieutenant, we have just one body in the living room, Elderly, Caucasian Female. Gunshot wound."

Just? Wasn't one dead body enough? Maybe the force should start these guys off with a course intact before they segue on to gunplay and chokeholds. "If you don't mind, Lieutenant, I'll stay here."

He looked at me for a moment and then seemed to agree that I'd be better off closer to a sink or a toilet bowl. Kathy, unfortunately enough for my male ego, lingered behind.

"I… I'm sorry, Sam." Kath put a hand on my arm. "I heard the call and thought maybe—I mean, I was worried that you had been—"

Kathy was having a rough go of it. I turned to face her but hung my head.

"I should have been. What the hell good is a man who can't protect the people he loves?"

"Don't say that. Don't ever say that. You didn't do this to her."

"I didn't stop it either."

"What happened?"

I shrugged and felt my stiff neck grab and hurt. I ran my hand up over it. "I got bashed. Out cold. I came to in there with" I nearly lost it. I took a deep breath, "With my Aunt Gladys at my side."

"Oh Sam, how awful for you, do you have any idea who may have done this?"

"Yeah, lots of ideas. No proof."

Kathy was about to say something when Terrana came back and broke it up with lots of officious garbage, some of which vaguely resembled Kathy's own attempt to ask me what had happened, but only vaguely. His voice and expression held none of her concern and sincerity.

Within five minutes, the coroner and an investigative crew were swarming over the house.

Within fifteen, Terrana was cuffing me and reading me my rights. Then, we headed out for a nice little jaunt downtown.

"Lieutenant?"

"Yes, Mr. Ryan."

"I didn't do it." Then I thought of a shred of proof. It wasn't much, but it was all I could think of. "Lieutenant, I didn't even come home on my own last night. I got knocked out at a party on a boat at the Pacific Yacht Club. My car's still there. I rented a Caddy for the evening, and you'll find it parked at the south side of the lot under—"

"You parked it in the driveway, Mr. Ryan." He gestured over the hood of the squad car.

The sight of that elegant white hood nosing into the driveway made me feel sick all over again. "Jesus, they thought of everything. I did not drive that car back here last night."

"We'll dust it for prints. Right now, however, we have a dead body, along with your gun, and it's been fired recently. I believe ballistics will find that your aunt was shot with your gun." He smiled at me. It wasn't a nice sight. "What y' wanna bet?"

"Of course, you're going to find my gun shot her. That doesn't mean I did!" He put a hand on the top of my head and eased me into the back of the cruiser. "Whoever knocked me out shot Aunt Gladys and left me to take the rap."

"Yeah? Tell it to the judge."

All the way to the station, Kathy sat like a stone in the front next to Terrana. I could tell she was hurting. I knew she wanted to intervene, but there wasn't anything she could do.

I'd played a lot of different characters over the years but never a murderer. Now, here I was, sitting in a jail cell. Somehow, all desire to whip out my notebook and make notes for my future acting profession had deserted me. Perhaps it was the fact that it didn't look a lot like I would have a future.

I kept remembering that only five days ago, Aunt Gladys was standing in the kitchen with an apron on, making a homecoming meatloaf for me; now, she was dead. The one concentrated thought that kept running through my mind was that I had to find the real killer.

So far, I hadn't even managed to get an attorney, let alone an arraignment and bail.

***

Twice, Terrana had me dragged out for questioning. He hadn't wasted any time getting a report from the crime scene experts or ballistics. They confirmed what I had suspected. What he had suspected. My gun killed Aunt Gladys right where she was found. My paraffin test showed traces from having fired a gun. Naturally, my fingerprints were all over the weapon. Cut and dried. I'd gotten too close when I'd started checking things out at the yacht club party.

The only shocker was Terrana's idea of a motive.

"Come on, Sam. You killed her for the money, didn't you?" He eased around the interrogation room and came up in back of my chair. "Acting isn't doing too well by you, I hear."

"If you know about Gladys's money, you also know my Uncle Hobart left me eight hundred thousand dollars in his will. What the hell would I need to kill Aunt Gladys for?"

He shrugged. "You know all about greed and how it works, don't you, Sam?"

I slammed my hand on the table. "That's insane."

"Yeah?" He smiled. "I figure that with what you'd get from your aunt, you could aspire to be something better than a millionaire."

He leaned very close to my face, and I could count the hairs in his chin stubble and smell the over-coffeed breath with a tobacco twist. "You always wanted to be a millionaire, Sam?"

"What I wanted all my life was a family. Aunt Gladys and Uncle Hobart were as close to parents as I ever got."

He raised his hands in a gesture of ignorance. "You know how many people kill family for money?"

"I don't give a good God damn. I didn't kill her. I didn't kill anyone. You think I'd shoot her and then phone you and then whack myself on the head just so I could be found with the body when you arrived?"

"No, Sam. I don't."

I sighed. Maybe the man had some grain of sense after all.

"I think maybe you struggled with that old lady and hit your head hard enough to have passed out. Then, I think a good neighbor called us about the gunshot—which you weren't counting on. And we answered the call before you came to."

I threw my hands in the air. "Jesus H. Christ! I think you have a scape-goat, and you're just as happy to stop looking further."

"Listen. I already have your prints from Debbie Pittman's apartment. You say you went unconscious at her place, too. But the bottom line for me is that when you came back to the scene, she was in a body bag."

"So, why didn't you arrest me for her murder, too, while you were at it?" Stupid, I know, but he'd pressured me right into losing my Irish temper. Just like I knew he would try to do.

"I would have, but we got the perp who left that print on her skin in a body bag already. Remember? You picked his picture out of the Polaroid's. It was Debbie's supplier. We got an eyewitness."

Terrana didn't comment after that except to have me taken back to my cell.

It was late afternoon by the time Kathy brought in a lawyer. By six that evening, I had been arraigned and my bail had been set for twenty-five thousand dollars. Kathy, with some help from Lone Wolf and her dad, had come up with the ten percent the bondsman demanded.

After I got my personal belongings back, I followed Kathy to the front door. It was the longest walk I ever took. I wanted to turn the clock back to my arrival at Union Station and start over. I knew I couldn't. Aunt Gladys was gone and that was that. Kathy seemed to be fading fast as well. She walked stiffly, as if she hurt all over, and kept her eyes straight ahead.

I wanted to hold her, or at least have her hold me, but this wasn't the right time or place.

I was afraid the right time and place might never come again for us. "Kathy, I'm sorry for all this mess. I can't thank you enough for your help, you and your dad and Lone Wolf."

"Lone Wolf started it all. When you didn't' meet him this morning, he went to the house and a neighbor told him you were carried in. He made such a scene down at the station, I had to notice. We got to talking and…" She gave one shoulder an elegant lift that told it all.

"Your dad?"

"He was helping me. I think he likes you. Either that or he trusts my judgment which is more than I can say right now."

We climbed into a cruiser and Kathy drove me home.

"If you feel that way, then why bail me out?"

"Look, I may have dated you just twice, and you may have given me the bum's rush yesterday afternoon, but I do know you wouldn't kill your aunt. I'm fairly naive right up until someone in a robe pitch me out his door at midday, but I do know you loved your Aunt Gladys."

The shock wave that passed over me was as profound as any I have ever felt. It had never crossed my mind that she might think I'd given her the boot due to a little in flagrante delicto going on upstairs. "Kathy! I'll tell you exactly why I rushed you off my porch. They had kidnapped Gladys and Beth, and I had been warned not to go to the cops or they'd kill them! Someone was watching the house, and you show up with that police light on your dash."

"Oh, Sam, I'm sorry. I mean I'm glad I misjudged you. I was all set to think you kicked me out the other day because you had another woman." She threw me a look and went up a freeway on ramp. "My own insecurities, we all have weaknesses."

I put a hand on her shoulder and let my thumb trace the hard bulge of collarbone beneath her delicate skin. "After what we had together?"

A tear started down her cheek. "What did we have? Two dates, one roll in the hay. I thought maybe, just maybe, it was curiosity. You know, bed the lady cop. Then move on."

I slid closer to her, my arm across the back of her neck. "Please, don't ever think that. I meant everything I said and did when we were together."

"Thank you." She sniffed and seemed to pull up her courage a bit. "Why in hell didn't you come to us?"

I took a deep breath. Then I started. It took me until we reached our destination to tell her all about Margaret and the years that followed. When we pulled into Gladys's driveway, Kathy shut off the engine and came inside with me.

We tried to ignore the yellow tape stretched across the entrance to the living room. Sitting at the kitchen table, she put her hand over mine. "I can understand how you'd feel that way, Sam, but times have changed. Surely you couldn't have thought that I'd have done anything to endanger your aunt, if you'd only told me."

I shook my head. "No. Of course you wouldn't, but you don't run things. Terrana, I'm not so sure of. And my track record with cops is dismal."

"Sam, Terrana's a good cop, maybe a great one. If only you'd trusted us, maybe your aunt would still be alive." She had that stubborn Irish look. The one I see in my mirror now and again. It's hell to deal with.

I shook my head, "No way. All I can really trust is me. I know you have to feel that the cops can make a difference, but I don't have to believe it."

"I'm sorry to point it out, Sam, but you didn't do a lot better without us."

I looked hard at her. "I might have pulled it off. I know there were things on that ship that might have broken this wide open."

"Famous last words, now I want you to tell me everything. Show me what you've got, and maybe we can find the bastards." Kathy looked adorable as she offered to help. Like a terrier pup volunteering to go after the biggest rat in the pack. I wanted to scrub my hand over her hair and tell her how much I appreciated her enthusiasm, her belief, and her dedication. But I still didn't believe calling the police from the start would have made it work out any different.

"Sam, this is an open police case. You have to stop. Let me take care of it."

"I—" That was all I got out before the tears flooded me out. Kathy held me for a few moments, and I got myself under control. "Dammit. Don't you see that I can't just bow out?" My eyes searched hers. "If I bear any blame for her death, I at least have to be able to take part in resolving it, or I'll go crazy."

Kathy's eyes had an unusual shine as she looked at me. "Sam, I understand believe me. But I'm in a difficult place. The police aren't in the do-it-yourself justice business."

"You're a cop. I understand that this is your career. But I can't promise you I'll stay out. I know I won't. I can't."

"Well, I can't help you break the law."

So, there it sat. I felt like a Class A bastard for trying to make her choose between her job and her feelings for me. We sat in stony silence for a few moments.

"I'll make a deal with you, Sam. You give me everything you've got, and you and I will discuss ways we might go about catching these guys. Also, I promise I won't report you if you keep a hand in, as long as you promise to turn over what you find."

"That sounds like a great deal, for you. What do I get?"

"Look, I'd love to be some crazy romantic who says, 'forget the fuzz, darling, you and I will bring these killers to justice together.' But I can't choke out all that melodramatic twaddle. All I've ever wanted is to be a detective. It's been my life for so long. I can't just throw it all away. Not for anyone."

"I'm not asking you to. I wouldn't ask that. I just want to be able to bring them down myself."

"I can help you, but I can't keep the police out of it, and I can't promise you'll be in on it if we solve it."

"We could just call "us" off until one of us gets Aunt Gladys's killer." Her face went blank. No expression at all. I knew she was fighting to keep it that way.

"Is that what you want?"

"No."

"It's not what I want either. You're a damn fine detective. I'd like your help. But I can't let a civilian in on police business. We don't have many choices."

"If I give you all I've got, can I count on the same from you?"

She hesitated. "I can only say I will try to keep you posted on the case. I can't say I'll give you any access to evidence. We have to turn it in, you know. It's not mine to give."

I nodded. Then I went to the portfolio and got out everything I had. I laid it on the table.

"Did you find out who dropped off the photos yet?" Kathy asked when she'd finished looking at them.

I shook my head and pointed to the number on the envelope. "Got a call in to a friend who works for the telephone company in New York, but maybe I missed his call."

Kathy went to the phone and dialed. Moments later, she had the information. Nothing wrong with her connections. Boy did cops ever have it easier. The few connections I had for information like that had taken me years to build.

"It was registered to a Gloria Davis. The phone had been disconnected for nonpayment about a month ago." Kathy was writing in her notebook as she spoke.

I held the pendant up and dangled it in front of Kathy's face. "It fits."

She took the silver teardrop shape on her palm. "Sure does." She made a note. "I think I'll check out the apartment. Maybe Gloria will tell me why she didn't pay her bill."

"Maybe she'll tell you why she took these photos and gave them to a woman who ended up murdered on a train to Denver."

Kathy nodded. "I guess we could hope to get information that easily. But somehow it never seems to work out that way. I doubt Gloria will still be around."

"Me too, oh if you decide to check out anything about Sondra Chase, take a guard dog and keep your hand on your gun."

She nodded. "I think you found out about as much as anyone's going to right now. If they were so afraid of you searching their files on that boat, then chances of finding anything incriminating now are slim to none."

There was a knock at the back door. Lone Wolf stood with one hand on the knob. "Come on in, buddy. I understand you two have met in the name of a common cause: me. Thanks."

He grinned and clapped a hand on my shoulder as he passed. He draped his body over a kitchen chair turned backwards and nodded. "Yup, you look better out from behind bars."

"You didn't see me behind them; how would you know?" I asked, returning his grin as I said the words.

"I got a strong imagination."

Kathy laughed. "He's right." She looked at Lone Wolf. "It was a pitiful sight."

I pulled a beer from the fridge and tossed it. Lone Wolf plucked it gently from the air and popped the tab.

"We got anything more to go on?" he asked, before taking a swallow. Kathy filled him in on the new information while I made some salami and cheese sandwiches and brought them to the table. I got a fresh Coke for Kathy and one for myself.

By the time dinner was a memory, we had decided who would check up on what.

Lone Wolf, acting like the very soul of tact, offered to take the Cadillac back to the rental place. Kathy and I followed in her Honda, and we brought him back to the house so that he could borrow the Mustang again.

Unfortunately, once he'd gone home, Kathy and I were left standing awkwardly in Aunt Gladys's kitchen. I wanted her to stay with me, but I couldn't seem to find the words that would let me impose on her emotions like that. "Look, Kathy, I want you to know how much I appreciate your help."

She came close and hugged me, leaning her cheek against my chest. I could hardly hear her words when they came. "I want to help you, Sam. I know how hard this first night alone in the house will be, and if you need me to stay, I will."

Her voice sounded tight, and she felt rigid in my arms. "That's all right, honey. Maybe you should be home with your dad. I have a lot to think about anyway."

She turned grateful green eyes toward me and smiled. "Thank you, Sam. Thank you for understanding." She hesitated a moment and then winked. "Besides, I think I have time to check on that apartment of Gloria's before I head home."

EIGHTEEN

Kathy called early enough to catch me still sleeping. She sure knew how to wake a man up on the right side of the bed, even by phone. We had just finished coordinating our investigations for the morning when I heard the Mustang pull up and Lone Wolf clattered in through the kitchen door grumbling good-naturedly and seeking a big cup of coffee.

I finished my conversation with Kathy and hurried downstairs.

"Caught you napping?"

"Didn't sleep till nearly four?"

Lone Wolf nodded and spun a chair around before he straddled it. "What time you want to leave for the docks?"

"Right after coffee," I said, popping bread into the toaster and setting out a tub of butter. How's your car?"

"May be finished sooner than I thought, he'll let me know." Lone Wolf didn't look too hopeful.

"Work?"

He shrugged. "They call it that for a reason, buddy."

I laughed. "Rough?"

"Bo-o-o-ring. I swear, we got more money for doing less than anybody in town. Jobs run and we watch the screen. The only time we do more than breathe is if something goes wrong, which is practically never." He shook his head.

"That would make me nuts in about a minute and a half." I poured coffee for the both of us and sat at the table across from Lone Wolf.

"You get things straight with your lady?"

I nodded. "That was her on the phone when you came in. We're going to meet her here later. She's checking out the apartment where Gloria Davis may still live."

"You mean the name for the phone number on the snapshots?" Lone Wolf said.

I nodded and bit into my toast.

By nine, we were on our way to Long Beach.

Lone Wolf parked the Mustang in the first space we could find that wouldn't involve taking a bus to get us over to Barrington's neck of the woods. I wanted to see if he'd brought that yacht up from the club. If he had, I planned to find a way to get aboard again.

I hadn't overdressed for the occasion, but I had to admit that Lone Wolf fit in down here better than I did. For one thing, the muscles bulging out of his sleeveless T-shirt matched the look of the dock workers. Lone Wolf also had an uncanny ability to blend. Something in his manner changed subtly, and he was one with his environment in that special way I had seen in great actors. They became the parts they played. Olivier had it, so did Ronald Coleman. Lone Wolf was more the John Wayne type though—forever himself regardless of the part. After an hour of walking up and down Barrington's docks, we still didn't have anything to go on. We'd talked to a few people and learned just enough to validate what I already knew. He freighted between the States and the Orient a great deal. He had some luxury cruise ships that warranted a fairly wealthy clientele. His cruises ran from Mexico to Alaska. He stayed within the Pacific Rim, and apparently, the Caribbean and Europe held no attraction for him with regard to business. That much information hadn't been worth the price of gas—1961! At well over a dollar a gallon, we were definitely losing money.

We headed down to the Pacific Yacht Club in Newport, hoping Barrie's Babe hadn't taken the party out to sea.

Lone Wolf and I parked a good distance away and came up on the rear of the yacht club by way of the docks. We were still several slips away from anything the yacht club rented when I spotted a young woman who was obviously canvassing boat to boat.

She was tall, maybe five-nine, with the spare figure of a tennis pro or maybe a swimmer. She wore a peach-colored dress with a lace collar. It had about a million tiny buttons down the front and the last 100,000 or so weren't doing a thing to conceal her gorgeous long legs. She had long strawberry locks that curled and waved their way from a center part. She was a beauty, but obviously an unhappy beauty. I saw her showing something to people and watching them as a dog does a diner. Then she would almost physically droop and walk on, perk up, show the paper. Droop again.

I stepped closer, leaving Lone Wolf on the lookout for anyone who might act as if they knew me and wanted to try to leave a calling card on my face.

She pulled a dog-eared picture from an imitation leather bag. That's what she showed to a boat owner whose trimaran lolled in slip B-730.

The man shook his head. She shoved the picture back under his nose and said something else. She looked earnest. He shook his head. She gave up and came back along the dock like a small boy on his way to a date with a bathtub.

"You looking for someone?" I asked, as she came even with me.

She glanced over and smiled. At that range, I could see that she had incredibly pale blue eyes, almost invisible blonde lashes, and more freckles than a picnic has ants. Still, it was a wholesome, intelligent face and the figure was top-of-the-line. "I'm looking for my sister." Her hand groped in the bag with pathetic eagerness and pulled out the picture one more time. "Cheryl Scott. I'm Jenna Scott. Well, Jenna Richards, now, but my maiden name was Scott."

She turned a cherry hue. "Why am I babbling like this? Excuse me. Have you seen Cheryl around here?" She held the picture out to me. Her hand trembled with hope and fear in probably equal proportions. "She's a model."

The woman in the photo looked young, maybe nineteen or twenty, and she had apparently plunged into a very different part of the gene pool. Perfect teeth smiled out of generous lips beneath a nose like a Greek statue. The eyes were no one's idea of watered-down blue. The brows were elegantly arched, and thick dark hair shone and curled its way over one bare shoulder.

I had to glance up at Jenna twice to catch the resemblance. She noticed, embarrassing both of us by saying, "We don't look much alike. Cheryl and I had different fathers."

"I can see a family resemblance," I insisted, looking at her again and back to the photo. "You have the same nose and a similar jaw line. You smile like your sister, I think." I stared at Jenna and waited.

When the smile came, it was slightly self-conscious. "Thank you. Cheryl's a print model, so that's a real compliment." Her pride in her sibling showed even through the disappointment.

I could almost feel myself do a triple at her comment. "Who does your sister work for?"

"Well, I don't know if she's still there, but her last letter said something about the Sondra Chase Agency."

That would have stood my ears straight up even if I'd been a cocker spaniel! "When did you see her last?"

Jenna shrugged and dug in her purse. "These are the last few letters she wrote me. I haven't seen her in about two years. But she used to write at least twice a month, regularly. Her letters stopped coming."

Her face seemed to crumple at this, and she rooted in the bag for a tissue. "I'm sorry. I just know something's wrong. She didn't even answer the postcard."

"Postcard?"

She smiled. "Yes. When Cheryl got short of time, and I didn't get a letter, I'd send her a stamped, self-addressed postcard when I wrote to her. All she had to do was check a box and drop it in the mail back to me."

"Check a box?" Standing next to water, I was beginning to feel a little like an echo, but I didn't want to miss anything or misunderstand. I had a feeling this was too important.

"Oh, I'd make up silly categories and draw little check boxes. You know. Check here if you are alive. Check here if you are not, that sort of thing. Our mom started it when Cheryl and I were away at summer camp. She'd pack a whole bunch of these postcards in our duffels, and we'd just check off silly stuff." Her lip trembled, and then, the whole thing got away from her. Suddenly, she was crying and turning that tomato color only a real redhead can manage.

I put a hand on her shoulder and offered my handkerchief when her tissue finally gave its all for flood control. "Why don't I take you for coffee? You could use a break and I could use the caffeine deal?"

She made a heroic effort to pull herself together. Then, she stared down at my sodden hanky. She stuffed it in her bag. "I'll launder it and get it back to you. I promise."

"No need. You can keep it."

She was adamant. "Mama always said: 'If you borrow, you give it back in as good or better condition than it came to you.'"

"Well, in that case, you do need to join me for coffee. I'll have to give you, my address."

She looked a bit wary.

"So, you can mail my handkerchief."

She smiled then and we walked away from the yacht club and over to the coffee shop where I had taken Leslie.

I was happy to see that Jenna needed a minimal amount of coaxing to order an early lunch with her beverage. She asked for iced tea and that sounded so good that I changed my own order. Then I added a burger, fries, and an iced tea to go, so I could take something out to Lone Wolf.

I quickly explained that I was a private detective and that I, too, was looking for a missing person. I didn't tell her my most important missing person was also dead. I didn't think it could possibly help her lunch go down any easier to know it. Then, I excused myself to take the food out to my partner.

"It's mighty warm outside," she said when I got back to the table. "Doesn't your friend want to come in here?"

"He's doing some surveillance for me," I said, investing the word with as much drama as I thought traffic would bear. It bore a lot.

"Oh, you really are a detective. You have a badge or something?"

I showed her my New York P.I. license, and she made noises, suitably impressed. "You probably could help me find my sister if I had the money to hire you." She looked a little uncomfortable just mentioning the subject.

"Maybe it won't cost you anything."

She gave me a skeptical look. "There's a price on everything, Mister. And I sure hope you aren't about to suggest some sort of a trade."

I laughed. I couldn't help it. She looked so much like what she was: a country girl who had been warned over and over about wicked, big city ways. "No, listen, I'm already on a case. If your sister's vanishing act has anything to do with the case I'm already on, maybe I can find your sister, and it wouldn't cost you a thing."

She looked at me for a long moment, and then she smiled. "You mean sort of two for the price of one?"

I nodded. "And we'll just let my current client pay the freight. He can afford it. True since I had a letter from Mr. Firth indicating that probate was moving right along. I shuddered inwardly wondering how I would tell him about Aunt Gladys. He had known her for so many years.

"Well, it doesn't sound quite honest," she said, hesitating. "To let someone pay for me but right about now, I'd do almost anything to find Cheryl. I just know something's happened."

"You tell me everything you know about your sister, and I'll tell you if I can help fair enough?"

She nodded and told me the story. It wasn't too unusual. Pretty country girl goes to the big city in search of fame and fortune and gets a little lost along the way. Only this country girl had a sister to whom she wrote long, homesick letters, letters that, while not frequent, were almost painfully detailed.

Cheryl wrote of attending fancy parties on a yacht and meeting lots of wealthy businessmen from foreign countries. When I read through a few of the letters, it wasn't hard to see that most of the bigwigs were the sort of Asian business moguls I had seen on Barrie's Babe. It also wasn't hard to identify that particular floating brothel from her descriptions.

Then, Cheryl mentioned a special job she was going to start on. She didn't spell it out, but she hinted that it could make her really big money, enough so that "my sis won't ever have to work at the five-and-dime again." Cheryl wrote that she was going to get a cover shoot soon and that she was really happy at her new agency: Sondra Chase.

I asked Jenna who her sister had been with before Sondra Chase, but she couldn't remember. She was sure it had been in some of the earlier letters, but she hadn't brought them all with her to Los Angeles.

"I don't have a whole lot of time to find Cheryl," she said, wiping her mouth with her napkin. "Joe—he's my husband—is expecting me back in McCook. McCook, Nebraska. That's where the farm is." She nibbled a French fry. "Joe and I run things. Now that dad passed on. That's when Cheryl left home. If Daddy had been alive, he'd never have let her go to Hollywood."

She sipped at her tea. "Now, I wish someone had been there to stop her. We lost our mom when we were little, but no one ever expected anything to happen to Daddy. It was such a shock."

"So, your sister is your only family?"

She nodded. "Only close blood family. I think Daddy had a brother somewhere in the East, but he didn't even come for the funeral, so I guess I can't count him."

I paid the check and walked with Jenna back to the docks. "You find anyone who's seen Cheryl, you call that number I gave you."

She nodded and then went back to canvassing the boats. It was hot, dull work, but at least she had a meal inside her now. I met Lone Wolf and we headed for a pay phone.

I gave myself a few minutes to climb back into character. Then, I dialed the yacht club and asked for Leslie. I was curious to know if she had said anything to Sondra Chase about me. I also wondered if Mr. Barrington had attended that party. I'd left a little early and without the benefit of introductions.

I have to say that it gave me a small jolt to be told that Leslie Norton no longer worked for the Pacific Yacht Club. When I expressed a hope that she hadn't been fired because she had yet to land me as a member, the receptionist assured me that Leslie had gone on to better things with Sondra Chase's agency. It led me to believe her big break had come through a little sooner than she'd thought it would.

It took me some fancy talking to get a line on her, but I managed, saying that poor pitiful country-boy me just had to thank her personally with some flowers or something before I could even think of joining their wonderful club.

All in all, it was a flattering and heart-rending story. At least it seemed to rend the heart of the receptionist sufficiently. She told me what I wanted to know.

Lone Wolf and I took off to find Leslie's house.

Since there was hardly a square inch of Los Angeles that Lone Wolf didn't seem familiar with, it didn't take us long to find the quaint two-story on a side street in Venice.

As we drove around looking for a place to park, I had flashbacks of my last trip to Venice. I had left sadder but no wiser, courtesy of Curly, Moe, and Larry.

The sidewalks along the waterfront were still alive with vendors. The fortune-teller still sat in a swirl of colored cloth, but Curly, Moe, and Larry were thankfully absent.

Leslie wasn't home. Unfortunately, her roommate said she had come back from one of Sondra Chase's fancy boat parties and packed a bag.

"Where did she say she was going?"

"She said she was going to visit her family."

"Are they local?"

She shook her head. "I think there's just her brother. He's stationed in San Diego for now. The Navy, I guess, maybe the Marines. What's the one with the cute dog as a mascot?"

"The Marines," I said, thinking of the statue of the pit bull at El Toro Marine base.

We thanked her roommate, and I found a pay phone.

I quickly learned that Leslie was not signed on with Sondra Chase Agency.

I was definitely worried. Leslie had been adamant about her career goals. She had said Sondra was the one giving her the break at the Yacht Club so she could start modeling sooner.

Leslie had talked with me at the yacht party. Then she'd talked to Sondra. Had she said something that made Sondra think she might be a threat? After all, soon after that, someone knocked me out.

"What'd you find out?" Lone Wolf said as soon as I hung up.

"We may have another pretty missing person."

"No shit?"

I explained as we drove back to Gladys's. It was almost time to meet Kathy.

"What I can't figure out," said Lone Wolf, "is what Marilyn Williams and her murder and that stuff in the gym locker has to do with a whole different rival agency?"

"That is the key question, my friend. What is the connection between this Gloria Davis who took the photos and seems to have vanished, and Marilyn, who was not only worth killing, but had Gloria's photos and what would seem to be her pendant hidden in her gym locker?"

"Also, the card from Sondra Chase at the Pacific Yacht Club," Lone Wolf added, "Although she worked for Taylor-Brown."

"Yes. And not an agency card but a yacht club card." It was making a little more sense.

Something was right at the edge of my brain. I fought to pull it all the way into focus. "Marilyn left that other stuff with a yacht club card even though, being a model, I would have expected her to have a card from Sondra's agency instead."

Lone Wolf perked up. "So, she was definitely trying to point out something fishy with Sondra's other investment."

"Right, we're off track if we go from the modeling angle. This has nothing to do with the feud between the Chase Agency and the Taylor Brown agency. So, what's the connection between the girls?" I asked, turning up a side street.

"All I can guess is that they met on a shoot and struck up a friendship. They do hire from more than one agency, don't they?" Lone Wolf looked out of his depth.

I pulled into Gladys's driveway and set the brake on the station wagon. "I'm pretty sure they do. I mean agencies don't set up photo sessions, advertising people do. They probably pick and choose the products, so to speak."

Lone Wolf got out and called across the roof of the wagon, "Except this product is human."

NINETEEN

had the door to the kitchen unlocked when I stared at Beth's wagon.

I reached inside, plucked the keys off the counter, and tossed them to Lone Wolf. "You want to take this heap back to Beth's for me? We don't need it now, and I'd rather there was a car in her drive. I'll stay here and wait for Kathy."

Lone Wolf nodded. "Want me to whistle when I come back?" He grinned lasciviously.

"Suit yourself. I'll kiss her once for you."

"I can handle that myself, man." He slid in behind the wheel of the station wagon and pulled from the driveway.

"Over my dead body," I called to him, and then shuddered at my choice of words.

I had just poured a beer and was sliding a grilled cheese sandwich onto a plate when Kathy came into the kitchen and slumped into a chair. "Thanks, you're a lifesaver," she said, sipping at the beer and reaching for my sandwich.

"Hey! I thought you cops didn't drink on duty," I said teasing her a bit.

"Not on duty. Not anymore."

"What?" I felt a little sick.

"Terrana felt I might be 'too close to this one,'" she said, gulping some more of the beer. "He put me on the night desk until your case is solved or closed." She was flushed and she was holding back a tidal wave of anger.

"Well, that's a hell of a note!" I wanted to strangle the guy for her, but it wasn't really Terrana who had done this to her. It was me.

"My fault honey, I'm really sorry." I stood behind her chair and put my hands on her shoulders. She felt tense, to say the least. I rubbed her neck muscles and she leaned into my hands.

"I'll give you an hour or two to stop that," she said gratefully. "And a lot less time to take back that apology. This is not your fault. It's just dumb bad luck. I wouldn't trade us for a crack at the case."

"But you only just got your try at plain clothes work."

She nodded. "I'll get another. Besides, this will give me more time to help you and Lone Wolf on my own."

"How?"

"I'm working the desk on a graveyard shift. The regular just went into the hospital with appendicitis."

"Kathy, I don't want you doing anything to jeopardize your job."

"Nonsense, if we solve the case, Terrana will have to admit that I've got the right stuff for his team."

"And what if he decides you're not a team player because of it?" She shrugged.

"It's a gamble. But it's one I'm willing to take."

Talk about feeling on top of the world. I had hardly ever been so down and out, and this beautiful woman was willing to risk her career to help me. I leaned down and wrapped her in my arms. "I know I shouldn't let you gamble in such a high stakes game, but I'm grateful for your support. And Lord knows I can use the help."

"If we solve it, I win. If we don't, and Terrana doesn't know about it, I win," she said.

"If you get hurt, we all lose." I hugged her closer. "Especially me, if I have anything to say about it, you will be nowhere near the line of fire."

Lone Wolf came whistling up onto the back porch. "You guys ready for company?" He called, rattling the aluminum frame of the screen door.

"Come on in," I said, pushing it open and waving him into the kitchen, "Beer?" He nodded.

"What took you so long?"

"I thought of a couple of calls I could make while I was dropping off the keys."

"Calls?"

"Local. James Hickey, a photographer I know. Something about those negatives was bugging me."

"You figure out what it was?"

"He wasn't at either of the places I called. I left a message for him to catch me here."

"So, Kathy, what did you find at that apartment?"

"The landlady hadn't kept much. When Gloria failed to make her rent payment, she packed it all up and called Goodwill. Hang on a minute." She ran out to her Honda and came back in with a small black train case.

"Was that it?" I asked, half afraid of the answer.

"This is it. But there are some good photos, a few commercial shots and jewelry."

"Things a next of kin might want?"

Kathy nodded. "She fudged a little on the time frame, I think. But she did report her missing after about a week, and she got permission to clean house after the rent payment failed to arrive on time."

She opened the bag and preempted our beer and sandwiches with the contents.

I picked up a dramatic shot of a lovely lady and held it closer to the natural light at the kitchen window. "This is Gloria?"

Kathy nodded. "The landlady said it was a pretty good likeness. Stagey, but accurate.

"Damn."

"What is it?" Kathy leaned close to me and peered at the photo.

"I could swear this woman looks like an older version of Jenna's sister."

"Jenna?"

"Oh, Lone Wolf and I ran into a young lady at the Pacific Yacht Club."

"The Yacht Club? Sam!"

"I didn't go inside, didn't stir up anything. I told you I had to keep a hand in. We agreed, remember?"

She shrugged. "I still wish you'd leave anything to do with those docks to the police." She sighed. "Well, what about this Jenna?"

I grinned at her and tapped her shoulder lightly with my fist, "Knew your curiosity would override your scolding. Anyway, Jenna Richards was searching the docks for her sister,

Cheryl Scott. The sister worked for the Sondra Chase Agency, but Jenna said that when she asked for her there, they denied knowing Cheryl."

"And you think Gloria Davis is tied in with this Cheryl Scott?"

"I think they're one in the same." I held the photo at arm's length and squinted. "In fact, maybe you should go talk to Jenna." I took her address and phone number from my wallet and gave it to Kathy. "You ask her to show you that picture she's got and see what you think."

"You can't tell for sure?" Kathy looked surprised.

"Listen, I've seen women change their hairstyle, hair color, and makeup so drastically for acting parts that their mothers wouldn't be able to pick them out of a lineup."

"Okay, I'll check it out. Ears don't lie. I hope Jenna's picture shows me a good ear shape."

I shrugged. "Can't recall let me know what she says."

"I'll be back as soon as I can."

"We'll be here. Lone Wolf's waiting for that call from his photographer friend."

Kathy nodded, but she was already halfway out the door and running for the Honda. She squealed from the drive and slapped her plastic bubble in her roof. Not completely kosher, but then, neither was using a siren to make a cigarette run, and I knew plenty of New York City officials who did it. She'd need that and more to get through mid-day rush hour traffic and back.

Kathy had been gone awhile when the phone rang. Lone Wolf grabbed the packet of photos that Marilyn had concealed in her gym locker and took off to meet his expert.

"Watch out for those. They're police evidence," I called after him, only half kidding.

"Not 'til Kathy turns them in," he said, grinning and jumping into the Mustang.

I felt suddenly stranded. I'd turned in the Caddy, Lone Wolf had the Mustang, and the station wagon was back at Beth's.

I finished my beer and went to see if some of the ball games were on television. I had hoped the Giants would be in some sort of pre-season scuffle with a local team and that the game would be televised. No such luck.

I flipped channels and paced around the den until Kathy came back later in the afternoon.

One glance at her expression as she came through the door was enough to tell me there was trouble.

"What's the matter, Kathy?"

"Oh, Sam that poor woman!" She fell into my arms, and I thought I felt a silent sob wrack her. Then she took a deep breath and let it out very slowly. "It's Cheryl. Jenna is sure. Gloria Davis is the sister Jenna's been looking for."

"Rough. I was afraid of that."

"I hate this part of being a cop. Dammit. I had to verify that her sister has, indeed, been missing for over a month and a half, according to Cheryl's— Gloria's—landlady."

I edged Kathy onto the sofa and clicked off the television, "Coffee, with a shot?"

She shook her head, "Just straight."

"The coffee or the shot?"

She smiled then, "The coffee please."

I got her cup, brought one for myself, and sat down next to her. "Jenna's taking it hard?"

"The worst, she's suddenly sure her sister's dead, and I couldn't say much to allay her fears."

I sipped my coffee. "I guess I couldn't either."

We sat quietly for a while, just absorbing each other's strength, at least I know I was getting that from Kathy. Words were unnecessary, and I appreciated that. In fact, I often found them incessant. I'd met far too many actresses who spent every moment being "on." It made for a harrowing date.

Suddenly, Kathy looked up and I saw lights in the drive. The Mustang's distinctive roar fell silent. Lone Wolf was back and judging from the pace he set coming toward the door, I guessed he had news. We walked out to meet him.

TWENTY

"There's news and there's news," Lone Wolf said, herding me back into the kitchen. He greeted Kathy with a wink, and she gave him a quick peck on the cheek. "First, my car's ready. Gunner is going to pick me up in about an hour so I can test drive it." He grinned like a kid. "Not that Gunner's work needs checking. The man is fine, but he likes his customers' input."

"That's great, Lone Wolf." I said.

"Yeah, it really is, especially now that we're down to one vehicle between us."

"What's the second bit of news?" I asked, wincing inwardly at the thought of my part in the reason for his current deprivation.

"I think we have a better clue in those photos than we suspected." Lone Wolf hurried into the den. "And it's a clue no one but a photo buff or an expert would ever have spotted in a million years." He turned on another light and spread the photos and negatives out on the coffee table. Kathy and I watched him like lions watch gazelles.

"Show me," I said, sitting forward on the sofa.

He carefully separated the negatives from the rest and handed Kathy and me one strip each. "What do you see?"

"At the risk of being obvious, the negatives to the photos from Marilyn's locker," Kathy said. "The ones I should have turned in to Terrana by now."

"You can have them tonight, as soon as we're finished here," Lone Wolf promised. "But this is why I wanted you to leave them for a little while longer." He leaned over and pointed to something on the strip Kathy held to the light. "See that?"

She squinted those lovely green eyes and held the strip closer to her face. "That little blurring of the edge of the emulsion?" she asked.

"That's it."

I leaned to look.

Lone Wolf pointed to the same on my strip. "It's on everyone. Find them on yours, Sam?"

We all sat squinting up into the den light like moles unearthed by a road grader. I could see that each square had one side that looked a little fuzzy.

Lone Wolf took a loupe from his shirt pocket and handed it to me, "Oops, ladies first." He took the magnifier back and handed it to Kathy.

She put the base against the strip and leaned into the eyepiece. "Oh, it's not a smudge! It's three little Vs."

She passed the magnifier to me. "So it is," I said, taking a gander at my own negative strip.

On the left vertical edge of each little square of photo, there were three small tepees of dark thrusting out into the clear boarder around the picture area. "Okay, what is the significance?"

Lone Wolf smiled and went to get a beer from the fridge. "Those marks are purposeful," he said, when he got back. "Jimmy says that photographers often notch the photo plane frame on the interchangeable back to their Hasselblad's. That way, if there's a light leak that shows up on a certain set of neg's, they can tell which back to have repaired, checked, or whatever."

"Even I can tell these negatives aren't from a Hasselblad." I said, setting my strip carefully with the rest.

"Right, so in these, it's a system to match the negatives to a specific camera." He waited for it to sink in, taking a long pull from his beer bottle.

Kathy was smiling. "You mean someone was tracking the camera that was used to take the photos?"

"Exactly, more likely tracking what photos that certain camera took." "And without your spotting this, no one would ever think these photos could be any kind of evidence once Gloria and Marilyn were dead?" I asked.

Lone Wolf nodded. "I'd say that would be a safe bet."

"There must be some important tie-in with these photos, or why bother tracking the camera that was used?" I offered.

Kathy pulled the photos from the envelope again. "Okay, let's really take these apart. What's in them?" She leafed through them slowly while we looked on. Then, we divided the packet and each of us stared long and hard at what we had before switching packets with someone else.

"Just stare at them and say anything that comes to mind," Kathy directed.

"Well, none of these girls looks like Jenna's missing sister," I said. "That would seem to rule out Cheryl/Gloria taking them as candid shots of friends."

"Why?" Lone Wolf wanted to know.

"Well, I've taken a lot of candid's at cast parties, and I've known a lot of other people who have. It's highly unusual for the photographer not to be in at least one of them."

Lone Wolf nodded, "Yeah. You're right. Even if you bring the camera, you always get someone to take at least one shot of you with your friends."

"Okay, they're not candid's. What else is here?" Kathy prompted.

"Half-dressed ladies, or undressed, if you prefer," I said setting my shots down on the table.

"I always prefer," Lone Wolf quipped and tossed his batch on top of mine.

I picked up the whole stack. "We have girls. We have girls who are obviously models. We have one who is obviously a dresser and makeup person for these girls. We have lots of shots of the dressing room or shots of lots of different dressing rooms." I pulled out individual photos as I spoke, lining them up across the tabletop until they were all spread out.

Kathy stared for a long time. "I think it's the same room. The chairs all match, and the color scheme is the same. So, they're probably shots of different girls who used almost the same location to change."

"That means that these photos were all taken at one showing or at different showings held in the same place," I suggested.

She nodded. "I think it's all the same show. A fashion show usually incorporates a theme, but a designer likes to offer clothes for every occasion. See this one? It looks like part of a wedding dress." She pointed at a trail of white lace and satin that poked into the frame of a photo of a model that looked like an anorexic Audrey Hepburn. "See, a lot of designers, especially the classic ones, present a wedding gown as the grand finales."

"Look here." Kathy pointed to a photo of a young lady being zipped into a black cocktail dress. "This is an expensive, well-made garment. The insides are as nicely finished as what shows."

"That's it. It's not the girls." I said, wrapping an arm around Kathy's shoulders. "You've hit it on the head."

"Oh, Sam, it's the dresses! I know it. But these can only be worth committing a murder if they're espionage photos of originals." She hugged me, jumped up and down a bit, and then hugged Lone Wolf, who looked caught somewhere between enjoyment and alarm.

"Okay. It's the dresses," I interrupted. "Now, what do you mean by espionage?"

"Industrial espionage stealing designer's ideas, they're worth a fortune to a knock-off artist."

"Knock off?"

She nodded. "Remember that white dress I wore on our first date?"

"Do I ever," I said, smiling.

"Some people make their entire living off of putting out affordable renditions of expensive designer dresses. Victor Costa even bills himself as the Copy King of fashion. Of course, that's not to imply he's into espionage. Many manufacturers go to the shows or send their top artists to take enough notes at legitimate unveilings to go into production very soon after those first showings."

"That's legal?"

"Oh yes. They're reminiscent of the originals—but they vary just enough to keep the copycats out of court. There are only a very limited number of ladies who could afford the originals anyway. Then there are the rest of us who will still pay a very good price to get a copy that is adequately reproduced in less expensive materials by more cost-effective methods."

"Wait. You're losing me,"

Lone Wolf cut in, "What, makes a designer dress cost so much is the hand work, detailing, and costly materials, as well as the design.

Some designs don't work as well—won't ever work as well—in a cheaper fabric, but that's the job of the good copy artist: to know how much he can shave from the overhead without sacrificing the design. It's an art unto itself."

"You mean there's a lot of production cost in something like that zipper opening you pointed out?" I said, catching onto her line of thinking.

"Yes. Look through the loupe and you'll see that the edges are all smooth. That means hand overcast and French seaming. When they make a copy, lots of corners can be cut. No pun intended," she said grinning at me. "That zipper placket is hand-stitched, French seaming showing inside, probably throughout. And beautiful lace placed in the inset. Lace alone can be worth a fortune if it's handmade. I'd guess there's all sorts of hand detailing here that are definitely not cost effective."

I smiled. "And where is the best place you can think of where you could lower costs—especially labor—significantly?"

"The Orient!" Lone Wolf said, only a beat behind Kathy.

"And where does Barrington, business partner of Ms. Sondra Chase, ship to?" I asked, feeling a little like a school marm getting a class to recite in unison. Then I scooped up the photos and negatives and handed them all to Kathy. "Turn it in to Terrana now and look like a hero, sweetheart."

She grinned at me. "And what will you two be doing while this Kat's away?"

"I think I'll try to find out if the camera that took these pictures is in Sondra Chase's possession."

Kathy looked frightened. "Sam, you can't! Promise me you won't do that. Don't go anywhere near her office or her boat club, please!"

"And, why not?"

"This may be enough to get a search warrant. If you go without one, no matter what you find, we can't use it as evidence. She could say you planted it. It could end up your word against hers and blow the whole case."

"She'd never walk—not if we found the camera in her possession?"

"Rules of evidence Sam, the police can find it on her. You can't. And we can't find it without a court order to search her place. That's what I'm hoping this will give us," she said, waving the packet of photos at me. "It will show enough probable cause to get a warrant."

Unfortunately, she made sense. "All right, I'll wait. But if you can't get a warrant, I'm the first one you call, promise?"

She smiled and gave me a kiss. "Thanks. I will call if we can't handle it. You'll have to give me until morning though." She looked at her watch. "I don't think this is enough to get a judge out after hours for a search warrant. And I can't prove that Sondra Chase will skip if we wait until tomorrow. One good thing about my graveyard desk duty, I'll be there first thing in the morning to bug hell out of Terrana." She said her goodbyes and hurried to her car.

The house seemed empty, and time started to drag the moment that woman was out the door. I was definitely getting in deep with this lady, and it sure felt like the real thing.

Lone Wolf brought me back to the present state of affairs with a pat on the back.

"Gunner should be here any minute with my car, "You going to be okay?"

"Sure, don't worry about me. I'll be fine.

He must have felt the letdown, too, because he asked if I'd like him to stay over.

I definitely didn't want to be in that house alone, but I also refused to impose any more than I already had. This would be the second night without Kathy, and her absence as much my fault as anyone's, weighed heavily on me. I shook my head. I hoped our hard work would get her another chance at detecting very soon.

Lone Wolf and I had another beer while we waited for his car to be delivered. We were considering a third when we heard a purring roar from the driveway and a car door slammed shut.

Lone Wolf was off the couch like someone had hit him with a cattle prod. I couldn't have beaten him to that back door with roller skates. Before I cleared the threshold, he was pumping the meaty paw of a large blonde man whose Viking heritage showed as strongly in his bones as in his name.

There was a speedy introduction and brief sales pitch encouraging me to bring my vehicles to him if they needed work. Then Gunnar and Lone Wolf were gone in a roar of finely tuned Trans Am, and I was standing alone in Aunt Gladys's driveway. I went in, showered, and tossed the beer bottles in the proper bin for recycling. On my way upstairs, I looked at the dark, silent living room with the yellow tape across the entranceway.

It was going to hurt for a long time. I hoped bringing her killers to justice would help me heal. And I hoped we brought them in soon. I groped for the clock on the bedside table and set my alarm. If I was lucky enough to get to sleep, this might be one of the few times in my life when I'd overdo it. Exhaustion, both emotional and physical, weighed on me I lay in the dark and tried to imagine Kathy here with me.

TWENTY-ONE

I awoke wondering how Jenna was taking the news of her sister being one in the same with the long-vanished Gloria. It was too early to call her, so I did a few things around the house that had been let go too long, like vacuuming and laundry and dishes. I knew it was really all just busy work to keep me from looking into that living room and seeing Aunt Gladys with that small hole in her forehead. The one I was supposed to have put there. Then I went to a local market and stocked up. By the time I put the groceries away and got the clothes into the dryer, it was a more respectable hour for a phone call. I dialed Jenna's hotel. It was worse than I'd ever have imagined. The hotel clerk told me that Jenna wasn't in. Worse: she'd left me a message: she was going to the Sondra Chase Agency to confront them about Cheryl /Gloria. Bad idea, I could only hope Ms. Chase was elsewhere. I didn't want another pretty girl to disappear. As near as I could tell from the fact that Gloria--only a sister who was very far away; Marilyn--only a roommate; Debbie--only a father who was drunk most of the time; and now Leslie--who was also an orphan with a brother who was all over the globe with the military; were missing or dead, it would seem as if any pretty lady who had almost no relatives was fair game at the Chase Agency.

I called Lone Wolf and explained. He said he'd meet me at the agency. Before leaving, I tried calling Kathy. She wasn't at home. Neither was her father. I left a message on her machine about my following Jenna and why. I hoped she wouldn't be too furious, but I couldn't see any other course. Jenna was undoubtedly going to get herself into real trouble. With the still-heavy traffic, it took me about forty-five minutes to get to the Sondra Chase office. I looked at my watch as I pulled up in front of the agency and got out. It was eleven. The traffic problems of Los Angeles were growing by the moment. The lunch rush hadn't yet started and still I'd been bumper to bumper all the way in from Glendale. Lone Wolf was there ahead of me and waiting. Trust a biker to know all the shortcuts. We went inside and startled the receptionist; guess she didn't see many models dressed quite like he was. She told us that Jenna had not been here. I hoped this lady wasn't considering acting as a profession, she would never make it. To anyone who had ever studied the craft, it would have been obvious that she was lying. The untrained don't do it well. Her eyes took a sudden interest in the middle distance and all but glassed over, her voice sounded entirely too matter of fact. One hand had a problem with the fingers--they kept rubbing nervously against each other. I thanked her and we left. When we got outside, we looked at each other with the same thought and we spoke at the same time.

"She's about as transparent as glass," Lone Wolf said. And he was the soul of tact compared to my own comment.

"Let's check around the back," I suggested.

We turned the corner into the alley in time to see Jenna struggling with a big man in a business suit. Suddenly he hauled off and smacked her one in the jaw. She folded and he loaded her in through the van's sliding side door and jumped in the passenger's side. I thought I saw him move to the driver's seat, but there could have been someone else for a wheelman. Lord knew, Sondra had enough guys to do her dirty work. I ran toward the back of the van while Lone Wolf headed for his Trans Am. I tried to get my hands on that bastard before he had the chance to get away, but I was too late. The van's engine caught, and the tires laid several dollars' worth of rubber against the alleyway pavement as I grabbed for the chrome ladder on the back. My hand slid off the polished surface and the van fishtailed its way out onto the street with Lone Wolf's car coming up fast. I turned and pressed flat against the building as the Trans Am pulled alongside me. It was too close to pull the door open, so I did a dive through the passenger's window and tried to haul myself up-right as he gunned it. Lone Wolf squealed his tires effectively but to no avail. The light at the corner must have gone to red because a long line of Hollywood traffic quickly filled the lane across the opening to the street, bottling us in the alley. Lone Wolf threw it in reverse and barreled backwards as fast as or faster than some folks can drive forward. He was good. I'd have let him drive anything I owned. In fact, I had. When I saw the Mustang sitting at the curb, I put a hand on his arm. "Hang on." I scrawled Jenna's name and the word "taken" on one of the cards I'd been given at the Pacific Yacht Club, jumped out and slid the card under the wiper. Lone Wolf looked a question at me with his eyes as I jumped back into the Pontiac. "I left a clue for Kathy. Her message machine will tell her we came over here to collect Jenna. I'm betting they'll take her to the yacht club, so I left Kathy their card on the Mustang's window." He nodded and wove through cars until we spotted the van up ahead. There was no way to get closer in the crush of cars. Lone Wolf cut to the right and started across an intersection. A freak with a vivid green Mohawk and wearing silver-studded black cowhide everything, stepped off the sidewalk in front of us and Lone Wolf landed on his horn, skinned past close enough to put a high polish on the guy's leather pants. Thanks to his reflexes we were in time to see the van getting onto the freeway. Sure, enough the 10 going toward the beach, the yacht club, it had to be. Lone Wolf urged the Trans-Am up an on ramp. The black van was disappearing into traffic when we entered the flow. It was already over in the fast lane. I looked at Lone Wolf. He had a grin on his face that was saying this was going to be fun. He crossed over two lanes as the black van moved farther down the freeway. There was moderate traffic for this time of the day. We managed to stay within sight of the van, at the same time we were able to use the cars in front of us to hide the fact that we were following them. After about forty minutes of freeway driving the van pulled off and headed for the club. Lone Wolf parked the Trans Am in the club's lot but kept it near the exit. No sense getting ourselves boxed in. I could just see the roof of the van parked up near the buildings. I got out and headed for it at a trot.

TWENTY-TWO

"How we gonna play it?" Lone Wolf asked, jogging at my side.

"We see where they take her, and we get her back." I eased the gun out of the small of my back where I'd stored it and showed it to him. He nodded and we both saved our breath for more important things.

Creeping around the side of the building, I saw the business suit—Jenna's elbow in his iron grip—marching her toward the docks at the rear of the clubhouse. She was moving in a dopey, shambling sort of gait, her head hanging low and her chin almost on her chest. Either he'd hit her hard enough to do some lingering damage, or he'd used some sort of drug on her once he'd gotten her into the van.

Halfway there, Ponytail and Broken-nose joined him, and they practically dragged her up the gangway and onto the Free Sea.

Only the suit came back off the boat. I watched him move and wondered if he had been the third of the Three Stooges who had come to Venice to watch me jog, maybe had helped Ponytail and Broken-nose get Beth and Aunt Gladys away from Lone Wolf? It was probable.

He came toward us down the dock and as he turned to the building, I saw it, the flash of red and gold from his ring finger. The third Stooge. No doubt about it. I'd had the impression of that ring on my sternum   in shades of black and blue, now faded to an ugly yellowish brown that left the pattern harder to find. But it was there. I rubbed a palm over my chest as I thought about it.

Lone Wolf nudged me. "That leaves one on board for each of us, right?"

I grinned at him. "And you'll take the cost of your bike out of the hide of the one you get?"

He shook his head, "Won't be enough. You'll have to take the rest out of yours."

It was my turn to deny him his request, "Huh-uh. If either one of these guys killed my aunt, we're going to run out of hide long before either of us is paid up."

He nodded. "Let's go."

We stepped out from behind the building and walked casually down the dock. I held my automatic inside my jacket pocket. As we came closer to the Free Sea, I eased the safety off and Lone Wolf edged ahead of me. I'd cover him.

There was Ponytail just coming up to take his watch on deck. I touched Lone Wolf's arm. He stooped low and froze near the base of the gangway, while I stepped behind the bow of the Bay liner in the next slip.

Lone Wolf crept up the planking and onto Free Sea's deck. She hardly moved as she received his weight. In a matter of moments, he had flowed up behind Ponytail and grabbed him in a very adequate choke hold. That wolf-headed knife was out where Ponytail could see it. He nodded to me, and I joined them. "Where's the girl?" I whispered at him.

He kept quiet and Lone Wolf torqued him a bit. "One of those eyes would look real cute rolling along these decks," Lone Wolf said, resting the blade of the knife on Ponytail's cheekbone, the point in the soft skin that covered the lower edge of the socket.

He gagged and then said: "Aft stateroom."

We must have been standing right over them. I moved to the hatch and went below.

The ladder led into the saloon. I closed my eyes for a moment and recalled the layout from the brief early morning search that had netted me Aunt Gladys's earring and a look in the captain's log. I circled behind the ladder and put my hand on the doorknob of the stateroom. I listened a moment.

I could hear soft sobbing. Jenna was definitely in there, and she was more than ready to have me get her out.

I pushed through, went low, and darted to the right. No problem. Broken-nose didn't even have a weapon. I threw down on him and Jenna lurched over to me, her step uncertain. I gathered her against my side. "You all right?"

She nodded. "I'm so glad to see you. I guess I never should have gone to the agency, but I thought, what harm could it do to ask about Cheryl? I mean, I had that professional name she used as well as a photograph."

"Lots of harm if your questions embarrass someone, I think asking about your sister is a real embarrassment to Sondra Chase." I used my gun barrel to motion Broken-nose into a chair.

"All clear, Lone Wolf," I said, cranking open a butterfly hatch above me and calling out to him. I looked at Jenna.

"But, Sam, I didn't even see Sondra. I just talked to the assistant manager, Miss Carter. She listened to my story, looked at my photo of Cheryl, and then went to call someone. She never came back. Some big guy in a blue suit came into the office and grabbed me." She touched the bruise that was blackening the side of her jaw. "Then he brought me here, I guess. I was out cold."

Lone Wolf came in, wrestling Ponytail through the doorway. He pushed him down hard in the chair nearest Broken-nose. I could cover them both easily, but Lone Wolf moved to my side and kept an eye on them, also, the knife resting in his hand like a woman's breast.

Ponytail got a good look at my automatic and raised his thin arms over his head. His eyes narrowed like an animals with its foot in a trap.

"One of you best tell me who killed my Aunt Gladys. Otherwise, I'm going to make sure you both go down for it, kidnapping and murder one." I let my eyes drift over Jenna. "Multiple counts of kidnapping."

I was watching Ponytail because I was almost sure he hadn't been the trigger man. Sure enough. It was quick, but it was there, that little fleeting glance at his buddy that said: "He wouldn't let me hang with him, would he?"

I knew who to pressure. I advanced on Ponytail and reached for his namesake, tugging gently and letting the greasy length of the hair run through my palm. "The inmates in maximum security will just love this long hair. Makes you look real girlish, that and your skinny little ass."

I put the toe of my shoe against his rump and gave him a nudge in the tailbone.

He flinched and pulled away, but I was on him again, running his hair and talking to him about how it was going to be inside.

Lone Wolf put in his two cents, and Ponytail was ready to crack when the door behind me eased open and someone placed the hard round circle of a gun barrel in the middle of my back. "So glad you could make it, Mr. Ryan," Sondra purred. "Drop the gun."

Lone Wolf lurched around to face her, and as she encompassed him with her weapon, Broken-nose stood up and brought the full power of his fist into contact with the point of Lone Wolf's chin. He went down hard and didn't get up. The knife with the wolf's head landed on the rug a few feet away.

I dropped my automatic and turned around slowly to see a tall, tight-faced blonde. She had been a breath-stealing, jaw-clenching beauty once, not too long ago, and was still statuesque and striking with enormous presence. In fact, Smith and Wesson made her only ugly feature of metal. It rested in her left hand and gave a whole new meaning to the term bar sinister.

With Lone Wolf down for the count, Sondra again turned her full attention to me. "Suppose you tell me what you got from

Marilyn on the train, Mr. Ryan. It probably doesn't matter much anymore, but I'm a curious woman, and I can afford to indulge my curiosity now." The muzzle of her gun nodded at me in confirmation.

I shrugged. "She gave me the key to her gym locker."

Sondra must have been extremely startled by that revelation because she frowned. Models, and most of the pretty actresses I knew, worked very hard at never allowing intense expressions… so wrinkle inducing. I guessed Sondra didn't care about that so much anymore.

"And that set you hounding after my business interests? I hardly think so. What did that key lead you to?"

I didn't say anything, so she gestured to Broken-nose. "There's another gun in that vanity. Take it out and shoot his friend if he doesn't tell me by the time, I count to three."

Broken-nose found the weapon where she'd indicated, a nasty looking little Browning .38. He grinned, leaned down, and placed the stubby muzzle against Lone Wolf's temple.

"That only led me to her dance ear and some photographs."

"Photographs?"

"Yeah, candid shots of her model friends changing for a show." I tried to sound casual with a slight overtone of disappointment so that she would think the pictures had meant nothing, "Oh, and a necklace with the initials G.D."

She smiled. "So, that's what led you to little Gloria."

"Where is little Gloria?"

She lifted a lip in a sneer, "Happy at last? I can only assume so I gave her a trip to the Orient, One way."

Jenna gasped and turned stricken eyes my way. "She's dead? My sister's really dead?"

Sondra looked over at the pale eyes, the skin stretched tight over prominent cheekbones, the freckles that stood out against the milk of her complexion like ink on a white satin sheet. "I didn't say that my dear. Your sister could be having a marvelous time with some of Japan's elder businessmen. A lady of extreme leisure, I'd say."

Jenna's hand flew to her mouth, and she made a gagging sound just before she leaned over and threw up on the carpet.

"After that party aboard 'Barrie's Babe', I knew you weren't above pimping, but white slavery? Where do you draw the line?"

"What line? Gloria needed to be somewhere very far away. I gave her an extended vacation, and some nice Japanese merchants decided I should be recompensed for my expenses." She smiled, "It worked out very well for all concerned."

"Not all. Aren't you having a convenient memory lapse where Gloria and her sister are concerned?"

Jenna was still hunched over her knees, her lips trembling as she was wracked by the occasional retching. I saw Lone Wolf twitch and hoped he wouldn't come to so abruptly that Broken-nose would get alarmed and shoot him. Where the hell was Kathy and her search warrant and, I hoped, some well-armed back up?

Surely, she'd gotten my message and gone to the agency where I'd left the Mustang and the business card telling her where Jenna had been taken.

"So, Mr. Ryan, you never told me what you did with that locker key and the things that you found."

"The police have them."

She flinched, thought I heard something on deck, and I fought to keep Sondra distracted. From my angle, I could just see the navy of a uniform's pant cuff slide past the butterfly hatch I'd opened. It was time to drop a bomb on her and hope for the best. "They were quite interested to see that your models had been taking advance pictures of clothes they were about to model for the first time at swank unveilings. Worth quiet a lot as patterns for knock-off artists, I understand. Not the kind of crime I would have thought people would kill for, but I learn something new every day."

Sondra drew in a quick breath, and I prayed that help was listening at the door. "How did you figure out what the photos were for?" she asked, spitting the words, the gun wavering a bit as her hand trembled.

"Simple." I saw the handle of the door start to move. I let her have both barrels. "They weren't shots of the girls. They weren't shots of a setting. They could only be shots of the clothes. That's industrial espionage!" I had raised my voice considerably as I ticked off the thought processes. It must have hidden any small sound made by our rescuers because Sondra never noticed.

As the door flew open and her head began its turn toward imminent danger, I lunged down and under Sondra's pistol. I hit her as she turned and her gun went off with the deafening report of a .357 magnum with a maximum load.

She went down under me and Broken-nose jerked at his trigger like a true amateur, returning the fire of the police.

The sound of shots exploded and then reverberated within the small cabin. I felt a searing pain in my left leg and knew jogging was out of the question for the near future.

I released Sondra and rolled, grabbing the gun she had dropped and aiming it at Broken-nose. "Lose it!" I shouted at him. He was already raising his hands over his head, and a quick glance over my shoulder told me Terrana had him covered. A uniform stepped up to me, slapped handcuffs on Sondra, and hauled her to her feet. I was pleased to see that she limped when he led her outside. Broken-nose seemed to be bleeding through his jacket sleeve. Good.

One of Newport's finest looked at me and called out into the hall for an ambulance. I was about to say I didn't need one when I noticed the still figure lying in the doorway. A tossed mane of blue-black hair spread out against the cream carpet and bright blood flowering against the crisp white of her blouse.

I crawled to Kathy, but there was nothing I could do. She had taken Sondra's shot through the chest, and although it didn't look like a fatal placement, her body was pumping her life out by the liter. I tried to find a pressure point, but the hole in her slender torso felt endless.

"Kathy?" I slid closer and got an arm under her head. "Jesus!" The word popped from my throat, half fear half supplication. Her hair was fast matting with more blood. One of the shots from Broken-nose's .38 must have hit her in the head. I knew it had been his bullet that had gone through my thigh. He had racked up quite a score for all that amateur trigger jerking.

I lowered my face to hers and kissed her cheek. Her eyelids fluttered. There was a flash of green amid all that blood on white skin. God, she was pale, the color of the ashes smudged on the foreheads of the faithful on the Wednesday that begins Lent.

"Sam?" It was hardly more than a croak. I crouched close, but those green eyes vanished beneath lids grown heavy with pain and shock, and she said no more.

"I'm here Kathy. I'm right with you, Baby," I said, in case she could still hear me.

While I assured her, she wouldn't die, her life kept pumping against my hand. Then, the paramedics ran in and took over, lifting her onto a gurney, attaching electrodes, and an IV.

Someone put a pressure wrap on my thigh, but I hardly noticed. Then they carried Kathy out to the ambulance, and Terrana offered to drive me in his car. I declined as politely as I could and looked at Lone Wolf who was hovering in the background, a cold pack pressed to his jaw.

"Ready?" he asked.

I nodded and he tossed the ice pack. He helped me into his Trans Am, and we followed the cry of the ambulance through the tourist crowded streets to the trauma center.

I spent about an hour in ER where they diagnosed a through and through and bandaged the nice clean hole in my leg. They gave me a prescription for pain killers and a wheelchair ride to the front entrance.

Lone Wolf came out of the hospital pharmacy with my medication and a pair of crutches, and we went up to wait for Kathy to come out of surgery.

We bought bad coffee out of a machine and sat around on a scuffed green leatherette sofa until I began to hurt so badly that I took one of the pills Lone Wolf shook from the orange plastic bottle. I downed it but knew it wouldn't touch my real suffering. Only good news from the surgery team could stop that pain.

Before too long, Kathy's father and Terrana joined us. Terrana stayed long enough to get a current report: no news. Then he went back to the station. He assured us that Broken-nose was getting axed by Ponytail's lugubrious confession. He had killed Daddy Warbucks on Sondra's orders because old Baldy had muffed it with Marilyn on the train and again with Debbie, all without gaining any information whatsoever. He had been warned against killing me or mine until Sondra got what she was after.

Marilyn had done a first-rate job of trying to blackmail Sondra Chase. She had the photos that proved industrial espionage, and she knew Gloria had been frightened enough to give her those photos for safekeeping. Gloria had vanished after reporting to a shoot on a Barrington freighter. Terrana said that State Department investigators were looking into what might have happened to Gloria after she entered Japan.

Sondra was going away for a long time. The camera with the filed notches had been found in a safe in her agency office. A Japanese office worker was apprehended leaving the agency basement with two other cameras with different filed patterns. Pressure on him from the police and the Department of Immigration and Naturalization forced him to reveal that an encoded list in the yacht club office tracked which cameras had been used by which girls at what famous showings. Proof, he said, for the overseas investors, a double check on the girls for Sondra. None of the Oriental businessmen were ever named or discovered.

Sondra, ever vigilant about betrayal from her partners since her ill-fated association with Taylor Brown, had kept secret records incriminating Barrington and indicating that other very attractive young ladies—all with a conspicuous lack of living relatives—had gone to work for her as models before mysteriously disappearing via the Barrington freighters.

She was the driving force behind the other killings and kidnappings, and now had chalked up assault on a police officer with intent. I hoped that was all that particular charge would amount to, but it would be a while before we knew.

After five grueling hours, the surgeon came out to tell us that Kathy was hanging on by her eyeteeth. Mr. Kelly was allowed to go into ICU for five minutes out of every hour. Bless him; he let me take his second five.

Kathy lay beneath the sheet, tubes running everywhere and that ticking sound of the respirator measuring her life by the breath. I wanted to scream. I wanted very badly to hit something extremely hard. What I finally did was put my hand over one of hers—the one without the IV needle through the taut skin and let the tears run down my face unabated.

I spoke to her of my sorrow and my hope and my love, wishing I had more to say and she something to answer. Then the nurse came to tell me my time was up.

So, it went for much longer than it should have: Mr. Kelly and I swapping five minutes with the woman we each loved, every hour on the hour.

TWENTY-THREE

By the end of the first week, Kathy was still in a coma, but stable, breathing on her own and out of ICU. Mr. Kelly and I were taking turns sitting in her private room and talking to her. Some people say that those in a coma hear every word, and some medical people think it could help them come out of it. If there was any chance of that, we weren't letting it slip past us.

Needless to say, Mr. Kelly and I got a lot closer while we were sitting our vigil. I was calling him Liam; he was calling me Sam most of the time, but a "Son" was creeping into his speech more and more often. I liked it. It felt right.

When Aunt Gladys's body was released, I arranged for a cremation and then a memorial service. Mr. Kelly and I both chanced leaving Kathy's side for the time it took to say goodbye to my aunt. When I looked over at him during the service, I knew we were both thinking the same frightening thought: would we soon be here again to bury his only child? Both of us were scared spit less as we returned to the hospital.

Mr. Kelly was really an understanding man. He didn't hold Kathy's condition against me, even though I did. He believed Kathy was just doing her job, being a good cop, which was all he ever wanted for her. I saw it differently. Her job as a cop had put her on night duty at a nice safe desk in the station house. My blundering, and her willingness to help me, had put her out on the streets and eventually, on the Free Sea and in the path of Sondra's bullet. More specifically, it had put her in front of Broken-nose's wild shots.

It was the head wound that was causing the most trouble. They'd patched up the chest wound easily enough, but the neurosurgeon hadn't been able to remove that bullet from her skull. It had lodged in her forebrain near the thalamus.

Lots of people lived with bullets lodged somewhere in their bodies he'd assured me. I thought of all the old-time western sheriffs. So now we were waiting to see if our Kathy would be one of them.

One afternoon, as we sat watching our sleeping beauty, I told Mr. Kelly about the big decision I had been in the process of making ever since I'd come west to be with Aunt Gladys. He thought it was a great idea.

"So, you'll stay out here? Open an office as soon as your uncle's will is out of probate?"

I nodded. "And then I'll take one deserving case out of every three I work on as pro bono work."

"For people with just causes and no money, you will work for free?" I nodded. "Of course, a fellow wouldn't want to advertise."

He smiled at that. "And you'd want Kathy's help—and mine?" His eyes gleamed with an excitement I knew came from even the thought of getting back into harness again.

"You'd be willing to help, then?"

He yipped, a sharp fox's bark of laughter. "It beats hell out of painting the house again," he said winking at me.

Then he grew quiet. "Will ya be doing all this if Kathy…" his voice almost broke, "if she can't do the work with us?"

I nodded and gave him my solemn vow and a handshake on it. "In that case, we'll do it for her," I said.

"For her and my Aunt Gladys." We both knew what we meant.

That was as close as we'd ever come to speaking about the possibility of Kathy not pulling through. But I'm sure it wasn't the last time either of us thought about it.

We were well into the second week of pure hell when I went for what must have been my third gallon of coffee. When I came back to the room, Mr. Kelly looked up and grinned at me. "What's up, Liam?"

"Kathy is! She's back, Son. She spoke to me," he said, leaning to grab my arm, pulling me toward her even faster than I was already moving.

"Kathy?" I leaned forward, grateful that Mr. Kelly was standing back, allowing me the foremost bedside position. I took her hand in mine and stroked it.

"How are you feeling, sweetheart?"

Her eyelids fluttered a bit and then a steady green gaze wrapped me in hope. "Sam?" Her voice sounded rough, but I was glad to hear it and sounded so beautiful to me.

EPILOGUE

J ust before Mr. Kelly took Kathy home to that pretty little green and white house in Studio City, the neurosurgeon ran a bunch of tests on her. The doctor also wrote a nice big report that Mr. Kelly could take home. Explaining everything he needed to know about Kathy.

It seemed even when you win you lose. But I was glad to have my Kathy alive. The proposal will just have to wait until she is completely healed. And in my heart, I knew that she would be. Then we could get on with the rest of our lives.